# YOU HAD ME AT COUGAR

HEART OF THE COUGAR
BOOK 9

TERRY SPEAR

PUBLISHED BY:

Wilde Ink Publishing

You Had Me at Cougar

Copyright © 2020 by Terry Spear

Cover Copyright by Moonstruck Cover Design

Discover more about Terry Spear at:

http://www.terryspear.com/

Print ISBN: 978-1-63311-074-8

Ebook ISBN:978-1-63311-075-5

# SYNOPSIS

Master baker Ava Lamar has one mission in mind after baking tons of treats for the Fourth of July celebration in Yuma Town—swimming at Lake Buchanan on this hot summer's day. What she doesn't expect is to be saddled with running the fortune telling booth—using her real psychic abilities—and giving a hot, bachelor cougar a place to stay for the whole weekend.

Cougar Shifter Force Special Agent Chet Kensington has just finished a tough mission, been chewed up a bit by rogue cougars, and he's taking a break to be with his old team, but he has no place to stay, everything being booked up in Yuma Town for the big cougar celebration. When Ava reluctantly allows him to stay with her, he finds himself drawn to her the whole celebration long.

But back home in Wyoming, things are getting out of hand. A serial killer is murdering female cougars and he and some of his old team have to find him, pronto. The problem is all the trouble leads right back to Ava—and now he has to do his best to keep her safe before the killer adds her to his list of victims.

*To Lora Allen who loves cats and rescues them and helps to find them homes, this big cat book is dedicated to you!*

# 1

Heart pounding, Ava Lamar, cougar shifter and baker extraordinaire, was running away from a large male cougar. He was angry and in hot pursuit. She didn't know why he was targeting her, but she felt he was dangerous and if she didn't lose him before he caught up to her, she could die.

She needed to reach the river well ahead of him and hide her scent to escape the danger. But he was hunting her with fierce determination. If, as a cougar she could sweat, she would have been melting.

She made it to the river, no sign of him and she had hope that she could actually lose him. She started to swim across the river. Don't look back. Don't look back. It will only slow you down.

She wished she could swim faster, but the current was strong, and she was only making negligible headway.

When she finally reached the riverbank, she looked back. He was leaping into the water. Damn it.

She headed straight for the forest. He would be able to track her scent. She wished she was a wolf and she could howl her distress. She ran through the forest, her thoughts switching from where she needed to go to how far he had made it across the river.

Through the woods, the cliffs were looming ahead. She knew she *couldn't outfight him or even outrun him now. She wasn't sure what she was going to do, but she had to keep her wits about her. All she could think of was getting to the top of the cliffs and then deciding what to do next.*

*She was certain no one would find her missing until it was too late.*

The phone rang and Ava was suddenly yanked out of the world she'd found herself. She glanced at the phone. And blinked. She was in her living room, watching a movie that night, and she'd totally zoned out. She wasn't having a nightmare. She hadn't lived the experience. She'd been having a premonition, as real as it had been. And, judging by the color of leaves on the trees, it was still summer when she would be on the run for her life.

EARLY THE NEXT MORNING, a special agent with the Cougar Special Forces, CSF, who took down rogue cougar shifters and humans who killed cougars, Chet Kensington had finally finished up a big case of eliminating three cougar shifters who had been killing cougars for the sport of it, hunting out of season, without licenses, and leaving the carcasses behind. And they had killed five hunters who had tried to turn them in. It made no sense to Chet that anyone, especially shifters who understood how it felt to be in cougar form and hunted, would be so cruel to any of the cougar kind. But rogues were rogues, and they didn't have to have a lot of motivation to kill.

Chet was so ready to take a well-deserved break and enjoy a fun 4th of July holiday with the cougars of Yuma Town. They took care of their own and everyone got along exceptionally well. He envisioned swimming in Lake Buchanan at Chase and Shannon Buchanan's Pinyon Pines Resort, getting some fishing in, water sports, fireworks, visiting with his friends. That's what he was looking forward to. Besides, his boss, Chuck Warner, had put him on sick leave after being injured in the fight with the rogue cougars.

Chet called up his former partner and friend, Travis MacKay, in the Cougar Special Forces branch located in Yuma Town, to see if he, or someone else, could put him up for the next couple of nights. Chet usually stayed at the CSF safe house for special agents when he visited Yuma Town, but Travis had told him that they were doing a lot of renovations, so he was going to see if anyone else could take him in.

As soon as Chet arrived at Travis and Bridget's house—Bridget also worked for CSF—they had him come in and have a beer. He'd had the fleeting notion while he'd been working with Bridget on cases out of Cheyenne, Wyoming, where they had all worked until Travis and Bridget came here, that he could even date her. But Bridget and Travis had connected in a way that Chet and she hadn't. He was glad for them. Though he was still looking for that special cougar to be *his* one and only.

"So," Bridget said, "Stryker said his mate, Nina, is checking with her sister, Ava, to see if she can take you in."

Stryker Hill was their deputy sheriff and so was Nina. Ava was a baker at Fitz's Bakery and Coffee Shop.

"She's a single she-cat." Not that Chet was averse to staying with a single she-cat, but *she* might be averse to having a bachelor male staying with *her*.

"Right. But she's the only one we could find who might have some space for you to stay," Bridget said. "As far as we know, she has an extra bedroom and no guests. Now, you know she is psychic and that means she needs some alone time. Downtime, if she starts to get her premonitions."

He wondered about that since Bridget could read minds, and he had learned Ava's twin sister could see future events too. Did

Nina need the space from others after working all day as a deputy sheriff? Bridget would work long hours with the CSF too. Maybe it all had to do with using their abilities and if they didn't, they wouldn't need to take time to rest from them.

"I will give her the space she needs." That was saying she would even allow Chet to stay with her.

"I'm ready to head over to the lake now. What about you?" Travis asked Chet.

"I sure am." Chet was so ready to just have fun and let loose.

"Ava will be at the lake later. Tell her thanks when you see her, if she lets you stay with her," Bridget said.

"I will. See you in a little bit." Chet really hadn't expected to be staying with someone other than his good friends.

"You did a fantastic job taking down those three men who were killing the cougars and human hunters," Travis said to Chet.

"Thanks. I sure could have used your help. Or Bridget's. Leyton's too. I've been crazy busy out that way because I haven't had much backup."

"I hear Chuck's going to hire a couple of more agents to work that region."

"Yeah, he is. He just hasn't found anyone qualified enough yet." Chet was even hoping that one of the agents he hired was a woman. Chet had the notion that if Chuck did, maybe Chet would work with her and fall in love with the she-cat like Travis and Bridget had done.

"We have been really busy too, but hopefully next time, one of us can come out to assist you." Travis got a call and smiled. "Yeah, Nina, Chet's here. I'll tell him." He got off the phone and they climbed into his car. "Nina's going to talk to her sister at the bakery, if she can spare her guest bedroom. We'll have an answer soon."

"Okay. I mean, I could just sleep at the lake in my cougar coat, somewhere safe."

"You could, but we'll give you a room somewhere. Sleeping on the couch at one of our places even. We'll manage," Travis said.

AVA LAMAR WAS busy baking at Fitz's Bakery and Coffee Shop, preparing cakes for all the July fourth birthdays and party cakes and cookies for the 4th of July celebration. It was a sunny, 96 degrees outside and despite the air conditioning inside she was sweltering just doing all the baking in the kitchen. She was so ready to strip off her clothes and throw on a bikini and dive into the lake, lie around on a float for a few hours, and just enjoy herself. The heat was perfect for that.

Her brother-in-law, Deputy Sheriff Stryker Hill, was in charge of crowds for the morning, until everything was set up. Then she saw her sister bounce into the shop. Ava swore Nina bounced—her step springy because she was so excited about all the celebrations. She had the day off from serving as a deputy sheriff and was helping to organize all the events. Ava knew that gleam in her sister's eye meant she was about to ask her to do something for the celebration when Ava felt she'd done quite enough. She was helping to provide a lot of the baked treats for the event after all.

She wanted to just kick back and enjoy the rest of the day. The shop was closing in an hour and she was thrilled. The owner, Florence Fitzgerald, had already headed over to the celebration, to supervise the setting up of the tables to display their baked goods. Ava didn't think she'd ever worked this hard at the bakery since she started working there.

"Before you say no, I have a favor to ask of you," Nina said.

Ava rolled her eyes. "You know"—she motioned to all the cakes and cookies she'd made—"you could ask how I was doing first. Or say, happy Fourth of July to me or something." She loved her sister, but really...

"Happy Fourth to you."

Ava finished cleaning up. "What do you want me to do?"

"Well, if you really don't want to do it, I'll try to find someone else to ask, but—"

"Just spill it." Because her sister was so hesitant to just come out with it, Ava figured it was something she *really* wouldn't want to do.

"Just for an hour, if you can manage our fortune telling booth from one to two, I would be forever grateful. The proceeds go to the Big Cat Rescue and we had a couple of people who were willing to be the gypsy fortune tellers, but something came up. I would do it, but I've got to be in charge of the sack races for the kids and if someone else doesn't volunteer to take over the fortune telling job before you're done with your shift, I'll take over for you."

Ava let out her breath. "You know if someone comes up to the booth and I see something in their future that is going to affect them, I'll feel obligated to tell them what's bound to happen."

"Well, you can just fake it."

"Yeah, but everyone knows we have second vision, and if I just say something silly, they're going to think *that* will really happen." Because it had. Both Ava and Nina had done that when they were growing up, not wanting to tell people who plagued them about learning something about their futures— mostly because others didn't believe they could see premonitions of future events so they were testing them—just silly stuff —like so and so was breaking up with them, or seeing someone else. But making up stuff had really backfired. Boy, were others mad at them. So in Yuma Town, where people really did know they could see future events sometimes, they had to be more careful.

"Okay, well, I'll try to get someone else to volunteer then." Nina glanced at all the cakes and cookies Ava had made. "You've outdone yourself."

"Thanks. I'll do it, all right? Just for an hour. I need to get some float time in." Ava couldn't believe how Nina could always make her feel guilty if she didn't do something for her. Maybe because Nina was working her butt off during the festivities, when all Ava wanted to do was go out and play.

Nina smiled and gave her a hug, getting remnants of flour all over her. "You are the best sister in the world."

"You say so now, but if I see something someone doesn't like, I'm sending them to tell you all about it." Ava smiled.

"Works for me." Nina hurried out of the shop as if she were afraid Ava would change her mind.

Not that Ava would. Once she promised to do something, she would do it. She packed up all the baked goods and Florence picked them up to deliver to the resort.

An hour later, Ava turned the shop sign from open to closed and locked the shop up after finishing to clean up.

She drove home to her own little townhouse that she'd just moved into and couldn't be happier. The place was all decorated in turquoise with accessories of purple and light gray as the base color. Her own place. Even her garden was filled with purple flowers of salvia, sage, lupine, violets, bellflower, iris, veronica, buddelia, lavender, tulips, purple statice, lilacs, liatris, larkspur, columbine, and ageratum.

She arrived home and hurried inside, stripping out of her clothes from the front door, that was now closed and locked, and up the stairs to the bedrooms, kicking off her sandals, stripping out of her skirt, shirt, bra, and panties. Naked, she made it to the landing and raced into the bedroom to put on her swimsuit, shorts, a shirt, and shoved her feet into her flipflops. She grabbed her beach bag off the chest of drawers that she'd already filled with sunscreen, a beach towel, and a bottle of water. She hurried down the stairs to the kitchen, dropping her bag on the dining table, and then threw together a ham sandwich—off-the-bone sliced ham, white bread, lettuce, mayonnaise, and mustard and stood at the island counter eating it. She had every intention of swimming before she had to do her part as a fortune teller, passing along all kinds of good news, she hoped. And then swimming again afterward.

Then she got a call and looked at the caller ID. It was her sister's mate, Stryker, calling. Now what? She answered her phone. "Yeah?"

"Hey, I hate to ask, but—"

Ava sighed. "Nina already asked me to be the fortune teller for an hour."

"I thought we had that covered."

Uh-oh, if Stryker wasn't calling about that, then what did *he* want her to do?

"Apparently, someone fell through on the fortune-telling booth assignment," Ava said.

"Oh, okay. Well, no, that wasn't what I was calling about. But thanks for helping out with it. Nina was going to tell you that Chet Kensington needs a place to stay for the night, or two. She said she had forgotten to ask you and was headed out to the lake. Chet thought he would still be working on the case he was dealing with, but he managed to get free and wanted to join us, but everyone has got house guests and the Pinyon Pines Resort at Lake Buchanan and local hotels are booked."

Ava wanted to snarl as a cougar. She didn't want anyone to stay with her. She would have to pick up her place and be ready for a guest. And if she had a guest, she wanted to be the one who invited him or her. She'd met Chet before, naturally, as he came to see his old buddy, Leyton, who was her brother-in-law's brother, Travis, and his mate, Bridget, all of whom had worked with him in the Cougar Special Forces in Cheyenne, Wyoming. But he had always stayed at the safe house before.

"He can't stay at the safe house?" Ava knew the answer to her question before Stryker answered her, because if Chet could have stayed there, Stryker wouldn't be asking her if Chet could stay with her.

"It's currently under renovations."

She let out her breath in a huff. "All right." That didn't mean she wanted to take him in as an overnight guest or anything else, so when did she become such a pushover? What if she became interested in someone who lived in Yuma Town, and he learned she'd had a bachelor cougar stay with her? Ugh.

"I've got to go," she said.

"I'll tell him to talk to you at the fortune telling booth then." Stryker sounded vastly relieved that she would take Chet in.

"Great." And she didn't mean it in a good way. Of course then she felt guilty about being kind of a curmudgeon about it.

She quickly ended the call. If she didn't hurry, she wasn't going to have one minute to swim. She rushed to Lake Buchanan in her neon green Honda and arrived there with forty minutes to spare. Yes. She pumped her fist and hurried to get out of the car. Cougars were everywhere, in human form, naturally, at the by-invitation-only event. Which meant anyone there had to be a cougar to attend.

Everyone was hurrying to get ready for all the activities. Moms and dads were trying to keep track of all the little ones, most wearing floaties so they wouldn't get themselves in trouble in the shallower water at the lake's edge.

As soon as Ava headed for the water, she saw the dreaded fortune teller booth, all decorated in purples and golds and little castle flags, near the concession stands where people were already grabbing lunches to go. It looked like it belonged at a medieval fair, and she thought it appeared magical and entertaining. And that made her feel better about working there. Especially since she was going to get a dip in the lake *first*.

She set her mermaid bag down on the beach, kicked off her flipflops, tugged off her T-shirt and shorts, grabbed her mermaid float, and raced into the water.

"Hey, Ava." a male voice shouted at her.

No, no, no. She was going to get some swimming time in before she did anything else. She could just imagine someone telling her she needed to start even earlier at the fortune telling booth. She hadn't paid attention to see if there was a line at it, or anyone working it yet, just that the concession stands were crowded, and the booth was pretty. She just wanted to get away from the beach and into the water.

She continued to ignore the man belonging to the deep voice. When she was far enough away, she turned to see who it was. Chet Kensington, pulling off his shirt, kicking off his shoes, and pulling down his shorts. Her jaw dropped in surprise. Oh, he had board shorts on underneath his Bermuda shorts. And a gorgeously bared chest. He waded out into the warm water. She frowned. Where did he think *he* was going?

She wanted, needed solitude before she began to give up her psychic secrets. The problem with her serving as a fortune teller was that she made an awful actress. Keeping a straight face, if she thought something bad was going to happen to someone, and just making up something else that would be lame and not upset anyone wasn't something she could do—and make it believable. Part of the problem was they were all cougars and could smell fear or deception on someone.

She sighed. Even when she had seen Chet stripping out of his clothes, she had envisioned him wearing form-fitting boxer briefs, or...ahem, nothing at all and her mouth had gaped wide open. She was sure, if he'd seen her surprised expression, he would have been amused.

He began swimming out to her, powerful muscles flexing as he pulled the water past him and drew closer. If he'd been her boyfriend, she could imagine him reaching her, pulling her from her float into his arms, and kissing the daylights out of her. It was a good thing he couldn't read her mind and didn't have any psychic abilities whatsoever. But after Chet had worked with Bridget, who could read minds, he had become a firm believer in psychics. Which she appreciated. Skeptics were one thing. She understood when they wouldn't believe in her abilities. But when they tried to say she was a charlatan, that was another thing.

Maybe he was going to tell her that he had found a place to bunk, other than her place. Now she felt guilty for ignoring him when he was calling out to her from the beach.

When he reached her, he sent ripples of water her way, rocking her float, but it was in a lulling manner and that was nice.

"Hey, sorry about putting you out when you have to give me a place to stay for the weekend, but I really appreciate it," he said.

For the whole weekend? She sighed. "No problem." So much for getting a reprieve.

"Ava said that after spending the day with a lot of people, you need time to recuperate."

"I do, thanks, when I have psychic visions. It just wears me out. Baking in a hot kitchen does too." Which made her seem lame—here she was a powerful cougar with lots of stamina. Not only that but he had some tough cases to handle and here she was talking about being worn out from baking cookies and cakes? He must have thought she was an idiot.

"I'll spend some time with the guys I work with and come to your place just to sleep then."

Now she felt *really* guilty. "You can, if that's what you want to do, but if it doesn't work out, you're free to come and have a bite to eat with me at my house tonight, watch TV, or whatever you want to do." What was the matter with her? He just gave her an out, and she was telling him it was okay to forgo other plans and chill out with her? When it was the furthest thing from what she wanted to do?

"We'll see." He was treading water next to her, being nice, which he should be, considering she was giving him a free room for a couple of nights, and she felt grouchy—but mostly because all of a sudden she had to be a gypsy fortune teller and now allow a near stranger—male cougar hot--to stay with her. "Can I pay you something for the stay?"

Yes. He made a lot more money than she did as a special agent of the CSF when she just worked as a baker. But that wouldn't be very nice to make him pay for his stay. Though if he'd stayed at a hotel or one of the cabins, he would have paid top dollar for the summer. "No, thanks. I appreciate the offer though."

If he had been her boyfriend, and she had to admit he had the looks that counted—blond hair, blue eyes that peered right into her soul, and a nicely manly chin, and the rest of him wasn't shabby either, especially the rest of him—she could envision his arms resting on her float, his chin on top of them as he smiled up at her.

But he wasn't her boyfriend, and he wasn't touching the float or smiling. She would say he appeared to be at a loss of what to say or do next. She hadn't expected that of the special agent who, according to Bridget, was good at taking the bad guys down without a moment's hesitation. He never flinched. He was always up for the challenge. She knew he had been dating on and off in Cheyenne, Wyoming where he was from and worked out of, but she didn't think he would be so tongue-tied with her.

"Okay, well, I'll leave you to it," he said, hesitating, as if he hoped she would say something to encourage him to visit a while longer when here she thought he had come to Yuma Town to visit with his friends.

"Uh, they're having fireworks until eleven tonight. I'll be at the townhouse after that." She realized she wasn't going to be chilling at the house either, but out here all day, and until late tonight. Which meant no dinner plans at home, just grabbing barbecued chicken, ribs or fish, chips, and drinks, and watching the fireworks out here.

"Oh, sure, that's true. Okay, well, thanks. See you then." He began to swim away.

"Wait, do you know what time it is?" She wondered how much time she had to swim before she had to become a gypsy fortune teller.

"When I looked at my phone before I swam out here, it was a quarter of one."

Quarter of one already? That's when Ava saw her sister waving from the shore with a gypsy outfit in hand. *Great. Just great.* So much for swimming in solitude.

"I hope Nina is waving at you with that garb and not me." Chet cast a smile over his shoulder at Ava. He had a nice, sexy smile that said he could easily win a woman over and break her heart afterward.

She chuckled. She liked a man with a sense of humor. "She needed a volunteer and volunteered me when someone else couldn't make it. But I don't see why a guy couldn't be a fortune teller. Kind of like a genie in a lamp, except not granting wishes but glimpses of their future. Not for real though."

"Not like you can offer. I know I couldn't fit in that garb, so I'll give it a pass."

She smiled. Then she sighed. Okay, so with dating men, Ava hadn't had much luck. Not that she was interested in jumping Chet's bones. Well, maybe a little.

She flipped over on her belly, but hadn't judged just how much room she had, or kept her balance, and ended up in the drink. She was a cougar, for heaven's sake. She should have had better balance and sense than that.

She came up for air and found Chet treading water, watching her to make sure she was okay. That wasn't necessary, but nice of him, she thought. Though she was thoroughly embarrassed, and she felt like she'd received an instant sunburn, her face was so hot. She climbed back onto the float, settling herself on her stomach, and began swimming for shore.

He joined her. Though she figured he could swim faster than she could swim on a float, he was keeping pace with her.

When they finally reached the shore, she dried off and then took the gypsy costume from Nina. It had a bikini kind of top with tassels and sheer fabric on the arms, banded at the wrists. The pants were made similarly, and she felt like Jeannie in *I Dream of Jeannie* as she grabbed her bag and clothes she'd had over her swimsuit, went into the booth, closed the curtains and stripped out of her wet bathing suit. She pulled the towel out of her bag and dried off, then slipped on her bra and panties. Once she was wearing the gold and purple genie costume and her sandals, she brushed out her damp hair and wrapped it in a chignon.

When she looked at her phone, she saw it was showtime. She sighed and opened the curtains to the booth and found a dripping wet Chet standing in front of her booth, first in line. "Madame Ava, I wish to have my fortune read." Chet handed her a one-hundred-dollar bill.

"Is it real?" She couldn't believe he would give her that much money for a reading.

He chuckled. "I take down the bad guys, remember? So I wouldn't give you a counterfeit bill."

"Uh, sure." She smiled and put the money in a box on a shelf below the window of her booth. "And thanks. The big cats at the reserve will appreciate it."

"Anything for the cougars. So how do we do this?" he asked.

"I can make something up," she offered helpfully. She noticed a line was already forming behind him and she heard someone say, "One of the psychic twins is giving fortunes."

"Or?" He smiled at her.

She thought he was too masculine, too adventurous for his own good and would want to know the truth. And he *had* contributed a lot of money to the Big Cat Reserve for this. But she didn't want to learn that anything bad was coming up in his life and with the kind of job he worked, it could.

"I can read your palm," she said.

He reached his hand out to her, palm up.

She knew this wasn't a good idea one iota. Not if she learned something really bad was going to happen to him, though she figured if she did, maybe a warning would help him avoid getting killed over it.

## 2

C het sensed the tension in Ava as soon as he offered his hand for her to give him a reading. He knew she was a true psychic, and he wondered if she would give him a true reading or something that was just made up. He could handle it if she wanted to tell him his life was in danger or something like that. He lived for danger. It was all part of his job. Though he hoped she could tell him a bit of good news. Like if he had to appre-hend or eliminate rogue cougars, he would survive the mission.

She frowned as she took his hand and ran her finger over his lifeline. "It's good news. You're going to get a pay raise."

"Really?" He was so surprised at her reading, he wasn't sure what to think. Was it for real, or made up to disguise something bad? Maybe she'd just been tense because she'd worried she might see something bad and she couldn't see anything about him.

"Take the good news and go spend some more money on something else," Chase Buchanan said behind him. He was a part-time deputy sheriff and the owner of the Pinyon Pines

Resort on Lake Buchanan, and Chet knew he was just joking with him.

Chet arched a brow at him. "I just paid a hundred dollars. I need a little more of my fortune read."

"Isn't a pay raise enough?" Chase asked, frowning at him, but he was just playing with him. "Tell him what he wants to hear, Ava. He's going to be in a world of danger before he knows it."

Chet laughed. With the kind of work he did, that was a given.

"Tell him he's going to lose the canoe race to me if he doesn't paddle hard enough," Chase added.

Chet doubted she would see anything like that. It wasn't a situation that would be dire enough, as far as he thought.

"I can tell you right now, neither of you will win," Ava said, looking perfectly serious.

"Oh, so who does?" Chase looked surprised that she would know that, despite knowing she had real psychic visions.

"Me."

Chase laughed. Chet smiled, but he again wondered if she knew it for real or she was she just playing with them.

"You are going to be in the worst sort of danger," Ava said, looking really serious, frowning. Then she smiled brightly.

"Seriously?"

"Of course, with your line of work it's inevitable. Next."

Smiling, Chet moved out of the way and folded his arms, watching while Chase got his reading. Ava took his hand and said, "Oh, you are going to be in the worst kind of danger."

Chase smiled and shook his head. "I know. It goes with my line of work as a deputy sheriff." Chase left to let the next person in line get their fortune read, Mandy Jones, their nurse at the clinic. He was about to say something to Chet but stopped to hear what Ava had to say to Mandy. She was one of the newest members of the cougar family, having been accidentally turned by her former boyfriend Ricky, also a deputy sheriff, who had also been newly turned earlier—not born as cougar shifters like the rest of them.

"You are expecting twins in the fall," Ava said, smiling.

"Ohmigod, really? For real? No joke?"

"Yeah, for real."

"Ohmigod. I've got to get back to the clinic. I just had a break to have my fortune read. I guess I'm going to have to have a blood test then." Mandy reached into the booth and gave Ava a hug. Then she pulled out her phone and hurried off. "Ricky, we are having twins. No, I didn't know. Ava told my fortune. Yes, for real. No, she wasn't making stuff up. Aren't you glad? Yes, yes, I'm getting a blood test to confirm it. Aren't you glad?"

Chet chuckled. "Ricky is going to be experiencing fatherhood sooner than he planned, it appears."

Chase agreed. "So how are things going for you?"

"Oh, busy as usual."

Vanessa Rugel, the veterinarian in Yuma Town, smiled at Ava. "So what do you see for me?"

"You..." Ava frowned. "Have you ever heard of white cougars?"

"They're rare. I've never seen one for real. I've just seen them in books."

"So you save one's life."

Vanessa stared her. "Truly?"

"Yeah, really."

"Wow, thanks, Ava. A white cougar." Vanessa thanked her again and then moved out of the way for the next person in line.

Carl Nelson, the reporter who had been a pest in Yuma Town earlier as he tried to figure out what was going on with the cougars and was bitten and now was one of them and writing for the local newspaper, was up next to have his fortune read.

"You will be chased by a hunter all over the surrounding area as a trophy," Ava warned.

Carl frowned. "Seriously? Do I evade him?"

"Trees are covered in yellow leaves at the time he's after you. Then when it's snowing, I see you photographing snowmen sculptures for the newspaper. So I think you're good."

Carl sighed with relief. Now he would know how it felt to be one of them when a hunter was on their tail, just like when he was always trying to learn what was going on with them.

"How are things going with you with the cabins and deputy sheriff business?" Chet asked Chase as Ava continued giving readings.

"Busy too. It seems I'm always doing renovations on the cabins, updating them, doing some more woodwork and then we've got to deal with deputy sheriffing issues."

Chet saw Chase's mate, Shannon, waving at him and then pointing to their girls.

Chase waved back and smiled. "Looks like I've got kid duty. We'll talk later. I'm so glad you finished that assignment and were able to make it here to celebrate with us."

"Me too."

The next person in line didn't smell like a cougar, but rather like a bear.

Ava confirmed that he didn't belong here. "You don't have an invitation to be here. This is a by-invitation-only event. I'm afraid that you have to leave."

"My money is as good as anyone else's," the man gruffly said.

"That's not the point. This property is privately-owned, and the owner is hosting the private party by-invitation-only," Ava said.

"You smell like you handle bears," Chet said, getting involved when the guy didn't seem to be planning to take Ava's advice.

The man stood six-four, had curly black hair, a black beard, and dark brown eyes that focused now on Chet. "You smell like you handle cougars."

Chet smiled. "Fair enough. Why don't you come with me and we can have a private talk?"

"I heard the fortune teller is really psychic. I need to know where my sister is."

Ava was already texting someone, Chet figured Chase or one of the other deputies or the sheriff.

But he was surprised to see Bridget show up. Like Chet, she was CSF, not with the sheriff's department. Bridget nodded to Ava and she said, "Okay, I'll give you a reading. But that's it. Then you need to leave."

Chet saw Chase and Dan Steinacker, the sheriff, headed their way. Ava must have sent a text to all of them.

The man reached his hand out to Ava, and she held his hand and closed her eyes. "I see a woman breaking into a cabin and then a big brown bear trying to break in after her."

"Where? What does the woman look like? The bear?"

"She has long, chestnut hair, and she's wearing hiking boots, jeans, and a T-shirt, a light jacket tied around her waist. Her skin was perspiring."

"That's Ursula. Where is the cabin?"

"I don't know. It's in the woods. Predictions can be unreliable. It may happen now, tomorrow, a month from now."

"Autumn? Bare branches?"

"Green, summer. The cabin has a weathered red door."

"That sounds like Shutter's cabin," Dan said, frowning, his arms folded across his chest.

"So now, what about the bear?" the man asked.

"Big. Brown. Beady eyes. Long claws," Ava said.

"Dark brown? Light brown? Blackish-brown fur?"

Ava opened her eyes. "Brown. And big."

"Don't tell me you think all bears look alike."

Ava smiled and then she frowned. "I hope you're able to reach your sister in time to protect her from the bear."

Dan offered his hand to the man. "I'm Sheriff Dan Steinacker, and this is Deputy Chase Buchanan. We can help you locate your sister. Why don't you come this way?"

The man shook Dan's hand. "Jonathon Browning."

"Wait, you didn't pay for your reading," Ava said, then flushed furiously as if she realized he was worried about his sister, and she shouldn't be charging him.

"Proceeds go to...?" Jonathon asked.

"The Big Cat Reserve," she said.

"If the money went to a bear reserve, I would pay more." Jonathon fished out his wallet and gave her a five.

"Even though a bear is chasing your sister and I might have helped you to locate her?" she asked.

Jonathon only gave her a tight smile.

"If you need my help, let me know," Chet said to Dan.

"Will do," Dan said.

Bridget told Ava, "He's a bear. And the woman he is after and the bear chasing her down is some other bear but I'm not sure that she doesn't want to mate him," Bridget said. "At least that was something that Jonathon was concerned about."

Chet realized Bridget hadn't come to deal with Jonathon, but to read his mind. Chet would never get used to her doing that.

Shannon was back to watching the kids when Chase had to take off on the bear rescue mission.

Even though a long line of cougar shifters were waiting to see Ava, no one minded the wait, not when the cougars were all like family and everything that was going on concerning them interested them.

Dan's wife, Addie, was next in line and she held her hand out. "What do you see in my future?"

"Uhm..." Ava cleared her throat. How could she tell Addie

she would be in an emergency situation as a deputy sheriff, delivering Mandy's babies? Ricky was nowhere to be seen, though Ava only got bits and pieces, but Addie was definitely delivering a baby in the backseat of a car.

Addie frowned. "Maybe I don't want to know."

"No, it's just..." Ava sighed. "Okay, you're going to be delivering a baby in an emergency situation. You might want to get a book to read up on it."

Addie's mouth gaped. "Whose?"

"Uhm, Mandy's."

"Okay, so I'll talk to Kate about putting Mandy on bedrest for that last three months of her pregnancy." Addie sighed. "And failing that, I'll get a book on emergency deliveries. All of us at the sheriff's department could use that in a crisis."

Ava smiled. "That's just the ticket."

"Okay, I've got to get back to work." Addie shook her head and hurried off.

The next person in the line to get her fortune read was Dottie Barrington. "I see your booth is really popular, now that you have taken it over. Everyone wants the real news, not some pretend stuff, even if it can be bad news. But a bear shifter here? Now that takes the cake." She gave Ava twenty dollars for the reading.

"Yeah I know. I had a dream about a bear chasing me earlier this year, and maybe it was a shifter, not just a wild bear. Who would ever have figured, right?" Ava said.

"A premonition or a dream?" Dottie asked, looking concerned.

So was Chet. Even though he meant to get some swimming in or visit with folks, he couldn't make himself move away from Ava's booth for anything. He was fascinated with her ability to see future events in people's lives. Bridget smiled at Chet, patted his shoulder, and headed back to where Travis was taking care of their two-year-olds.

"A dream, I thought. And then I realized I'd had a premonition. It makes me wonder if it has to do with Jonathon and his sister. Now I'm not sure. So, let me read your palm."

Dottie turned her palm up. "Don't tell me I'm delivering anyone's babies or going to have any more kids of my own. As much as I love them, five is enough. And if we have more kids, Jack's going to have to go back to the clinic to have it snipped again."

Chet felt in pain for Jack all of a sudden.

Ava glanced at him and smiled as if she knew just what he was thinking about.

"Or," Dottie said, "Jack will think I've been seeing someone else."

"No, way," Ava said. "Okay, I see you are having a celebration in a little while of your own."

"A celebration. We're doing that all day today."

"Jack just finished his mission south of Yuma Town and he'll be here shortly."

Dottie smiled. "That's great. Thanks so much."

Tracey came up next. Her husband, Hal Haverton, was also a part-time deputy sheriff, ranch owner, and he was working with the U.S. Fish and Wildlife Service as a special agent with Tracey. She had quadruplets by her husband and the first thing she said to Ava was, "Ditto for me. Something other than I'm pregnant. I'm thrilled for Mandy though. So what do you see for me?"

"Your horse, Misty, is going to foal."

"What? We had no plan to breed her. Wow, okay, thanks." Tracey began texting away and left.

Deputy Sheriff Ricky Jones was standing in line after that, arms folded, looking cross. "Mandy's excited about having twins and mad at me because I sounded shocked instead of being as excited as she is."

Ava smiled. "Sorry, Ricky. I am just giving everyone a reading. It just happened hers showed she was pregnant with twins and they're due in the fall. I thought you had already both known. Do you want me to read your palm?"

Ricky kept his arms folded across his chest.

Kolby, Ricky's older brother, gently pushed Ricky's shoulder. "Get it done or move out of line. I want to get my fortune read and the new fortune teller is coming, and she doesn't have true insight."

Ava was so glad that her relief was going to be here soon. She was ready to swim again. She was getting hot.

"All right." Ricky gave Ava a twenty-dollar bill.

"An old girlfriend is coming to town and you'd better find a way to ditch her quickly."

Ricky's mouth gaped. "No way."

"Yeah, way, Deputy Sheriff." Ava smiled.

Ava could be so wicked. Chet knew she had dated Ricky too, until his old girlfriend, Mandy, turned up, ran into him with her car, accidentally, and he bit her, as a cougar, accidentally. He better not bite the new old girlfriend.

"Great. Her name?" Ricky asked.

"I have no idea, but she won't be easily thwarted."

Ricky ran his hands through his hair and glanced at Kolby, who winked at him. "Mel Paccato, betcha. And her dad has ties to the Mob. I told you she was bad news, and you shouldn't have dated her."

Ricky's jaw dropped. "Great. It just better not be." He headed off to do his deputy duties.

Kolby stepped up to the booth next. "Do you see anything for me?"

Ava looked tired, like she had seen about all she could handle. Chet wanted to rescue her.

Ava read his palm. "You will have some good news this fall."

Kolby frowned. "About?"

"I'm not sure, but you're ecstatic, and I see Jack-O'-Lanterns in the vision, so it will happen around Halloween, it appears."

"Are you sure? Hmm." Kolby brightened, "Ted is finally going to let me take on some more leadership roles at the ranch."

Smiling, Ted Weekum, Hal and Tracey Haverton's horse ranch foreman shook his head.

Kolby turned and grinned at Ted. "Thanks, Boss." Then he thanked Ava and hurried off.

"What about me?" Ted asked Ava, stretching out his palm after giving her a twenty. "Am I going to give Kolby more reign over the ranch?"

"You do. It will take a lot for that to happen, but it will."

Ted frowned. "So what's going to happen?"

Ava shrugged. "You know me and my visions. I just see bits and pieces."

"Okay, thanks, Ava."

Amy Mayflower, the sheriff's department dispatcher was up next, with her eleven-year-old son, Bobby, and her husband, Deacon, who was a news reporter and doing some cougar-human interest stories for the paper.

"Bobby, you go first."

Bobby was eager, but he was also looking a little apprehensive. Chet hoped Ava didn't have bad news for the boy.

"Your girlfriend is going to give you a great gift for Christmas, but I can't tell you what it is." Ava smiled.

The boy's jaw dropped. "I'll have a girlfriend." He pumped his fist and yelled out, "Yes." Then he ran off, calling to some other kids. "Hey, you don't know what I learned."

Amy smiled at Ava. "I hope that they don't have a terrible breakup in their future. So what about me?"

Ava touched her hand and closed her eyes. "You're going to win at some contest today."

"But I'm supposed to return to the sheriff's department as soon as I eat."

"Maybe you win something later." Ava shrugged, but she sounded certain it would be soon.

Deacon offered his hand then. "What can you see about me?"

She laughed. "Sorry. You're going to take in a stray kitten, and Amy and your son are going to be shocked."

Deacon laughed. "Okay, thanks."

"I'm here as your relief," Nina said. "Kolby's in charge of the canoe race and I heard you were going to beat everyone, so get to it."

When other cougars saw that Ava's relief was her twin sister, the line grew long again.

"RIGHT," Ava said to Nina, though she couldn't imagine beating all the guys. They were really gung-ho when it came to competitions. She closed the curtains, hurried to strip off the gypsy costume, her bra and her panties, then pulled on her damp swimsuit and put on a long-sleeved rashguard over that. Then she packed her clothes—including the fortune teller costume that she would wash later—into her bag, before she left the booth to her sister.

Chet hurried after Ava.

"I thought you might go swimming or something instead of just standing there while I had to be the fortune teller," Ava said to Chet, surprised he had hung around the whole time, watching her "perform." She thought he would surely visit with his friends some.

"Seeing you come up with your predictions, and observing the disbelief on the recipients' faces, and the joy they expressed —well, all except for Ricky—was fascinating. Pure entertainment. Everyone seemed pleased."

"Except for Ricky, well, and the bear shifter. I keep thinking we'll see a wolf show up around here again. But I never expected a bear." She picked out a bright orange canoe and Chet stayed with her. She frowned at him. "I have to beat you."

"I'm going with the winning team."

She smiled. "All right. I didn't see that in my vision, but it could work out, I guess."

"What exactly did you see?" Chet climbed into the canoe in back of her as the stern paddler.

"That I made it to shore before everyone else."

"With you in the bow."

"Maybe."

"Wait for us," Chase shouted.

"I thought you were helping out with the bear situation." Chet sounded surprised to see Chase back so soon.

"Jonathon said he would handle it himself, as soon as he knew where the cabin was. There was no arguing with a pigheaded bear." Chase and Shannon got into a bright yellow canoe, while some of the others watched their kids.

Eight other contestants had been waiting on Chase, then someone fired off a flare and the race was on.

va couldn't believe Chet would stand near her booth for nearly an hour until she was done, and that he had been ready to tackle the bear if he hadn't minded Ava and left. That was until they realized why he was there. She appreciated Chet's help. She still was surprised that Jonathon was a bear shifter and had come here looking for his sister and another bear. She hoped no cougars would be hurt in the process. Well, and that his sister would be all right.

"Why didn't you really swim or do something else while I was stuck in the fortune teller booth?" she asked Chet again.

"Everyone else appeared busy with kids and such. What you were doing was vastly more interesting."

She smiled as she looked back and watched him paddle, his muscles rippling like the waters about the canoe. "Well, thanks for being there for me in case Jonathon had turned out to pose a real threat. I visited Alaska last year, and by mistake I ended up in White Bear where shifters run the town. So it turned out to be providence. Amazingly enough, a polar bear couple are psychics too. It was fascinating to see polar bear shifters, snow leopards,

Arctic foxes and wolves, all shifters there. Oh, and they had grizzlies too. No cougars though."

"I would love to see it sometime. What made you go up
there?"

"I just wanted to take a trip up there. I had never been to
Alaska. They were surprised to see a cougar arrive. I was
surprised to see all the different kinds of shifters there."

"Sounds like a fun place to visit, as long as no one minds
cougars invading their territory." Chet was paddling hard,
expertly, as if he had been in competitions like this for years.

"They were thrilled to meet me." She glanced back at Chet.
"Have you done this before?"

"Paddled? Sure."

"No, in competitions," she said.

"No, but I'm a competitive sort. Besides, you said we were
going to win. So I have to do my best to prove to you that I was
part of the winning team."

Smiling, she glanced at the other canoes. Without him
paddling, she would never have won. She and Chet were way
ahead of all the others. She thought they had a good chance at
beating the rest of the competitors.

"Do your predictions always come true?" Chet asked.

"They do, but you never know the exact context. Like this. I
saw my boat coming in first, but I didn't see you in the boat
with me."

"Which is a surprise"—he flexed his broad, muscled shoulders—"since I would think it would be hard to miss seeing me."

She laughed. "Your muscles are getting a good workout.
What I saw was me getting out of the canoe and everyone
cheering me."

"So you didn't see me at all? Maybe I fall overboard, and you
made it to shore on your own."

She chuckled. "I'm sure if you fell overboard, we wouldn't win."

"Maybe we do this another time."

"We might, but the premonition was so clear that I'm sure it happens now. And from the looks of it, we're way in the lead." They turned the boat around and headed for shore.

Chase hollered, "Hurry, we can't let them win."

"Too late," Chet shouted. "We're on our way to first place."

To begin with, Ava hadn't even planned to paddle in the race. She had planned to swim. "So do you know what we're going to win?" She hoped it was something they could split between the two of them—a cash prize would be nice.

"A weekend at one of the cabins, and breakfast at Mrs. Fritz's bakery."

Ava's mouth dropped. Okay, that wasn't what she had in mind when it came to sharing her prize with her partner.

"We're going to win," he said. "You were so right on your prediction."

They reached the shore, and everyone was cheering them.

She was glad they'd won, if nothing else to prove her premonition was correct, though she still wished the prize had been something they could have divided up equally between them.

Chase and Shannon and the others finally made it to shore. "Hey, we couldn't win because we own the resort, so we're glad the two of you did."

Maybe Chet could pay her for half his win, and he could find a friend he wanted to share the cabin with.

Tracey handed Ava the gift certificate. "You're hanging onto it, right? Or is Chet going to?"

"She can hang onto it," Chet said. "We'll make plans later for our stay, when one of the cabins is available and we're both free to do it."

Ava wanted to roll her eyes at him, but she curbed the inclination.

Some of the adults and kids were flying kites. Some of the little ones were taking well-deserved naps on quilts under shade trees.

"What are you going to do next?" Chet asked, as if he thought he should tag along with her the rest of the day, just because he was staying at her place for the next couple of nights.

"Swim."

"You're not going to take part in the fishing contest?"

"Only if I got to do it as a cougar. I'm good at it, but not as a human."

"I can teach you."

"Are you lonely?" Did Chet think he had to keep her company because she was on her own? Or did he want to date her or something?

He chuckled. "I'm on my own. You're on your own."

"I'm going swimming." She headed for her bag, left the gift certificate in it, then made her way to the water.

He didn't follow her, but then said, "Do you want some company?"

She laughed, threw up her arms, and said, "Come on." She swore that half of the cougars on the beach were watching them. It was a good thing she wasn't thinking of dating some other guy she was interested in anytime soon.

Then Chet raced after her and she squealed. She was not a squealer, normally, but he just scared her in a fun way. She ran into the water and dove in. He ran through the shallow water, and where it dropped off, he dove for her.

They swam out to the floating dock and climbed onto it and sat down at the edge, kicking the water with their feet.

"I keep wondering if Jonathon has resolved the issue with the bear and his sister," Ava said.

"Everyone seems to be on the beach. Otherwise, I'm sure there would be a number of us going out to help him. I'm sure he feels it's a bear issue and a bear fighting a bear is a better match than some of us cougars."

"A tranquilizer gun always works." Ava noticed the kids were up from their naps and were building sandcastles.

"True, but sometimes the shifter kind have to take the rogue shifters to task using their animal instincts."

"Do you often have to do that?" She didn't. Not while working in a bakery.

"Yeah. Since the CSF deals with rogue cougars, that's often how they want to fight the special agents determined to take them down."

"What about the case of the three men you just had to deal with?" Ava asked. "You had a partner, right?"

"No. Anyone who could have been a partner on the mission was on another case. And Leyton and Travis were working their own cases. Bridget is still home with the kiddos."

"So you took on all three men at once?"

"We're cougars. We learn to prowl, stalk, and take advantage of the situation. The three of them figured they had the lead. Three of them to one of me. They never thought I would get the best of them. It was a cat and mouse game for several weeks. I should say cat and mice—because I was hunting them."

She was captivated by the idea, as much as she told herself she preferred baking to hunting, but it was in their blood—cougar blood. "Okay, so how did it all go down then?"

Chet rested his hands on the floating deck and looked over at her. "One of them was hiding in a cabin. The other two were waiting for me to come, sitting in trees, having the advantage of height."

"But you still took all three of them down by yourself." She figured he had to be really clever and outwit them to do that, not just stronger than all three cougars combined. She admired him for that.

"Yeah. I was wearing hunter's concealment."

"They didn't need to smell you, just see you."

"Right. I was at the cabin before they arrived. I overheard them talking about the cabin, its location and that was why they had to pick up food at the Chinese restaurant. It was the closest fast-food place to the cabin. Now, the problem was, were they telling the truth? Or did they know I knew they were going there, and it was a ruse?" Chet said.

"They weren't that smart." Ava figured it wasn't a ruse because he got his men.

"Right, not a ruse."

"But how did they know you were coming? I mean, they could have sat there for days before you caught up with them."

"True, but they knew I was only a short distance behind them. Every time I caught up to them, they got out of my reach by the skin of their teeth. This time, I was going to be ahead of them. I reached the cabin first, looked it and the surrounding area all over, and then picked my hiding spot. As much as it doesn't sound very brave, I hid under the bed, waited while they ate Chinese dinners at the cabin, and then they split up. Two went outside to sit in the trees on either side of the cabin to have the vantage point where they could see the door to the cabin and the windows in front and back. They planned to trade off, keep watching for me, and take me down. No more running.

"That worked for me. I was ready to finish this. I was tired of hunting them down."

"So you took out the man in the cabin first."

"Right. He was pacing across the living room floor as a cougar. He was the ringleader of the three men, murderers, all of them. When I was sure the others were gone, I came out and took him out before he warned the others."

"It wasn't a fair fight for you when you had so many to take on," she said, knowing she would never be able to do something like that. Managing even one male cougar on her own would have been difficult enough.

"Yeah. No doubt about it. I waited for a while, thinking that maybe one of the cougars would come into the house, but remember how I told you that the one inside was the gang leader? I suspected that they were waiting for him to give them the word to switch off."

"But if you went out the front door, the cat would look and know you weren't the boss man. And then he would warn the other."

"Exactly, and then I would have been facing two cougars instead of one. I might have still come out on top, or I could very well have been dead. The only thing I could do was wait for one of them to come into the cabin to see why the boss didn't replace one of them on duty. He was supposed to go out there in three hours. So I had three hours to wait. Waiting can be the toughest job."

"Then one of them came to the cabin?"

"Yeah, the cat out front. He waited fifteen minutes after the time he was supposed to be replaced. I figured he thought the boss was sleeping too long because he didn't alert the other cat. Anyway, he came in by himself, I'd hidden the boss under the bed, and then when the cat closed the door and called out for the boss, I attacked."

Though they healed twice as fast as humans, she noticed claw and bite marks on Chet's shoulder and neck. She ran her hand lightly around the wounds. "He got you here?"

"They're fading already. But yeah. The other cougar got me elsewhere."

"He came inside?"

"No. I waited for about twenty minutes, recuperating from the last fight and then went outside and around the cabin to take on the other. He cried out to the others, telling them to come join them and take on the sole cougar."

"But he was alone too."

"Yeah."

"But you had already fought two cougars."

"I had. Which is why he had gotten a bite on my flank."

She glanced down at his board shorts.

"It hurt like the devil, but it's feeling better now."

"And you did all that swimming and rowing? You poor thing."

He smiled. "You know we heal fast."

"Ava. Chet. Come have some birthday cake," Shannon called out.

"Okay, coming," Ava said. Then to Chet, she said, "Do you want me to return with a canoe for you?"

"No, I'm good."

"Has Dr. Kate or Dr. William looked at your injuries?"

Chet smiled, rose to his feet, and dove into the water.

She still didn't believe he was perfectly okay, or he would have answered her about seeing a doctor. A cougar doctor preferably so that he or she would understand the faster healing genetics and human police wouldn't get involved in trying to locate where the cougar was that had bitten him. Male cougars were so macho and the worst patients. Ava was going to tell Kate as soon as she could locate her.

∿

CHET WAS AMUSED that Ava wanted to have his wounds checked out. He wasn't about to see the doctor about it. The bite marks would go away soon enough. Ava could sure be persistent.

He was ready for cake and ice cream and singing happy birthday to the little ones—Bridget and Travis's twins, Theo and Phoebe, and Addie and Dan's twins, Mitchell and Maddie.

Then there was the fishing contest, and he was ready to challenge the competitors on that. Later tonight, a big barbecue and fireworks were on the schedule.

As soon as he reached the shore, Ava was right behind him.

They all sang happy birthday to the two-year-olds, then everyone began getting cakes and cookies and ice cream.

"Chocolate?" Shannon asked.

"You made all these?" Chet asked Ava.

"Yes."

"Which is your favorite?" Chet asked.

"Chocolate cheesecake."

"That sounds good to me." Once Chet had his slice of cheesecake and a scoop of vanilla ice cream, and Ava had hers, they went off to sit at one of the resort tables that Chase had made.

She was watching Chet when he sat down this time and he was amused. Was she making sure he hadn't fibbed about his injury? It was higher up than that and he wasn't sitting on it.

Ava was looking around at all the cougars gathered, then suddenly spied someone who got her attention. He looked that way and frowned. *Dr. Kate.* Ava better not call her over. The doctor was here to enjoy herself just like everyone else. She didn't need to give resort beach doctor visits to potential patients when he was all right.

As soon as Ava caught Dr. Kate's eye, she motioned to her to come and see her, and Kate nodded, finished talking to someone, and then headed their way.

"I hope you are asking her something about yourself. It better not be about me." Chet took another bite of his ice cream.

Once Kate had joined them, Ava motioned to Chet. "He has an indelicate cougar bite mark that his board shorts are hiding."

"It's going away and healing. There's no need for you to check it out," Chet said.

Kate smiled. "All of you guys are the same. We'll run over to the clinic right after we finish eating our cake and ice cream. I'll grab mine too. And then we'll be back here before the fishing contest. You're fishing against the others, aren't you?"

"I am. I know Leyton is fishing and I have to beat him." Chet and Leyton were always in competition. He still couldn't believe Leyton would get himself wounded, then he would take Kate hostage and end up mating her. Some guys had all the luck.

Ava was eating her ice cream before it melted, looking as innocent as could be.

He wouldn't tell her any other war stories, if he ever had the chance, about current wounds he'd received in combat. He wouldn't trust her not to tattle on him to a cougar doctor again.

"It's really not any big deal," he said to Kate when she returned with her apple pie and vanilla ice cream and sat down next to Ava.

"I will be the judge of that. Did you tell your boss and give him an incident report?" Kate said.

"He gave the orders to have a cleanup crew take care of the bodies."

"That's not what I asked you." Kate wasn't going to be bamboozled.

"I told him that I had been scratched. I didn't tell him I was bitten. What do you think would have happened? I wouldn't have been able to come and play with the rest of you at the party today. After what I went through, this was all I could think of."

"I won't report that you need further time off, if I look you over and determine you're fit for duty." Kate took a bite of her apple pie.

Chet gave Ava a cross look. Ava cast him a small smile. "Just think. After Doc looks you over, and says you're well, you won't have to worry about it any longer."

"I haven't been worried about it. Just about getting a room for the next couple of nights. And since you said yes, that solved that problem. But that's the only thing I was thinking of."

Dr. Kate finished off her pie and ice cream. "Come on. Let's get this over with."

"Are you coming too?" Chet asked Ava. "You instigated this."

She chuckled. "Of course not. I'm not a nurse. Good luck with him Doc. Don't let him give you any grief."

"You're going fishing with me," Chet said to Ava. "Payback."

She sighed. "Fine."

Then he left with Dr. Kate. "You know this is a waste of your party time."

"Are you kidding?" Kate said. "I would be up half the night worrying about you."

He chuckled.

Kate smiled.

When they arrived at the clinic, he saw Mandy. She was glowing.

"Was the pregnancy test result positive?" Chet asked Mandy as she showed him to an exam room.

"Yes. I think Ricky's still in shock, but hopefully by the time we have the twins, he'll have come to terms with it," Mandy said. "What are you in here for?" She weighed him, took his temperature, and checked his blood pressure.

"Cougar bite in the ass."

Mandy tsked. "You guys sure know how to play rough. I hope the other guy paid for it."

"He did. But I don't really need to have this looked at."

Kate came into the room wearing scrubs and looking like she was going into surgery. He could face any foe, but seeing a doctor who looked like she was ready to operate on him? That was another story.

"Okay, drop the shorts," Kate said.

Chet smiled. "I bet you tell Leyton that all the time."

Kate smiled.

Once Chet was up on the exam table with his ass on display, Kate said, "Oh my."

"What?"

"That's one nasty bite. It's healing, but it's showing signs of infection."

"No way. I'm going fishing and I'm beating Leyton."

Kate readied a syringe and gave him a shot in the butt cheek. "Hell."

Kate smiled. "Antibiotics. I'll give you a prescription for more and I'm going to drain the infection, so I'll give you a shot to numb the area."

He might be all tough about some things, but when it came to cutting on him, he was ready for any numbing she would give him. As long as he could still fish.

Kate and Mandy worked on him, cleaning up the infection, suturing it, and bandaging it.

"No more swimming in the lake. If you go for a run as a cougar tonight, someone needs to bandage your wound again. The same thing with showering tonight. If you begin running a fever, come in to see me right away."

"It's going to heal up, Doc."

"It sure is. If you do as I say. We might heal faster, but little things like an infection can cause real problems, even for us."

"Congratulations, Mandy," Chet said, "and thanks, Doc. I've got to get back to the party." He pocketed the bottle of antibiotics in the pocket of his board shorts.

"Let's go."

Okay, so he might have been a little annoyed about having the doc check him out and felt it was all Ava's fault when he didn't need any help, but he realized she had good instincts. Then he frowned as Doc took him back to the party. Unless Ava had already had a sixth sense that something had been wrong.

# 4

Chet rejoined the party at the lake. He shouldn't be looking for Ava and just leave her in peace, but he couldn't help himself. He'd enjoyed the time he'd spent with her so far and he felt he had to say something to her about the business of siccing the doctor on him.

He maneuvered around a group of people playing soda crate ring toss and another group doing a bean bag toss.

"Remember to tell me if you have any problems with your wound," Kate told him, then headed off to be with her mate, Leyton, and their twin boys who were playing a game of tag.

Then Chet saw Ava and paused to watch her playing with some of the kids, running after them, grabbing them up, swinging them around and laughing. He smiled.

Travis joined Chet and slapped him on the back. "So what was the deal with seeing Doc?"

Chet glanced at Travis. "Isn't that supposed to be in the realm of patient confidentiality?"

Travis laughed. "Not when we work together on a mission. Something might be going down while you're here, and we'll need you. Leyton and I have to know that you are all right."

"All right. I'm good. I just got a cougar bite, but it didn't turn me."

Travis smiled. "You were born a cougar."

"Right. It's fine." Chet switched his attention back from Ava to Travis again. "Do you have a case you need me to help with?"

"We could."

"Okay, I'm ready. Just say the word and I'll let Chuck know I'm working on this with you." Chuck Warner was their overall boss, and he needed to know if Chet was going to be staying in the area and not returning to Cheyenne right away.

Leyton headed their way. Chet frowned at him. He better not ask about Chet's visit with his mate.

Leyton shook Chet's hand. "Okay, there's a rumor you were injured on your last assignment."

Chet shook his head. "Doc told you."

"No. I saw you leave with Kate. I just put two and two together. I figured you wouldn't leave the party for anything once you got here. When you went with my wife to the clinic, I didn't figure it was for updating your immunization records."

Chet chuckled. "All right. Do I have to tell everyone the cougar I took down at the last mission bit me in the ass?"

Leyton smiled. "No wonder you didn't want to talk about it to anyone. So how is it?"

"Good." Then Chet saw Ava headed their way. He knew she was going to ask how he was doing.

When she joined him, she reached for his hand. "I hope you are not talking shop after just coming off of a difficult mission."

"Not us," Leyton said. "I've got to go play with the kids."

"You're not fishing?" Chet asked.

"Yeah, I'm fishing. Someone has to beat you." Leyton smiled.

"I'll beat everyone," Ava said.

Travis frowned at Ava. "Did you have a premonition of it like you did about the canoe race?" He looked like he was about ready to cancel on fishing if Ava already knew she was going to win.

She patted his shoulder. "You know I can't fish. Not unless I can do it as a cougar. But Dan says no cougar stuff until after the fireworks and it's quiet and dark."

"And we'll go running together?" Chet asked.

"With whoever else wants to go...uhm, how's your injury?" Ava said.

God, he should have known that was going to bite him in the butt...again.

"I'm good."

"Okay, well, see you out there fishing. May the best cougar win," Travis said, then left.

"You really didn't have a premonition about the fishing contest, did you?" Chet asked Ava.

She laughed. "No. I told you. Unless I'm a cougar, I never catch anything. Of course,"—she gave him a little evil smile —"I've never fished but once with a pole before."

"Good thing we don't have partners in this." After Chet said it, he realized he shouldn't have made it sound like she was the only one he should be partnering up with, if they'd had partners, or that he would only partner with her if she could help him win. Of course, if she had never fished but once before, maybe she would be really good at it, despite saying otherwise.

All those who were fishing in the competition began to get ready with their tackle and bait.

Chet took Ava in hand as they got ready to fish though, and told her, "You don't want to head straight for the edge of the water and cast as far as you can. You want to make short casts and fan it from side to side. Then do the same with longer casts."

"Oh, wow, okay, great. I'll try it that way." Ava sounded thrilled.

Chet was glad he had offered to assist her in fishing, even

though they were in competition. He really wasn't worried she would beat him. Leyton and Chase were another story. Bridget could give him a run for his money, if she got someone else to take care of the children. Maybe Shannon or Kate. There were several others there too.

And then he watched Ava fish. Everyone was starting.

"Good catch." He couldn't believe it when she felt a tug on her line and stopped to pull in a bass.

"Oh, wow, oh, I can't believe it. That technique really works."

He cast in the same manner as she did and didn't have any luck catching anything. This reminded him of when he was younger and helped a boyhood friend study for a test that he was having difficulty with. Then the friend ended up making a better grade than he did.

With his friend, Chet couldn't help but have been perturbed that he hadn't made at least the same grade as his friend. But with Ava, he was pleased he could help her enjoy fishing as a human. Though he would love to fish with her as a cougar too.

In the end, Chase won, just like he had at an earlier fishing contest and Chet had only caught a small fry.

"I told you I didn't see that I won," Ava said.

Chet smiled. "I would have cheered you on if you had."

"Sorry yours was too small and you had to toss it back."

He chuckled. "You don't look sorry at all."

She smiled.

THE FISH that had been caught were taken to the cooking area and then it was time for some more games.

"I want to do that first." Chet pointed to the strongman game.

Ava figured he wanted to show off his hot muscles at work.

She was watching them more than she was watching what he was doing as he struck the sledgehammer and sent the puck up to ring the bell with a clang.

"You won! But you knew you would, or you wouldn't have done it in front of me."

He chuckled. "What would you like?"

"If it was for me, I would pick out a stuffed cougar. But wouldn't your mother love it?" Ava was sure his mother, Wendy Kensington, would be happy he was thinking of her while he was in Yuma Town.

"It's for you, hard-earned for putting me up for the week-end," Chet said.

Ava smiled. "All right." She hugged the cougar and then put it at the table where they would sit to eat, along with her bag. No guy had ever won a prize for her at some contest booth. She felt...special.

Then they went to the tables to dish up some of the food at the barbecue. Barbecued ribs, fish, and chicken were ready. Corn on the cob, watermelon, coleslaw. Just the perfect dinner for the Fourth of July celebration.

Chet and Ava grabbed a couple of plates, filled them with food, and sat down at the picnic table.

"What are you doing tomorrow?" Ava had tomorrow off after all the hard work she'd put in at the bakery this morning and planned to work on her garden. She'd gotten behind on it and desperately needed to weed it.

"I don't have to stay another night. I thought I would be spending it with one of my former CSF agents, but since they're kind of busy with families, I might just grab a bite at the bakery in the morning and head out. What are you planning on doing?"

"Weeding the garden. I might go swimming at the lake tomorrow afterwards. It's been so hot, swimming really appeals."

"That sounds good. If you don't mind, I could go swimming with you before I leave."

"What did Dr. Kate say? But we can have lunch before you leave."

"That would be great. Thanks." He was ready to take another bite of a barbecued chicken leg. "The food here is sure good." He smiled at Ava. "I've had a great time." Better in a different way than he ever thought he would.

"Me too."

"Will you dance with me when the music starts?" Chet asked.

"Yeah, sure. I'd love to."

Yeah, really a great time.

THEN THE MUSIC STARTED, and Chet wiped the barbecue sauce off Ava's chin. She groaned, amusing him. She was so carefree and unpretentious. He'd been so amused when she'd rolled off her float by accident in the lake earlier, he'd waited, in rescue mode, in case she had swallowed too much water.

"Come on, let's dance," he said and led her to the beach where everyone was dancing who wanted to. The music was fast paced, and kids and adults alike were dancing to the music. Some of the younger kids were sleeping on picnic blankets, oblivious to all the noise. Chet suspected moms and dads would take them home before the fireworks started.

When a waltz began to play, Ava wanted to sit it out. He didn't blame her. He'd spent enough time with her already and he didn't even work or live here, so it wasn't like he could date her or anything. And he was certain she didn't want to give anyone the impression he was really with her.

As soon as the fast-paced music was playing again, she grabbed his hand and pulled him onto the beach where everyone was shimmying to the music. The last dance before roasting marshmallows and shooting off fireworks was upon them, and couples danced to the slow music.

This time Chet snagged Ava's hand before she could leave the "dance floor" and he danced with her nice and slow, his hands on her back, her hands on his shoulders, and he kissed the top of her head. He didn't know why he did it. He wanted to, sure, but he didn't want her telling him off in front of all the partygoers.

She smiled up at him. "Happy Fourth."

"Happy Fourth." And then he kissed her on the lips. Nothing really wild or passionate or deep. Just a kiss that said he'd really enjoyed being with her the whole day. And she gave him the same kind of kiss back, but no matter how unassuming it was, he was already hot and eager to do more about it.

"Marshmallow time," Florence said. "S'mores."

Chet smiled at Ava. "Ready to roast marshmallows?"

"I'm making s'mores. But I need to make a run to the little girl's room."

"I guess I'll make a pit stop too." When Chet came out of the restroom, Ava was still in line. He saw Ricky and went over to talk to him, curious about the business of his fortune telling.

"So who's the ex-girlfriend everyone needs to be watching out for?" Chet asked Ricky.

"Do you really believe Ava saw it?" Ricky cast a glance in her direction as she waited in line for the restroom.

"Did you date a girl whose father had Mob ties?"

"Uh, yeah."

"Then I believe she saw it. So who is the girlfriend?"

"Mel Pallotta from Cody, Wyoming. As soon as I began

working for Tracey as an informant, I stopped dating Mel. I mean, I didn't know what her father and his friends were up to, but they all looked like they were straight out of the movie, *The Godfather*. And Tracey was going after Fish and Wildlife kinds of crimes, so I didn't want to try and get involved in whatever they were doing and have to report their criminal activities to a different handler."

Which easily could have gotten Ricky killed. "Okay, so did you have any more than a gut instinct that these guys were doing something illegal?"

"As soon as I went over to pick Mel up for a date, they shut up, like they didn't want me overhearing what they were talking about. And I saw that the men were armed. They wore jackets but when they moved, I saw they were packing. Anyway, after that, I ditched her. She didn't care. She was running around with some other guy behind my back. In the business I was in, I watched and learned. And when I was trying to learn stuff for Tracey, I caught Mel seeing some other guy. Hugging and kissing on him like she didn't even know I was dating her. So I didn't make a big deal of it, just said I wasn't ready for anything permanent, not that she was either, and I wanted to date others if I found anyone else to date. Then she could too. She didn't care. She had the new guy in her life.

"And then a few months later, I met Mandy in Durango, Colorado. She'd been from Cody, Wyoming also, and I began dating her. We were in high school together, but I hadn't dated her back then. Now, Mandy, I wanted to keep. I truly cared about her. But in the line of work I was doing, I was afraid if anyone tried to come after me, they could go after her too. I didn't want her to get hurt. Then you know the rest. I was up here on a job for Tracey, got bit, bit my brother and then Mandy runs me over with her car and I bit her—accidentally. True love." Ricky smiled.

Smiling, Chet shook his head. "I still can't believe she mated you."

"Yeah, I guess I really got lucky."

Then Ava came out of the bathroom, smiled at Chet, and joined them. "Don't tell me you don't believe my premonition about your old girlfriend coming here."

"Nah, I mean, yeah, I believe it. I just didn't *want* to believe it. We went our separate ways; my brother and I even moved out of Cody and went to Durango and I never had anything to do with Mel again. I can't believe she's hunting me down."

"Don't you figure she'll drop the whole issue if she learns you're married to Mandy and you're a deputy sheriff? If her father has Mob ties, she's not going to want to have anything to do with you."

"You saw that, didn't you? That her father is connected with them? I mean, I figured they were, but I didn't have any proof and I wasn't about to snoop around and try to get anything on them either. Not when I was on other dangerous missions working for Tracey. I know she wouldn't have wanted me to either."

"I agree with that. I didn't see anything about the father's Mob connections. Is everything all right between you and Mandy? As far as the babies go?" Ava asked.

"Oh, yeah. I'm going to be a daddy. And everyone said they'd help us out in every way they can."

"You know it. Hey, Chet, are you ready to roast marshmallows?" Ava asked him.

"Yeah, but I might just make some s'mores too. See you later," Chet said to Ricky. If Chet was still here when Ricky's ex-girlfriend came to town, he planned to help him, and the rest of the law enforcement officers from the various agencies as they dealt with it.

Then Chet and Ava got their marshmallow roasting forks out, skewered marshmallows, and began to roast away.

Ava had the best time this Fourth of July. The last two years, she'd watched the fireworks with Stryker's dad and mom, Henry and Marybeth, but being with someone her age, who was a single cougar, was even more fun. She really hadn't expected that. Chet had helped to make it special. Though she had to admit when a very pregnant Bridget broke her water and so did an equally pregnant Addie, each of them having twins two years ago, that was some wild night. Even Vanessa Vanderbilt, the vet, had to be there to help with the deliveries, since the ladies had decided to have the babies as cougars.

Mrs. Fitz was herding everyone around the campfire as the flames glowed orange yellow, the slight breeze fussing at the flames.

"I'm really going to get a pay raise?" Chet asked Ava, roasting his marshmallows over the fire.

"Yeah, really. Unless you royally screw up and you don't get the pay raise right away. Are you sure you're all right?" She was roasting two marshmallows also, her plate with her graham crackers and chocolate bar was waiting to turn her marshmallows into a tasty treat.

She swore he had winced when she moved her hands to his waist from his shoulders while they had slow danced. She had never planned on doing that with him, as much as she'd really wanted to. No way did long-distance relationships ever work out. Besides, her sister was going to have twins someday and Ava wanted to be close by to watch over them and play with them as they grew up—and not move to someplace like Cheyenne,

Wyoming, where they didn't have a lot of cougar shifters to interact with.

Now that she had found a town full of cougars to work and play with, she wasn't giving it up for anything. Still, he was hot, and she'd had so much fun spending the day with him. She would enjoy swimming with him tomorrow.

"So about tomorrow, we could grab some pastries at the bakery and then go to the lake and have coffee and eat our treats, then swim?" she asked.

"Yeah, I would like that," he said.

Then she remembered the weeding she wanted to get done. "Okay, but before we do that, I'm going to pull some weeds. I have to do it first thing when it's cooler out. Normally, I have to work early in the mornings and keep missing out on doing that. Then by the time I get off work, I'm too tired and lazy."

He smiled. "Well, if you don't think I'll pull up the wrong plants, I'll help you. Maybe the two of us can make the work go faster."

"Sure, that would be great." As long as he pulled up the grass and weeds and not her flowers. Her garden wasn't big, but she still couldn't seem to keep after it.

One of her two marshmallows caught on fire and she quickly blew on it to put out the flame. He chuckled.

"I like it like that. Cajun style. Blackened," she said.

He laughed while she put together her graham cracker, blackened, melted marshmallow, and melting chocolate sandwich.

"Hmm, this is soooo good. You're not going to have one?" She only had them a couple of times a year and it was well worth it.

"Yeah, sure." He got up and got some fixings for s'mores and stuffed his browned, melted marshmallows sandwiched between a chocolate bar and graham crackers and began to eat it. Chocolate and melted marshmallow was dripping down his chin and she ran her finger over the chocolate and ate it.

"Hmm, now that is good," she said.

"It sure is. I haven't had these in years. I've had a great time. I knew I would when I was considering the drive here from Cheyenne, but I didn't think it would be *this* much fun."

Then the fireworks started to go off, and they finished up their s'mores and washed up. She meant to sit next to him on the resort bench, since she hadn't remembered to bring a picnic blanket, but he pulled her onto his lap on the beach and they cuddled while they watched the sparkling lights shoot off in a barrage of colorful fireworks all reflecting off the dark lake. It was truly beautiful.

She sighed and watched the sparkling lights bursting against the dark sky. The air was cooling down and she appreciated the warmth of Chet's lap and his arms around her, though again she wondered about his wound. She would have to make up a little fib and tell him Doc told her she was to check it out and make sure it looked okay tonight. She didn't want him pretending it was all right when it wasn't.

What a spectacular night though. No rain in the forecast for the next couple of days and this was just perfect.

Orange, yellow, blue and red, green, purple, and white fireworks shot up into the air, setting the sky on fire.

Once the fireworks were finally over and everyone helped to pick up the debris, Chet asked Ava, "Are you still game for running as a cougar tonight?"

"You bet. I run whenever I can. I swear that working in the bakery adds calories to my daily diet when I haven't even touched one pastry."

He smiled down at her.

"Okay, so maybe a couple of pastries."

Then they headed into the woods where most others were

ditching their clothes in the dark. The newspaper reporter, Carl, was watching her, and finally came over. "Do you think that a hunter will be after me tonight?"

"Not tonight, Carl. In the fall. The leaves are yellow and orange and red. So this fall." She pulled off her shorts.

"Okay." He moved back into the woods to strip and shift.

Then she finished ditching her clothes and shifted.

As a cougar, Chet was right behind her and then the race was on. She loved rock climbing best of all and she led them in the direction of the waterfalls. They should have named them Shannon Falls after Shannon rescued a human boy who had fallen in the pool of water beneath Carver Falls. Ava would always think of it fondly that way—even though she hadn't been in the area at the time, but she loved hearing Chase tell the story.

The rest of the cougars had scattered, finding their own perfect spots to race each other and play. She sat at the top of the rocks watching the waterfall spill down below. Chet joined her, pressing his cougar body next to hers. She looked longingly at the moon reflected in the water, then leaped from boulder to boulder to the bottom and jumped into the water.

Chet was following her all the way, like two choreographed cats that had practiced the moves for years. She dove through the waterfall and he joined her. For a few minutes, they sat on the mossy stone floor just watching the water cascading over the rocks. It was a beautiful sight and lulling too. Which made her sleepy. She yawned, her long cat tongue curling up. She had to get up so early in the morning, she was always tired at night.

He smiled at her, licked her face, and yeah, she was ready to go home after a beautiful day.

She ran through the waterfall, and he chased her out, both of them landing in the deep pool of water and coming face-to-face with one big black bear—male, who looked just as startled to see them. He was sporting blood and looked ready to kill anyone who got in his way.

He stood up on his haunches. She knew it wasn't Jonathon since she had smelled his scent and this bear's was different. Was it a genuine bear—not of the shifter kind? Maybe he was the one who was hassling Jonathon's sister.

Chet snarled and growled, ready to take the bear on. Ava swore she was having heart palpitations.

## 5

C het's first thought when he and Ava saw the bear by the pond was that it was the one Jonathon was after and he had wounded him and rescued his sister. They had startled the bear when they had shot out through the screen of the waterfall and saw him on four legs, drinking from the water, his head jerking up to see what was coming at him. Water droplets had collected on his snout and his small, dark brown eyes were as wide as they could go.

The fur on his leg and neck bloodied, he stood up on his hind legs and snarled at them. Chet wasn't about to back down when he was protecting Ava. She smelled of fear, her heartbeat racing. So was his, but he smelled of anger.

They were at a standoff, neither of them advancing.

The bear could kill a cougar, but two cougars might be a little too much for him. Still, Chet wanted Ava to leap onto the boulders and go all the way to the top of the waterfall and get out of harm's way and he would follow her if he thought he could do it without getting into a fight with the bear. The bear couldn't climb the steep rocks fast like they could with their long-legged leaps and bounds.

But Ava wasn't budging from where she stood next to him, as if she knew the two of them as cougars stood a better chance against a wounded, angry bear than one of them.

The bear huffed at them, threatening to charge them. The bear wasn't Jonathon because Chet knew his scent from the fortune telling booth situation. If this was the troublemaking bear, he might not know that cougar shifters ruled over this territory.

Chet took a deep breath, let it out, and shifted. Taking the chance that the bear wasn't a wild bear was the best thing he could think of to protect Ava under the circumstances.

Ava's jaw dropped. So did the bear's. Then the bear dropped to all fours and took off. Ava swatted at Chet's hip, her claws retracted, and he shifted into his cougar and looked at her and smiled.

She growled at him, and he knew she hadn't liked that he had shifted into his human form in front of an angry bear. He wouldn't have if she'd just climbed onto the rocks like he had hoped she would.

Besides, it worked, didn't it? The bear took off, which was just what he'd hoped for, and nobody got hurt. Chet suspected the bear thought they were real cougars at first, and he was angry about being wounded and he was just defending himself. But when the bear saw they were shifters, Chet figured the bear's beef wasn't with them but Jonathon. Chet, by turning into his human form, had proven they didn't intend to harm him.

Chet licked Ava's face, but she still appeared annoyed. He raced up the rocks. She swatted his tail twice on the way up after him. He smiled. At least she didn't stay mad. At least he hoped not, or he might be sleeping under the moon and stars tonight.

AVA COULDN'T BELIEVE Chet would shift into his human form in front of a wounded and angry bear. She had been certain he was a wild bear. But she had to admit Chet's action had made the bear back down and go away without anyone getting hurt.

Despite her attention being on the bear initially, watching the threat in front of them, when Chet startled her by shifting, he'd caught her eye momentarily. Then she'd turned to see how the bear would react. To her surprise, the bear just left, and she suspected he was a shifter.

In that instant, she had seen the cougar bite on Chet's back-side that Kate has stitched up. So it wasn't just nothing, like he had pretended it to be. It looked red and irritated. He shouldn't have even been running tonight. Then he had shifted into his cougar form, waited to see what the bear was going to do, then turned to see her growly expression, and licked her face, as if trying to make it up to her.

But now she was worried about his wound and the fact he should never have gone running with her in the first place. When he began to climb the rocks to the top of the waterfall, she had swatted at his tail. Not in play though. Because she had still been annoyed with him. If the bear had attacked Chet when he had turned human, she would have had to attack the bear and she was sure the bear would have won out.

FOR A MOMENT, Chet and Ava just sat there on the boulder on the top of the world and enjoyed the view. Chet thought about the bear and thought about her. Then he nuzzled his face against hers and luckily, she didn't stay mad at him for long. She nuzzled him back, and then they headed down the rocks again and raced each other back.

As soon as they reached their clothes in the woods, he

shifted and grabbed his phone—all business, alerting Ricky of the bear incident since he was still the deputy sheriff on duty tonight. "All right, Ricky. Yeah, Carver Falls. Okay. The bear left, but he had been wounded—looked like he was wearing a bear bite, and if he dashes into the path of any others running as cougars, they might have a different outcome."

"Okay, I'll notify everyone," Ricky said.

"Okay. Thanks."

AVA WAS GETTING DRESSED, eyeing Chet's hot physique. What could she say? He was standing there frowning, talking on the phone to the deputy sheriff and fully nude. So yeah, she could have looked away, but the view was just too good.

Chet smiled and winked at her, making her blush, then he put his phone in the pocket of his shorts and began getting dressed. "I know you think I shouldn't have shifted to confront the injured bear, but I was certain he was that rogue bear shifter Jonathon was after."

"And if he hadn't been?"

"I would have shifted back in a flash and tackled him, making a hell of a lot of racket. Then others would have come to our rescue, and he would have known the battle was lost and he would have raced off like he did anyway. I take it your swatting at my tail a couple of times while I was leaping up the rocks to the top of the waterfall weren't love pats."

She snorted. "Hardly."

He took her hand and walked with her back to the resort where her car was parked. "I came with Travis, if you could drop me off at his place, and I can follow you to your home."

"Sure. That will work."

"You're not still mad at me? I was afraid I might be sleeping under the big sky tonight."

She frowned at him. "You weren't in any shape to fight. You shouldn't have been out running." Then she softened her expression. "I thought we could have leaped for the boulders and gotten out of the bear's path without any further trouble. But no, you were being Mr. Macho Cougar and had to tough it out with the bear."

He smiled. "I was hoping you would make the move to leap onto the boulders, but when you didn't, I had to do something. I wasn't leaving you behind." He climbed into her car. "What do you mean I wasn't in any shape to fight?"

"The wound on your backside. Don't tell me it doesn't hurt."

"You were supposed to keep an eye on the dangerous bear, not me."

"Both of us were shocked to see you shift."

"Well, the wound will start to itch soon, meaning it's healing up," he said.

"But it's not yet."

Changing the subject, he said, "Didn't you see the trouble ahead for us?"

She scoffed. "As if I would let us face the danger if we hadn't needed to. You're talking about having a premonition of it, right? It doesn't work like that. I can't see every occurrence of everything that might happen. If I had seen any sign of a bear in a vision, I would have..." She paused.

He looked at her. "What?"

"I had a dream about an angry bear last night."

"At the waterfall?"

"No. I mean, I didn't see anything but him standing there on his hind legs. If I'd known the bear was going to be there, I would have made us stay where we were behind the waterfall. He didn't see us, and we didn't see him. Neither of us smelled the other. The thing about my predictions is they're wholly unreliable. And they can be about anything—like your pay raise. Then I miss something important like us facing down a wounded bear. And you getting naked to scare him off."

Chet smiled, then frowned. "But it sounds like you did have a premonition. You just hadn't realized you had. I figured he was a shifter, and he would know we weren't wild cougars defending each other, and ready to give him any more wounds."

She pulled into Travis's driveway and Chet got a call from Travis. "Okay. I'm just picking up my car at your place and following Ava home. No. Ava's okay. She's pissed off at me, but otherwise, safe." He smiled. "Talk later." He got out of her car. "I'll follow you home."

He followed her car in his own, but then she got a call from Nina. "Are you all right?"

"Yeah. Can you believe Chet would shift into his human form while confronting a bear?"

"Oh, wow, no. It's a good thing the bear didn't attack him then. But I'm glad you are both okay. I heard you told Ricky his MOB ex-girlfriend is coming to see him and cause trouble for him."

"Yeah. He wanted a reading. I could have made one up for him, but I figured he would be glad to at least be ready for it. We're almost to my place. I'll talk to you later, Nina. Thanks for checking on me."

"What are sisters for?"

"I agree, but I still owe you one." Then they ended the call.

When Ava and Chet finally got home to her place, Ava let Chet in, his overnight bag in hand. She had forgotten about tearing her clothes off when she came home and throwing them all over, leaving them in a trail all the way up the stairs in a rush to change into her swimsuit and get to the lake. Her lavender bra and panties were strewn about just like the rest of her clothes. Ugh. She began grabbing them up and Chet smiled at her.

"You didn't know you were going to have a visitor staying with you," he said, excusing her.

"You're right. I didn't, though I usually don't toss my clothes all the way through the house. I was in a hurry to go swimming. I had a great time, didn't you?"

"Yeah. You made it truly special."

"You did too." She frowned at him. "You look like you had a little too much sun today." His face was really flushed, and she reached out and touched his forehead. He was hot to the touch. "You are burning up."

"I'm just a little sunburned."

Ava looked skeptically at him. He felt feverish to her, but her thermometer wasn't working, and she hadn't gotten a replacement yet.

He let out his breath. "I'm fine."

"Drop your pants."

He chuckled. "No she-cat has ever asked me to do that before. Are you sure you want to go there?"

Now *her* cheeks were burning. "Let me see your wound."

He pulled down his shorts and boxer briefs low enough that she could check out his bite mark.

"It's infected. You need to take a shower, and I'll put an antibiotic on it, then cover it with a bandage. Did Dr. Kate give you an oral antibiotic?"

"Yeah, a shot and some pills. I need to take a pill before I go to bed."

"All right. The guest bathroom is between the two bedrooms. You can put your bag in that room. I'll bring you a fresh towel."

He lifted her face to him and kissed her. She wrapped her arms around his neck. "You are so hot."

"Yeah."

"I mean—you are feverish," she said.

He smiled down at her and kissed her again. This time she opened up to him and their tongues licked and stroked. He sighed. So did she. But she needed to find a cougar who lived and worked closer to home. Still, she hadn't been this hot for a guy in forever.

"Okay, off to bed for both of us—separate beds—but after we shower—separate showers, I'll bandage your wound." She figured she needed to make sure he knew all the rules.

"All right." He sounded amusedly resigned, pulled up his pants, and ran up the stairs.

She went to the kitchen to grab a glass of water for him so he could take his medicine and once she was upstairs, she set it on the dresser in the guest room. She grabbed a towel out of the linen closet and while he was soaping up with his manly soap, looking glorious through the glass just starting to steam up, she set the towel on the bathroom counter.

Ava left the bathroom and got some antibiotic cream and a fresh bandage for his wound. When he turned off the shower, she came to the bathroom, waited outside the door, and asked, "Are you all dried off yet?"

"Yeah. I forgot to bring a change of clothes in with me."

"I'll try not to peek." As if she hadn't been eyeing his physique all along. He was sure one hot, muscled cougar. She'd never seen him with these many clothes off this many times.

He opened the door to the steamy bathroom, the towel around his hips, and he was so sexy, she almost changed her mind about him sleeping in the guest room by himself.

"Why don't we go to your guest room and that way I can do this where we won't feel like we're in a steam bath."

He smiled at her. "Sure." He led the way and in the guest room, he pulled off the towel and dried his hair while she covered his wound with the antiseptic and then bandaged it.

She figured that would be it, but he put the towel on the chair in the room and pulled her into his arms. "I want to know that you're not angry with me."

She scoffed. "You are running a fever. What were you thinking?"

"That I wanted to go with you on a cougar run."

"Yeah, well now you're going to have to have bed rest until you get better."

"I'll be fine by tomorrow. You know how we are."

"You had better be." Sure he could be, since their healing genetics made them heal up twice as fast as humans, but they could still get worse and could die. They weren't immortal. And how would she feel if he became even more ill just because he went with her on a run? Awful.

No one would blame her though, because he was trying to prove he was all manly, but it didn't matter. She would still feel it was partially her fault. She should have known better.

Still, she kissed him, and he kissed her back in a way that made her feel she wanted to get to know him better. That made her wish he was living in Yuma Town and not Cheyenne, Wyoming. Though she wondered if she moved there to be with him, and she knew she was getting way ahead of herself here, what would it be like?

Okay, she guessed, if she was with the man she wanted to be with. But she did love working for Florence at her bakery, and she loved being near her sister and if her sister and her mate ended up with kids, Ava wanted to be there for her. She smiled at the thought that she would be an auntie. "Get some rest. Don't get up early. Sleep in. I'll make you some breakfast in the morning when you're up."

"Breakfast in bed?" He gave her the most devilish of smiles.

What, breakfast in bed with her? Guys were all the same. She smiled, shook her head, and patted his chest. "Only if your fever makes you bedridden. And then? You're going to be in a hospital bed."

"No way."

"Well, then get your sleep and no more wild running around. But I have to say I did have fun, so thank you for the run tonight."

"Yeah, I feel the same way." Then he gave her a hug and kissed her again before she left him alone.

She shook her head at herself. She knew not to let this go anywhere between them, but she sure had enjoyed the time with him. Running with a single, male cougar who intrigued her was a lot different than just running with cougar friends and family. There were just different nuances about it. The playing was more—intimate, just...different.

She took a shower, then pulled on a long, T-shirt and climbed into bed. She was supposed to work a half day tomorrow afternoon, but what if she needed to look after Chet? Actually, anyone who could, would, so there was no reason for her to take off from work. So why was she calling her boss then and asking, "Florence, did you know Chet is staying at my place because there was no room for him to stay anywhere else?" She didn't want to let on that this had been her idea, should anyone think there was more to this situation than there was.

"Right, because of the celebration."

"Correct. Anyway, he was bitten by a rogue cougar while on a mission and the bite is infected. He's running a fever and—"

"Say no more. You need to watch over him." Florence was trying to sound strictly professional about it, like she didn't believe there was anything more to it than that, but Ava could hear the amusement in her words even so.

"I could have anyone else keep an eye on him if he needs watching and you really need me to be at the bakery." Though

Ava was supposed to be off and weeding her garden and whatever else she wanted to do for most of the day.

"No, you go right ahead and take care of him. If you need time off the next day, just let me know."

"I'm going to drop him by the clinic if he doesn't get better by morning, and then I'll be in at my regular time. So he has to behave himself."

Florence didn't say anything, and Ava figured she was assuming something she didn't want her boss to assume.

"We went running tonight and I didn't know he was feeling poorly," Ava said.

"Oh, typical of one of the special agents with the Cougar Shifter Force. Well, males in general. I'm sure Bridget wouldn't be like that if she were feeling poorly."

"I agree," Ava said. "Anyway, then he came down with a fever and the wound doesn't look really good. So just in case...."

"Don't think anything of it. Just take off however long you need to. Just like you said about someone else taking care of him if I was in a bind, which I'm not, any number of cougars would come to help me out so you could stay with Chet. Tell him to take it easy for me and I'll drop a special breakfast off for the two of you in the morning."

"Oh, you don't need to."

"I want to. You've been invaluable as my master baker and now when I have an opportunity to help pay you back, you've got it." Florence was always that way.

Ava had the sneaking suspicion that Florence was thinking that she would need to be baking a wedding cake for them next, and Ava didn't want anyone to think that. Heck, she hadn't even been the one to invite Chet to stay at her house.

"Well, thanks, Florence. We'll see you in the morning."

"You're welcome. Good night."

They ended the call and Ava stretched out in her bed, not

believing how fun the celebration and the run with Chet had been, until he got all heroic against the bear. If she had jumped onto the rocks, would he have followed her?

He might have, but she had worried that he would have stayed below to fight the bear. She would never have left him to do that on his own.

She closed her eyes and all she could see in her mind's eye was one hunky cougar with chiseled abs and muscular biceps, with muscled legs and the rest of him was just as hot. She sighed. She needed to sleep but then she envisioned the wounded bear looking all ferocious and she groaned.

When she had a premonition, she wished she knew that it wasn't just a dream.

## 6

Because of the wound infection, Chet felt horrible. He'd taken his antibiotic and even some fever-reducer medicine, but he was hot and sweaty, then cold and shivering. No way was he going to tell Ava that though. Hopefully, by morning, he would be fine. He didn't want to end up in the hospital for any reason. He did feel like his injury was healing and with the antibiotics, that should help speed things up.

Then his mother called.

He sighed. He had wanted to just go to sleep. "Hey, Mom."

"Hi, honey, did you have a good time at the celebration?"

"The best."

"You know I keep telling you I'm going to be old and gray-haired by the time you ever have kids. I've given up on your twin brother. Kenneth is so busy working as a park ranger at Fort Collins, he has no time for girlfriends. Have you met anyone yet?"

Chet smiled and changed the subject like he always did when it came to girlfriends. His mother always asked whenever he went to Yuma Town. "How's everything going up there?"

"Good. You said you were having trouble finding a place to stay. But you must be staying with someone."

"Uh, I am."

"One of your agent friends? Leyton? Travis and Bridget? Jack, the new guy?"

"No one you know." That was the thing he loved with working with the CSF. Family was important and his mother had had all of them at one time or another over for dinners and special occasions when they had been in the area. She had been hopeful he might have ended up with Bridget. His mother really loved her, though she had worried Bridget would get herself into trouble being a special agent and dealing with rogue cougars. But it would never have worked out between Chet and her. The guys all treated his mother like she was their mother too.

"A woman. A she-cat. I knew it."

"Now how do you figure?" His mother had an uncanny way of knowing about things even when he hadn't told her enough to give her any clues. She had taken over as the director of CSF some years earlier and finally retired, but she was just as sharp as when she had been in charge of the agency.

"Because you didn't just come out and say who you were with. Some new agent, or some family. No name at all."

"She's—"

"I knew it." His mother sounded positively excited.

He smiled. "She's Ava Lamar and she's the head baker at Fitz's Bakery and Coffee Shop."

"Oh, not a special agent then with CSF."

"No, and they just asked if she could put me up because no one had any room. There's nothing more to it than that." He didn't want to worry his mother that he would move to Yuma Town and leave her all alone in Cheyenne, if there was no chance of that.

"Well, it's good she's not a special agent. That can be such a deadly business."

They all knew that only too well when four rogue cougars ganged up on his dad and had killed him while he was on a mission, trying to take down one that he had thought was a lone cougar involved in the murders. Chet and his brother had lost his dad when he was ten, and his mother had continued to work to earn their keep. Ultimately, she'd ended up finding the rogues and contacting other CSF agents to help her terminate them. Eventually, she'd even been in charge of the CSF for several years before she retired, and Chuck Warner took over after she'd mentored him for some years. She had loved her job, but she had also been so lost when Chet's dad had died. Well, Chet and his brother had too. His dad had been such a great role model for them. But his mother's work had convinced him he wanted to take down rogue cougars for a living also and for a time, they had even done that together. Whereas his brother hadn't wanted that life. Not that Kenneth hadn't had some harrowing times as a park ranger.

"Well, you'll have to bring her here to Cheyenne sometime so I can meet her."

Yeah, if he was seeing her because they were going to be a couple, sure, but if not? He didn't want his mother seeing anything more to it than there was.

"We aren't seeing each other as a couple," he clarified, thinking his mother might believe he'd been seeing Ava every chance he had when he had visited Yuma Town before and kept it a secret.

"What did you do with her today?"

He smiled. As soon as he mentioned all the things he'd done with her, his mother would assume otherwise. "A few things."

"Well, that's a start and since you're being so secretive about it, there's hope for you and the she-cat yet. As to another matter, how are your wounds after that cougar encounter you had?" His mother was still always checking up on him as if he were a kid and living at home, but he loved her for it. If she didn't care, she wouldn't have been his mom.

"They're healing like I told you they would."

"Okay, well, if they don't, you get in right away to see the doctor down there. Leyton did all right by marrying Kate."

"Right."

"Or William Rugel. Or even his mate, the veterinarian, Vanessa. At least in Yuma Town, you have lots of options. You know your father—"

"Yes, he was too stubborn, and it killed him." At least that's what his mother had always said. In truth, no one could have come out of the fight he'd had with a group of four cougars and lived.

"So what are you doing with Ava tomorrow? Or are you returning to Cheyenne?"

"I'm not sure what the plans are for tomorrow. I'll let you know if I'm heading home right away. I might have a mission that takes me a while."

"Down there?"

"Yeah, one that involves a bear shifter though."

"Oh, my. In my day, we didn't have anything like that to deal with. It was strictly cougar shifters. I don't know what this world is coming to. So what's the case?"

"A bear is trying to rescue his sister."

"Okay, well, it's a worthy cause. Don't you get yourself killed over it though."

"I won't, Mom. I'm about to go to sleep now. I'll call you sometime tomorrow to let you know if I'm returning tomorrow or might be busy with this mission."

"All right, son. Talk to you tomorrow."

He knew she was just concerned about his welfare, plus she

planned to have him over for dinner tomorrow night if he'd been home. "Night, Mom, love you."

"Love you too."

Leyton and several of the special agents of the Yuma Town branch of the CSF had wanted Chet to join them down here. He would love to partner up with them and to live among a community of cougars, but he still had his mother to think about. He wanted to ensure she was happy with him doing so, though she said often enough he needed to do it so he had others to watch his back. But they'd really never talked about what she would do then. Move to be close to him? He would want that. They'd always been close. But he wasn't sure she would want to give up her home and move to a different state, a different town. Though she did know several people in Yuma Town already, all of whom had wanted her to move there too.

He closed his eyes and saw the cougar fight in his mind again, wishing he'd gotten the best of the cougar who had bitten him before the deed had been done. He supposed he shouldn't be swimming until it was healing up and he had no infection any longer. And he figured he shouldn't be running as a cougar, unless he could have someone bandage him up again after he shifted back. He suspected, if the other guys knew he was sick, they would take him off the team. But he didn't want that. He was running a fever, sure, but he could still complete a mission. Especially if they really needed him to back them up.

Then he was thinking about Ava and the kisses they'd shared and how much he had liked that. She was funny and fun to be with. A spitfire too.

Sometime between thinking of holding her close to his body during the dancing, and becoming aroused then, and kissing her the other times, and becoming aroused again, he was even aroused now. So he couldn't be all that sick, right?

She had mentioned gardening, weeding tomorrow and he

was bound and determined to help her with her garden chores while it was still cooler in the morning, to pay for room and board. Even though she wouldn't accept any money for it.

He drifted off to sleep then.

*He felt submersed in water, first warm, then cold and he shivered. Alaska. He must be in Alaska, surrounded by cold wetness and he had to find warm, dry clothes or he'd freeze to death. Yet he was hot, burning up again and that didn't make any sense. Had he gotten some warm clothes on after all? Too hot though. He felt he was sitting in a sauna, the steam surrounding him, and he was soaking wet. He pushed something aside and felt the cold return as if he'd found his way into a warming hut and then he was back out in the cold again. He shivered incessantly. Where were his warm, dry things? Everything was pitch black out and he didn't know if it was day or night, only that he couldn't get warm. He had to find his way back to the warming hut, to dry, warm clothes. To a fireplace and a hot fire roaring. Then it was hot again, and he realized he'd accomplished his mission, found warm clothes and the heat of the room again. Before he was ready for it, he was cast out into the wet cold like a never-ending nightmare.*

Then, sometime later, he heard someone moving in the room and he was immediately sitting up, gun in hand, the hazard of being an agent, but also, the concern the threat was real.

Ava moved toward him in the dark room, her cougar eyes seeing all. "You are perspiring. Nina dropped off one of their thermometers for us so I could make sure you're okay." She took his temperature. "You're running a fever. It's time for you to take some more fever-reducing medicine, though a fever can help to kill off the bug. Come on, climb out of bed. I'm changing your damp sheets. You're shivering. You must be having chills."

He realized that was why he had been dreaming about being in Alaska in winter, about not having warm, dry clothes, because he was shivering in sweat-covered sheets. He was grateful to see Ava and he was glad to get something dry to sleep on.

"I'll help you," he said, not used to having anyone do things for him when he was sick.

She looked like she was going to tell him no, but then she seemed to think better of it. She went into a hall linen closet and brought out sheets and a blanket. She handed him the blanket. "Wrap this around yourself. I'll pull off the sheets."

Then he did and she started to pull of his pillowcase and sheets.

He started to help her as she removed the sheets, but she gave him a stern look to stay put. "Keep the blanket around you and once I've remade your bed, you get into it and let me know if you need me to change out the sheets again later in the night."

"What if I use a couple of towels?"

"Sure, I can get you a couple of bath towels."

No way did he want to keep disturbing her sleep so that he would stay dry and warm. He did want to help her make the bed, but he didn't have a stitch of clothes on underneath the blanket and maybe she wanted to do this herself because of it. Once she had remade the bed, she hauled off all the damp linens and left the room. He heard her slam the door on the wash machine and start the wash. Then she returned with two oversized towels. She laid one on the bed and once he set the blanket on the bed and climbed onto the mattress, she put the other towel over him, then covered him like he was a small, sick child. He wished he wasn't sick like this, or that she had to cater to his needs. She was probably right in saying that he shouldn't have run with her as a cougar, but he had been feeling just fine at the time.

She smiled and kissed him on the forehead, as if letting him know that she didn't mind helping him out in the least.

"Thanks, Ava."

"No problem, and Florence said she would bring us over something for breakfast, so we can just chill—well not literally, hopefully in your case—and watch TV or something."

"You were going to do your gardening in the morning."

"Uh, yes, I was. But you are *not* coming out there with me."

"Unless I'm perfectly fine."

She gave him a long, stern look. "All right. But you'd better not be fibbing about it."

He smiled. "I don't fib."

"I'll check your temperature," she said, as if she still didn't believe he would be honest with her.

He figured with Ava, he wouldn't be able to get away with anything. "What made you come and check on me?"

"I had a premonition you were in the Arctic and freezing cold, and then in the desert, dying of thirst. I had to check on you and make sure you weren't getting sicker. And of course, you were experiencing fever and chills."

"Did your premonition tell you I was staying for longer—so you could take care of me?" He was only half joking.

"I'm sure they would tell me I had to sign you into the hospital."

He smiled and shook his head. "Thanks, Ava."

"You're welcome. Sleep in."

"Will do." If he could.

A va returned to bed, glad her premonition, which she had thought was just a nightmare, had stirred her from sleep so she could check on poor Chet. She'd been through the same thing when she'd been shot while running as a cougar. Once she'd been patched up—as a human —she had thought she would be fine. But wouldn't you know, she ended up with an infection and she'd experienced the same symptoms as Chet. She didn't want him to have to feel as bad as she had felt that time.

She wanted to keep him here, truth be told, as long as he was feeling unwell, and not have to send him to the clinic. She guessed his job with the other CSF agents to help them with the bear situation—if they needed his assistance with that —was out.

She closed her eyes and took a deep breath and let it out. She'd really had fun with him, yet hadn't expected this at all, but at least everything else had been great.

The next morning, she woke and hurried to get dressed and check on her guest. He was still sound asleep, but when she checked his temperature, loving how she could do that without touching the patient, she found his fever must have broken during the night. She left the room and made herself some hot lavender tea in the kitchen, threw the sheets from the washing machine into the dryer, and got a call from Florence.

"Are you up?"

"Yes. Chet's still asleep. He had a rough night with fever and chills, but the fever broke, thankfully."

"Do you want me to wait to bring over the breakfast?"

"No, you can bring it. Then when he gets up, we can eat. I'm going to work in the garden for a while until then."

"All right. I'm on my way over."

It didn't take Florence long to get there and she handed Ava a box of baked goods. Ava knew she was giving them to her for free, but she was going to offer to pay for them anyway.

"No, it's one of the perks for working at the bakery. If I get sick, you can make a special delivery for me."

"You know I will," Ava said.

"Enjoy your day off."

"Thanks, I sure will."

Then Florence left, and Ava set the box of fresh baked kolaches in the fridge, grabbed her garden gloves out of a drawer, and headed outside to work before it got hot. Right now was the perfect time to pull weeds and maybe even dig up some plants that weren't getting enough sun or water and move them. That was the thing about a garden. When she planted everything, the plants were tiny. Then other plants volunteered, appearing out of nowhere—bird dropped, or wind driven. And then plants that needed sun, suddenly weren't getting enough of it.

She puttered around in the garden for a good hour, then noticed movement in the kitchen window and saw Chet looking out at her. He smiled. He looked well-rested. She hoped that he was all right. She pulled off her gloves and went inside. "Hey, how are you feeling?"

She went straight to her drawer that had the thermometer in it and whipped it out.

"I was going to say fine, no fever, but it looks like you're not going to take my word for it."

"You're right. I'm not." She checked his temperature, and it was normal. "Okay, you're fine. How do you feel hungry-wise? Could you eat something?"

"Yeah. The baked goods smell great."

"Kolaches. And I suspect you want some coffee?"

"Yeah, that would be great."

"Did you sweat anymore in the night?"

"I might have, but if I did, the towels helped to absorb it. I stripped the bed and threw them and the towels in the wash. I hope you don't mind, but when I saw you outside, I went ahead and started the wash."

She shook her head. "I would have done that. Can I check out your wound?"

"This is getting to be a regular thing between us."

She smiled. "Only as it pertains to me either keeping you here with me or taking you to the clinic and seeing the doc again."

He pulled down his pants so she could check out his wound.

"I don't know. I'm calling Doc anyway. I don't want to have to worry about you if it's not any better."

"All right." He sighed. "But I'm hungry and can't wait any longer to eat." With coffee in hand, he sat down at the breakfast table, and she warmed up the kolaches and set them on plates for them.

After she made more tea for herself, she called Dr. Kate. "Hey, I'm calling about a patient of yours."

"Chet? Is he worse?"

"He was running a fever last night and had chills. His fever is gone this morning, but I checked his wound and I'm not sure about it. Maybe you should check it again?"

"I would be happy to. Just bring him over."

~

CHET WAS GOING to drive himself over to the doctor's office, but Ava wanted to go with him, he figured so she knew that he truly was okay, not trusting him.

She was going to sit out in the lobby of the clinic though, but he told her to come back with him. He figured she'd seen enough of his butt not to be shocked and if she was going to watch out for him, what the heck.

Dr. Kate had him pull down his pants so she could check the wound, and he smiled at Ava.

She smiled back at him.

Then Kate said, "It looks much better than it did to me last night. Ava tells me you were having fevers and chills last night."

"Yeah, but then they were gone, and I slept well after that."

"Get plenty of rest, lots of fluids, and take it easy. You don't want me to have to confine you to a hospital bed. I hear you plan to help chase down a bear in the woods. I would say no to that. Not for another day or so. If you have no fevers tonight and the wound looks more healed up by tomorrow, then we'll see. But I want to take a look at it again."

He sighed.

Doc smiled. "You guys are all the same. I thought only Leyton made for a bad patient, but I've learned all you guys do. Make sure he comes in to see me before he goes off on any missions, Ava."

"I will. We were going to swim, but I think that is out, don't you?" Ava asked.

"Yes. He doesn't have to wear a bandage now, but I don't want him in any kind of water unless it's to shower."

"Okay, thanks, Doc," Ava said, giving Chet a look that he'd better mind the doctor.

He sighed. "So what *can* we do?"

"No running as a cougar," Doc said. "You don't want to scratch the area against tree branches and what not. Just heal, Chet, and you'll be all better in no time."

"You can watch me garden some more this morning," Ava said.

"All right."

"You can sit with a cup of coffee at my table on the back porch."

He wanted to help her, and he would, if she would let him.

Then they left the clinic and returned home. He got a fresh mug of coffee and she got a thermos of iced water and her gloves and she went outside with him.

"I guess you don't have another pair of work gloves for me," he said.

"Not man sized and you're not working. Sit," she said, pointing to a chair at the table.

He sat on the patio in the shade then to watch her, but he really wanted to help her. He folded his arms. "You know helping you to weed won't bother the wound."

"You're my guest. You don't need to work. Just enjoy the day. You're not a workaholic, are you?"

"I don't consider myself one, but I hate seeing someone working when I can help and I'm just sitting around watching."

She clipped some shrubs. "You might pull up the wrong plants you think are weeds when they're not."

"Ahh, there's the truth of the matter."

She smiled.

He got a call and she looked up to see who it was from, probably suspecting it was from Leyton, and it was. "Hey, Leyton. I'm on the patio resting."

"Doc said you can't go with us."

"Yeah, Doc said no running after bears in my current condition. So she called you?"

"Yeah. How are you feeling?"

"Great now."

Ava rolled her eyes.

"I have a pretty she-cat to watch while she's gardening and a great cup of coffee I'm drinking while I do it. What a life."

"Kate said you're to be watched at all times. I'm under strict orders not to let you go on a mission until she verifies you're good to go."

"I should have gone to Dr. William."

Leyton laughed. "He would have been under strict orders from Kate too. Just enjoy your vacation. Ava will take good care of you."

"I would rather be helping you guys."

"You will, if we don't catch up to the wounded bear today. We'll let you know how it goes."

"All right, talk to you later." Chet called his mother next. "Hey, Mom, I'm going to stay awhile longer here. I won't be going on the bear hunt today, but probably tomorrow. Or worst-case scenario, the next day. I'll let you know when I'm getting in though."

"Okay, that's fine. Thanks for letting me know. I'm off to get some grocery shopping done."

"Okay, love you, Mom."

"Love you too, honey."

Chet set his phone on the table. "You know I could clip the shrubs back like you're doing. I couldn't make a mistake in doing that. You could continue to pull weeds."

"Thanks, but if you get sick again, I would feel it was all my fault. Just sit and relax."

"I wonder if we could go boating."

She gave him a look that said he couldn't be serious.

"If I stay out of the water."

"No."

"We could take a walk on a hiking trail, no cougar coats. Just as humans."

"The walking could cause friction between your pants and your wound, I think."

"I could call Kate and see if that would work."

"How about we play board games? In a nice clean house, no chance of getting your wound infected."

"Yeah, that could be fun. Sure." He never thought of things like that. He tended to be all about the outdoors, especially in the summer.

"Okay, then it's decided. We can watch movies later."

"You've got a deal." Then he felt better. He wanted to do something and if she had fun doing the things with him, all the better.

Once she was done with her chores, she went inside with him and she got them glasses of ice water and set out a stack of games. One that looked interesting was all about a dragon who was hoarding his gold coins until one of the players put him on a tile and a player could control the dragon with a certain move and force his or her opponent to lose a coin and be sent back to the beginning tile. The dragon could be moved up to three spaces in any direction, and Ava was the one controlling the dragon. No matter how many times Chet tried to move beyond the path of the dragon, Ava kept getting him, via the dragon.

Chet smiled. "You're good at this."

"I just got lucky. If I hadn't picked up that tile to summon a dragon, I would never have been able to control him and sic him on you."

It was an entertaining game and he thought it would be fun to play with even more people. They played several games and then she checked his temperature, even though he said he was fine, just in case. "You're good."

And then she went to fix lunch.

"What can I do to help?"

"I've got a roasted chicken in there and I'm going to make homemade chicken soup with the chicken from that, shredded carrots, rice, onions, cook it all together, and we'll have that. We can figure out dinner later."

"Okay, sounds good to me."

He helped her while she pulled all the chicken meat off the whole chicken and he shredded carrots and cut up the onions. She made the rice and then they put all of it in one big saucepan, added spices, and finished cooking everything.

She heated up rolls and once the chicken was done, they had lunch.

"This is great. I've only eaten chicken soup and rice that came in a can," he said.

"Yeah, it's great when you're sick, or it's cold out. Though it's not cold, I thought it would be nice because you're—"

"Not sick."

"Well, true, just under the weather."

When they finished eating, she started to clear away the bowls. Then they sat down to watch a movie, but he said, "You really don't have to stay with me and watch over me the whole time."

"I know, but I'm enjoying your company. When you're gone, I'll be alone again. So this is nice for a change. Oh, I need to get the stuff out of the dryer and dry the sheets."

"Here, I'll help you with that." Chet wasn't about to sit around while she worked, especially after he was the one that caused her to have all this extra laundry.

She didn't seem to mind his help and when she pulled the clean clothes out of the dryer, she handed them to him. "You can take them into the bedroom, and I'll help you make the bed again."

"You don't mind me staying another night?"

She shook her head. "I know you want to help the other guys with the bear issue. If they don't resolve it before you can join them on the hunt, you're welcome to stay here at my place."

"Okay, I appreciate it."

"That means you get to grill chicken tonight if you're up to it."

"Oh, yeah, I can do that." He would love to do anything to help pay Ava back for all that she'd already done for him. He noticed she'd put the stuffed cougar on one of her chairs in the living room as if she were showing it off. He smiled.

"So what did your mother think about you staying with a she-cat she didn't know in Yuma Town?" Ava asked.

"She's already getting ideas. She has hoped for a long time that I would settle down. So I'm sure she's dying to meet you, even if there's nothing to it."

"What about with Bridget?" Ava threw the wet linens from the washing machine into the dryer and started them.

"I was Bridget's partner, but Travis was the one who charmed her into mating him. Bridget and I were a great team together, and we are great friends, but we didn't have what it took to make a couple. Of course, my mother wanted to meet her, and I had to tell her that there was nothing going on between us, as much as I had hoped for more. If you didn't know, both my parents were CSF special agents."

"Aww, so your mom probably is more interested in you

TERRY SPEAR

hooking up with another CSF agent and not someone who just works in a bakery."

"On the contrary. She would be worried about a mate of mine who was in such a dangerous occupation. Now for Bridget and Travis it works out great. They work together on missions, see each other all the time, but then again, they have kids now and that makes it harder. She's at home while he's on missions, and she really wanted to go on them too."

"I'm just a baker and I enjoy learning how to make new treats. Sometimes I create really unusual stuff, to challenge myself like they do on those cooking channels. I made the coolest zombie girl for Halloween that actually glowed in the dark. Florence loved it so much, she wants me to make a whole bunch of different ones to put on display in the windows for different occasions. That one sold right away for the Halloween party the town was putting on. But I can see making more for individuals who have a thing for zombies. Or, really, anything that I can paint with florescent icing for Thanksgiving, Christmas, and other holidays."

She pulled out her phone and showed him a picture of the zombie.

"Now *that* is cool."

"Thanks." They made up his bed then. "I'll leave a couple of towels out for you on your bedside table, once they have dried, in case you have any night sweats this evening."

"I appreciate that. It really did the trick last night. I probably would have been freezing again, if I hadn't used those to help absorb the moisture."

"I've done that before, when I finally realized I was sweating in the middle of the night and making my sheets and nightshirt all wet repeatedly after drying them out."

While they grilled chicken that night, they enjoyed the cooler air and listened to the cicadas and crickets in the woods.

She rarely sat on her back patio but with Chet it was really relaxing.

"You didn't tell your mother you were injured and feeling poorly, did you?" Ava asked then as they looked up at the stars sparkling and the full moon all aglow.

"No. There's no sense worrying her unless I had to be hospitalized."

Ava scoffed. "Even then, you probably wouldn't have told her."

Chet just smiled at her.

They finally cleaned up after dinner, and she had been halfway considering allowing Chet into her bed, but instead, she came to her senses and kissed him good night and they retired to their own beds.

But in the middle of the night, she was being chased by a bear and she woke with a start. She rubbed her forehead. Was it a nightmare? Or a premonition of things to come?

## 8

The next morning, Chet woke to see Ava leaning over him with a thermometer next to his forehead, checking his temperature. He smiled at her. He was feeling like his normal self and he was ready to tackle any mission. He realized just how much he didn't want to leave Yuma Town. As much as he liked working with all the CSF agents, Ava was the one who made him want to stay there longer.

"How are you feeling?" Ava asked as she made them eggs, ham, and toast for breakfast.

"Great. No fever, chills, no pain." He pulled his pants modestly down to show her the wound. "The wound is healing nicely."

She smiled. "Good. I won't have to have you drop your pants any longer to inspect your injury then."

"Not for that reason, anyway."

Smiling, she raised a brow.

"I mean, if we want to strip and shift and run as cougars. Which, now that I'm able to, I'm ready. Did you want to run?"

It was light out, but they didn't have to worry much about hunters in the area.

"Okay, sure, I would love that."

"Good." Chet called Leyton, "Hey, Ava and I are going for a cougar run. If you need me, we'll be back in a little while."

"We haven't found the bear yet, so enjoy your run. We can get with you later to make some plans to hunt him down."

"What about Jonathon's bear sleuth? Shouldn't they be the ones handling this?" Chet had wondered about that after they had offered their help.

"It's our territory. I believe he was afraid of infringing on our territory, should a bunch of bears suddenly start running through the area. But you're right. I need to verify why they aren't handling it."

Then they ended the call and Ava asked, "Are they wanting you to run with them instead?"

"No, not until later. I think Leyton is getting some clarification as to why Jonathon's own people aren't dealing with this."

"What are you thinking?" Ava asked.

"I wonder if they don't know about it. That something deeper is going on."

"Like?"

"Maybe his sister *wants* to be with the bear and it's just Jonathon who doesn't want her to be."

"Oh, a family feud. That would be awful. Especially if we involve ourselves when they need to handle the matter themselves."

"I agree."

"Are you ready to run?"

"I sure am."

"Wait, weren't you supposed to see Dr. Kate first?" Ava asked.

He slipped his boxer briefs down to show her his wound again.

"Okay by me, but if you get worse again, it's all your fault you didn't have it checked out again."

"She has real patients to see and doesn't have time to waste with me every day. Besides, if I do get sick, it *will* be my fault for not going in to see her again."

"All right, just remember that."

They stripped out of their clothes, then shifted and ran through the condo to the cougar door. Then they bolted outside. He wondered, offhand, what the bear shifters did about leaving their homes if they wanted to run. How would they get out of them in a hurry? A couple of the ones up on the North Shore of Lake Superior had gone into one of the resort cabins through the cougar door, but as humans to get inside and then outside again. As bears, they would have been too big.

He and Ava ran through the woods and paused only to look up at a mountain of rocks, then both of them began the climb, leaping from one rock to another until they were at the top. He was glad they were cougars and could climb like this with ease. His wound wasn't bothering him at all, though when Ava looked at him with concern, he suspected she had been worried about it.

He just nuzzled her face to let her know he was good and that he was glad they were up here enjoying the view as cougars. She nuzzled him back, reciprocating the affection. Then they looked out across the land and saw the lake off in the distance, mountains, forests, the beauty of the area. He took it for granted, he realized, when he was running through it just for sport and not really seeing the vast splendor. With Ava at his side, he wanted to take a pause and enjoy all of it.

But then she saw something, heard something, her ears perked up, twitching one way and then the other, listening to whatever sound she had heard. He'd been concentrating on being with her and had missed hearing what she had heard. Then she bounded down the rocks and he tore off after her.

That's when he heard a cat snarl—a big cat—and he wondered how he'd missed it.

They ran together to help the cat—it was the reporter, Carl Nelson, who had been more recently turned—which had been a good thing for the residents of Yuma Town since he'd been looking for a story about them before he was turned.

When they reached the area, they realized a bear had treed him. Chet would have laughed, if he could have as a human, though the bear could be dangerous too. It was the same injured bear they'd seen before. What the hell was it doing in their territory and now treeing their cougars?

Ava glanced at Chet with a warning look not to shift and talk to the angry bear. He was sitting on his haunches, eyeing them warily. Carl wasn't moving from the tree.

Chet had to communicate with the bear. He just hoped that Carl and Ava would take the heat off him if the bear charged him once Chet shifted.

Chet shifted. "We need to know what's going on with you. If you and Jonathon have a beef between the two of you, we need to know that."

The bear grunted and shifted. The guy was big, six-four or so. "Jonathon is the one who is at fault in all this."

"He says you stole his sister away from him. Why not go to your sleuth to resolve this?" Chet glanced at Ava since she was the one who had seen the event in her premonition.

"He has lied about all of it. He doesn't have a sister. Just a brother. Jonathon and I have been squabbling over a she-bear."

That made sense.

"And that's why you haven't involved your sleuth?" Chet asked.

"Yeah, they tell us to deal with issues like this on our own."

In the bear's way, Chet suspected. "Okay, well, Jonathon solicited us to help track you after he turned us down at the beginning. I'll let the others know that this is an issue between you and the she-bear, but don't kill Jonathon in our territory or we'll have to deal with it." And they needed to verify if this bear was telling the truth. "I'm Chet Kensington, by the way, special agent with the Cougar Shifters' Force, CSF. We normally go after rogue cougar shifters."

"I'm Blue Bearsden. But this issue between Jonathon and me needs to be settled between the two of us, no one else."

"Where's the she-bear?"

"Ursula Brownstone has vanished. I thought Jonathon had her, and he thinks I have her, but I don't. We got into a fight a couple of days ago, and he got the best of me."

"Do you think she doesn't want to have anything to do with the two of you?"

"No way. I'm sure she thinks if she's out of sight, we'll cool down over her."

"Will you?" Chet asked.

"What do you think?"

"No." If Chet was fighting with another cougar over dating Ava, he would feel the same way. Though he hoped he would go about it in a better way. He was sure everyone in their town would shame him and another cougar into doing so if they both were too hot-headed to see the truth. Why wouldn't the sleuth do that? "Are you sure she's not in trouble since neither of you know where she is?"

"No. She threatened to disappear. I just thought she was telling me that so I wouldn't fight Jonathon."

"Why did you tree Carl?"

Blue looked up at the tree where Carl still sat, not making a move to come down and join them.

"He was chasing after me and what was I supposed to do? So I treed the pesky cat."

Chet raised a brow at Carl. He snarled in response, sounding annoyed that the bear got the better of him.

"Are we good?" Blue asked Chet.

"Yeah, for now, sure. We won't interfere in dating squabbles between bears unless someone is killed, then that's another matter." Chet shifted back.

The bear did too, inclined his head and ambled off. When he was far enough away, Carl finally came down out of the tree.

Carl greeted them, looking thankful Chet had taken care of the bear, but Carl looked a little foolish that Ava was still standing near Chet and hadn't escaped to the tree like he had done.

Then Chet nuzzled Ava and she nodded. They took off for home so he could call in what he'd learned from Blue.

Carl ran behind them, as if he was ashamed to run beside them, or maybe he was just cognizant that Chet had been running with Ava as though they were now a couple, and he didn't want to intrude. But he wasn't going back to town on his own, rather, sticking with them in the event they ran into any more angry bears.

When they finally were near town, Carl ran off in a different direction and Chet figured he was going for his clothes wherever he had left them. Chet and Ava finally reached her place and inside, they dressed.

"I'm glad you heard Carl snarling. I didn't right away," Chet said. "So what's the deal about the sister/girlfriend angle?"

"I guess when I saw a she-bear in the vision, I was sure it was a sister, not a girlfriend because Jonathon said it was his sister."

"Was Blue lying? Or was Jonathon?" Chet slipped his shirt over his head.

"I'm not a mind-reader like Bridget is. She didn't say for

sure." Ava pulled on her shoes. "I knew you were going to shift in front of the bear again."

"Yeah, well, I knew you wouldn't jump into the tree for safety. I had to learn who the bear was and his side of the story if it had to do with Jonathon. Also, why he had chased your reporter up the tree."

She laughed. "I have to admit, it was funny. I wonder if Carl was looking for a story. He was doing such a great job baking for Mrs. Fitzgerald, but once he had the opportunity to go back to being a reporter, he jumped at the chance to work for Roger and Milly Haverton. He's a good reporter, now that he's a cougar like us and not trying to get a story about us that would tell the world what we really are."

"I'm calling Leyton to let him know what the story is—according to Blue."

"I'm going to make some iced tea. Do you want some tea or something else?" Ava headed into the kitchen.

"Water would be good." Then he called Leyton and once he had him on the phone, he said, "Ava and I went for a run and we ran into the wounded bear again." He told him all about it and then added, "I'm still not sure whose story is true." Then he mentioned the bear treeing Carl.

Leyton laughed.

# 9

Ava had a blast running with Chet as a cougar. She sure hadn't expected to see the bear and that he had treed Carl, which, if she hadn't been really worried about him, and the bear, she would have thought was hilarious. Of course, now she did, knowing that everything was okay, and that Blue hadn't been a dangerous wild bear.

But the business with the sister/girlfriend bothered Ava. What worried her the most was what if the woman was really in trouble, and she wasn't just trying to get away from the two male bears so she wouldn't cause any more trouble between them, where was she?

"Are you going to look for her?" Ava asked Chet, handing him a glass of ice water.

"If the other guys are going to, sure."

"What if the other guys *aren't* going to? Don't you want to know that she's all right?"

"Are you having a premonition of her now?"

"No." She led him to her back patio that looked onto the woods. It wasn't her woods, but it was nice that the condos had a nice woodland view. She couldn't imagine living someplace

where all she saw were wooden fences and other homes or
apartments marring the view of the wilderness.

Chet took a seat next to her at the patio table. "But you're
worried about her."

"Yeah, aren't you? It would be one thing to keep out of sight
of the two male bears, but why not let someone in her sleuth
know that she's safe? I would want to know that it's as Blue
suspects, rather than speculate she could be in trouble."

"So what you're saying is if the other guys think there's not a
case for us to get involved in, I should still look into it."

She smiled at him. "That's exactly what I was thinking. And
I'll help."

He looked doubtfully at her.

"Okay, listen, I might not be a hot shot special agent like you
and the rest of the cats in the CSF, but my senses are just as good
as the rest of yours, and I'm good at doing research. I don't have
to help you though." She tilted her chin up. "I can do my own
sleuthing."

He smiled at her.

She frowned at him and took a sip of her tea. "What? You
don't think I can do it?"

"Oh, hell, no. I think you can do it for sure, but I wouldn't
want you to do it by yourself."

"Just in case there *is* something wrong and she is in trouble."

"Exactly. I wouldn't forgive myself if something untoward
happened to you."

"So what's our first step?"

He chuckled. "I'll check with the other guys and see if they
want to investigate this further." Then he pulled out his phone
and called Leyton back. "Hey, it's me, Chet. Ava's worried that
something might have happened to the she-bear and wants to
look for her just to make sure she's okay." He glanced at Ava. "No,
she doesn't have a premonition about it. I know she's not one of

us in the CSF, but she's got our cougar senses and she wants to do this with me if the rest of you guys don't think there's anything to it...okay, thanks. I'll let her know." Then he ended the call. "Leyton said he would talk to the others in his branch and let me know."

A few minutes later, Leyton called Chet back and Chet put the call on speaker so Ava could listen in on the conversation. "Okay, here's the story. I got in touch with Jonathon, and he says that Ursula Brownstone is like a sister to him. That's why he called her his sister. That she doesn't have a brother to watch out for her and he's always been that for her. Blue is bugging her when she doesn't want him to. So Jonathon was trying to chase him off and stop him."

"And you asked him about the business with her disappearing?" Chet asked.

"Yeah, she does that when she gets tired of Blue pestering her and Jonathon trying to look out after her, Jonathon told me."

"So Jonathon isn't going to look for her now? He doesn't want us to help them?" Chet asked.

"Yeah, he says it's a bear thing like it's probably a cougar thing for us."

Chet glanced at Ava. She smiled at him. "Okay, are you going to send out a team to look for her?"

"No. Not unless we're asked to do so. We've got cougar cases to look into. But by all means, if you want to check into it on your own, do so. And if you need backup, don't hesitate to ask for it," Leyton said.

"Okay, that sounds good to me," Chet said.

"Are you and Ava going to look for her then?" Leyton asked.

Chet glanced at Ava to see her take on it.

She nodded. "We're doing it."

"All right. Well, if anything looks dangerous, you're responsible," Leyton told Chet.

He knew Leyton was referring to taking a civilian on the mission. "Yeah, if it looks at all like we're going to have any trouble, we'll call you." And then Ava would be sidelined because Chet wouldn't risk her safety if it looked like they were bound to have trouble they hadn't expected.

Then they ended the call and Ava said, "I know you all don't think I should be involved in this because I don't usually carry a gun and I'm not law enforcement like the rest of you, but you never know if I might end up having a premonition about something regarding her and then my being with you will be invaluable."

"I totally agree, or I would say no to your coming, only because I don't want to risk your safety for anything. But if the bears are telling the truth, then she's okay, just cooling her heels," he said. "And if she's not, we can hopefully locate her and help her out. You know, even if she's fine, I wouldn't mind learning the whole truth of the matter because I'm not sure Jonathon is telling us the truth still."

"Okay, I agree since he has changed his story once already. So where do we go first with this?"

He smiled. He liked a woman who was ready at a moment's notice to go on a mission. He just hoped the she-bear wasn't in any trouble and he didn't get Ava into a mess. Or that he didn't rile up a couple of male bears who wanted to keep the cougars' noses out of the whole business. He wouldn't blame them if they were annoyed with them. He wouldn't like it if a bear made cougar business his business. Then again, if a cougar was in trouble, he would welcome a bear's assistance.

Chet said, "We find that cabin you saw in your vision and follow her trail. Though I'm sure the bears would have done the same thing, we can start there."

"Let's go check it out. I've got some time off and I want to make sure she's okay."

"Then let's do this." Chet and she left in his car to see what they could learn about the female bear.

"I had a premonition before you came, that someone or something was chasing me. Before I could make it up a tree and out of danger, a bear came after me. I had to climb the tree and try to get away from him."

"Bears can climb trees."

"I know that. And fast. But I stripped out of my clothes as fast as I could and then I shifted and leapt out of the tree and headed for the cliffs."

"Here?"

"Yeah. It had to be here. The premonition where I hear and feel sensations that make it so real mean it happens soon."

"You think we could be in that situation here? If we go looking for the bear?" Chet asked.

"Maybe. I wouldn't discount it."

"Where am I?"

"I don't know. Maybe you were behind me. But I couldn't see you. I don't know who it was."

When they reached the cabin, they found that no one was there, but they smelled both a female bear had been, and also Jonathon and Blue—the one who was interested in mating her, they suspected.

They hoped all was well between the three bears. Ava wished they could have at least spoken with her to learn her side of the story. In this case, there were three sides to the story. What if Jonathon was the only one having a fit about Ursula seeing Blue? What if she left to keep the peace? Or maybe even was trying to secretly rendezvous with Blue there. Oh, that could be bad. Then Ava could have interfered when she hadn't meant to. Here, she thought she was helping out when she could have caused a worse situation to occur.

She told Chet what she was thinking.

"Don't overthink it. They're gone and maybe everything's acceptable with all three of them now. They could have worked their differences out. If we get another lead on them, we can look into it. But I think for now, this is all we can do."

Ava had to agree with him. She was a baker, not a special agent like him who dealt in all kinds of stuff like this. Still, she wished she knew Ursula's side of the story. She wondered even where the bear sleuth was located. "All right. Let's go home. But I do have a question about this whole sordid affair. When we talked to Jonathon and Blue, they both indicated they hadn't seen her."

"She must have already left the cabin before they arrived."

Ava wished they knew what was going with the bear, but when they returned to the condo, Chet got a call, and she knew it wasn't the greatest news the way he glanced at her. "All right, yeah, I'm on it. No, I'm well. All rested up. I'm on my way within the hour."

"Chuck?" she asked, when he hung up the phone.

"Yeah, another day, another dollar. I knew the fun wouldn't last."

She smiled at him. "You love doing your work."

"True. I do. And I love taking down the bad guys and helping our kind out. Normally, I would be eager to get back to work. But this time, not so much so. Truthfully, you are the reason for my change of heart."

She smiled. "Well, I'll miss you too. I've had a great time also. I guess you've got to go now?"

"Yeah, I need to pack and leave."

"Did you want me to fix a quick lunch for us while you're packing?"

"Yeah, sure, that would be great. Thanks." Then he headed into the guest room and she went into the kitchen to make them grilled ham and cheese sandwiches.

It was quick, but a little fancier than a plain cold sandwich for the long drive ahead of him.

"So what's the case about?" she asked as she worked on the sandwiches.

"A cougar stealing cars in Cheyenne. We just can't let them get caught and become incarcerated," Chet said from the bedroom.

"Has he injured or killed anyone?"

"Not that we're aware of, but I have to stop this before he gets himself caught by the regular police."

"Okay, so what do you do when you catch him?"

"If he only has stolen cars, not harmed anyone, he could be incarcerated here. If someone has died as a result of his illegal activity? He has made his bed."

"Well, you be careful."

He smiled. "But if I have a disaster like the last time, you'll take care of it for me, right?"

She laughed. "I would rather we could just have fun together."

"Yeah, I agree."

After Chet ate lunch at her place, he kissed her goodbye, but it wasn't as much a kiss goodbye as it was a promise of more—sizzling, passionate, needy, and she was giving him as good as she got. She realized he wanted more, and she was feeling the same need. She really was going to miss him.

Then he finally pulled his mouth away from hers, kissed her on the forehead, and squeezed her arms and left and she didn't know what to do with herself. That had never been a problem for her.

When it was early evening, she stripped off her clothes and went running as a cougar. She had to do something. Everything reminded her of Chet now. What was up with that? Eating meals here? Watching movies? Even sitting on the back patio watching the sun set.

She sighed. She just had to get out of the condo and run, but that reminded her of Chet too.

She headed toward the cabin where she had seen the vision of the she-bear, not that she thought Ursula would return there, but she just couldn't quit thinking of her. And of course, she thought of doing that with Chet.

Had it been a mistake to have done so much with him while he was here?

No way. He'd really made everything so much more fun. The only regret she had was that he didn't live and work here.

She had been running for awhile when she saw movement out of the corner of her eye. She turned and saw a male coyote coming out of nowhere. If a coyote thought to tangle with her, he'd better rethink his position. She was not in the mood for playing games. Then she thought she smelled the female bear's scent trail. A fresh scent trail. The same one they had smelled at the cabin. But what if it was some other bear's scent? Not the she-bear they were looking for?

She hurried to track the bear trail, but the coyote was following her. Ava turned around and ran at him. She didn't want to waste her time on this. He turned tail and ran. Good. She hoped he would listen to reason. She wondered why he would even come after her. He had to realize that wasn't a good idea. Then she smelled the scent of a female somewhere close by. Oh, great. She smelled young ones too. He was trying to chase her off because they had little ones nearby.

She took off in another direction, planning to make a wide sweep around the area where the den must be. She heard the small cries of the little ones then. Crap. She was headed toward the den, not away from it. Then she raced off as if the hounds of hell were after her, when she wasn't afraid of a couple of coyotes.

She just didn't want to upset them. She had to let everyone in Yuma Town know that coyote pups were out here and not to come into the area. They respected other animals that had found a home here, and they didn't want to disturb them. The male coyote chased after her. Darn it. She didn't want to climb into a tree, though if she did, he couldn't reach her.

But then Ava would have to sit him out and she didn't want to have to do that. It was one thing for her to leap into a tree because *she* wanted to. Quite another to be treed by an animal. Then she saw a bear racing toward her and the coyote. She frowned. What now?

The bear was running so fast, she was impressed. She realized he would be impossible to outrun as a human. She hadn't seen Jonathon in his bear fur coat, and she wondered if that's who it was. Or maybe the female he had been after? Or it could be just some full-time bear. She couldn't smell his scent on the breeze. The wind was carrying Ava's scent to the bear instead.

She leapt up into a tree.

The coyote was so busy barking and pawing at the tree, trying to reach her, he hadn't yet noticed the bear's approach. Then he suddenly must have heard the bear or felt the bear's heavy weight pounding on the earth, or seen him in its peripheral vision, because the coyote suddenly turned and then ran off, leaving her alone to face the bear threat. If it was one. Cowardly coyote.

The bear finally reached the tree and shifted—Jonathon. "You're the one who gave me a fortune telling reading earlier. I smell your scent."

She nodded but she didn't shift. She didn't need to. She wasn't going to talk to him in her naked human form when she really didn't have anything to say except thank you. With another cougar, she might have, but not with a male bear she really didn't know.

Then again, she wanted to warn him there was a coyote den nearby, so he wouldn't disturb them too. She sighed and shifted. "Thanks, a coyote den of pups is over in that direction, just to let you know."

"Okay, I wondered why a single coyote would have treed you."

"Did you find your sister?" She arched a brow.

"Not yet. Do you need an escort home?"

"No, thanks. I smelled a she-bear had come this way and I was hoping to track her down in case she's the one you're looking for. I'm circling way around where the coyote den is to avoid them though. But Chet and I ran into Blue a little bit ago, and he told us you don't have a sister. You have a brother."

Jonathon opened his mouth, and then closed it and smiled. "Okay, you caught me. She's like a sister."

"That you want to date."

Jonathon smiled again.

"Okay, what are you doing here?"

"I smelled her scent also. I've been searching for her still."

"So am I. I'm looking for her, to learn her story and make sure she's all right." Ava hoped she wouldn't need Jonathon's help with the coyotes after she had turned him down.

"Okay, maybe we'll both find her at the same time."

She shifted back into her cougar and leaped down from the tree. Then she inclined her head, and took off running, away from the coyotes' den of pups.

She finally lost the she-bear's scent at a creek. Jonathon had been right behind her the whole way. She let her breath out in exasperation. She needed to return home and let everyone know so no one would kill the aggressor male coyote by accident, and she needed to update those involved in searching for the she-bear about Jonathon's comments.

She headed home and Jonathon watched her for a bit, then

he left in the opposite direction. She should have asked him where the bears were from. When she arrived home, she slipped in through the cougar door, shifted and headed for the bathroom to take a shower. She got a call before she could do that and saw it was from Chet and she hoped everything was okay.

"Hey, missing you. I tried calling earlier," he said.

"I was out running as a cougar. And I came across a coyotes' den and had some issues, but mainly I met up with Jonathon while I was looking for the she-bear."

"Without me?"

She figured he might be upset with her if she mentioned it, worried about her safety. She could handle herself on her own. She told him about what Jonathon had said.

"Okay, so a guy doesn't call a woman a sister and then say he's interested in her."

"So you figure he's been interested in her all along."

"I would say that's a good bet."

"All right. Well, I miss you too. How are things going for you on your case?"

"I just got home so I haven't had time to investigate the cougar. But I wanted to call you and check on you."

And here she was out running as a cougar.

"As soon as I finish this job, I want to see you again," he said.

She shook her head. "You'll have another job after that."

"Probably. But I still want to see you."

She chuckled. "We'll see."

"You can always come see me."

"You'll be busy working," she said.

"Probably. Well, I'll let you go. Miss you."

She smiled. "Yeah, I miss you too." But she wasn't going to tell him how much and make it worse for them both.

"Okay, call me anytime, and...hell, Ava, don't go out alone.

You know some bear's going to be chasing you because of the premonition you had."

She sighed. "Yeah. Good night."

"Night, Ava."

She stared at her phone. If Chet kept calling her, telling her how much he was missing her and wanted to see her there or here, she wasn't going to be able to put this all behind her like she thought she might.

After she took her shower, she called Dan. "Hey, I was out running by the old creek and I came upon a coyote den with pups near the old Calvert Silver Mine. Just a heads-up so you can let everyone know not to run there. Oh, and I ran into Jonathon."

## 10

A fter apprehending the car thief, Jasper Holliday, a sixteen-year-old cougar who had been stealing the cars and selling them, whose parents were done dealing with him, Chet sent Jasper with another agent to Yuma Town to have Jasper incarcerated.

Dan had told him they'd do a trial with their cougar judge, and Jasper would be sentenced to supervised probation while working at Hal Haverton's ranch, mucking out horse stalls and such for four years. As a parttime deputy sheriff, Hal did a good job straightening out wayward male teens, of the cougar persuasion. He was fair and expected the work to be done, and he and his family provided the love and support the teens needed. Not to mention their foreman, Ted Weekum, kept them in line.

Chet was given the mission of chasing down another murderous cougar shifter, this time a suspect by the name of Joe Sharp. He figured he needed to call in reinforcements. Thankfully, he was able to get some help from Yuma Town, though he was surprised Travis *and* his mate were coming. Bridget hadn't taken on a mission since their twins were born.

Chet was waiting in the lobby of a hotel in Cody, Wyoming

for them. They were due any minute. Then he saw them coming into the hotel and he hurried off the chair to greet them. Of course as soon as he saw them, they reminded him of what he was missing in Yuma Town—being with Ava.

Chet motioned to the steak restaurant off the lobby. "I've got reservations for dinner at the restaurant."

"Oh, good," Travis said, "We're starving, and I know they have good food here."

"Yeah, that's why I said to meet here." Chet led them into the restaurant where they took their seats in one of the red vinyl booths. "Joe was spotted seven miles east of Cody, fifty miles east of Yellowstone National Park. But I knew I needed backup assistance this time because the other newly hired agents are gone, working on other cases."

"You asking for backup is saying a lot," Travis said. "And we're glad to have your back on this one."

Chet, Bridget, and Travis had worked out of Cheyenne, Wyoming, so all of them were familiar with much of the state and of course working with each other.

"You know, the first thing I thought of when you mentioned the assignment and coming to Cody was that our two more newly turned cougar brothers in Yuma Town, Ricky and Kolby, are from Cody. Would anyone know of them from here?" Bridget asked.

Travis smiled. "I asked Ricky before we left. He told me no, but he said he didn't want us looking anyone up. Mostly because they are cougar shifters now and Cody, Wyoming was their past life. But I suspect the Jones's brothers hadn't wanted us to learn of their past shenanigans in the city either," Travis said.

Chet laughed. He could understand that feeling.

"I still feel like I'm neglecting the babies," Bridget said.

Chet had been afraid of that and that she wouldn't be able to remain focused on the job when she was worried about the kids.

"Your mom and dad are thrilled to take care of Theo and Phoebe for a couple of weeks. This is the first time you've been back to work, and they've wanted to take care of them since they moved down from Ely, Minnesota to see more of them anyway. Besides, Benjamin and Bernadette said you could call them night or day to check up on the kids. They'll be good. But if you're too worried and don't want to leave the kids for that long yet, you can fly home or take the car and I'll fly home once this is done." Travis rubbed her back.

"No, it's okay. If I don't do this now, I might never return to work, and I really do want to work again."

A pretty, redheaded waitress, her name tag saying she was Irena, brought glasses of water and their menus. They smelled her cougar scent and their mouths gaped. She was a cougar shifter like them.

Irena smiled. "Well, *this* is a surprise. We don't get many of our kind passing through here."

"You wouldn't happen to know a Kolby and Ricky Jones, would you?" Bridget asked, on the off-chance Irena knew them from the small town. She was just curious.

"Kolby Jones. Yeah, he and I went to high school together before his father was shot in a hunting accident. It was a real shame. Everyone felt terrible for the family. The mother moved them to Durango, Colorado, the last I heard. A lot of us had a crush on one or the other of the brothers, but their lives were shattered by the death of their father. Their mother couldn't cope. It was a real tragedy."

"THEIR MOTHER DIED from a prescription overdose, and they believed she'd committed suicide, unable to live with losing her husband. The brothers were turned and are now living in Yuma

Town among more of our kind. Cougars run the town," Bridget said.

Irena's mouth gaped and Bridget read her thoughts. Irena had immediately thought of going to Yuma Town to give them her regrets about them losing their mother. Especially Kolby. "They're cougars like us?"

"Yep," Chet said.

"Ricky just mated a girlfriend he'd known from here. A Mandy Richards."

"Oh, my, she and Ricky were born at the local hospital practically at the same time. My mother helped deliver Mandy while the doctor ran between delivery rooms, trying to catch first one, then the other baby."

Bridget laughed.

"What would you all like to drink?" Irena asked.

"Caffeinated coffee for me," Travis said.

"Coke for me," Chet said.

"Tea for me," Bridget said.

Irena brought over a pot of coffee and poured a cup for Travis.

"I'll get the rest of your drinks." Then Irena hurried back to the kitchen.

"It's a small world, isn't it?" Travis took another sip of his coffee.

"I'll say. I hadn't really expected Irena to know the brothers." Bridget watched as Irena brought a tray with glasses of water, a tea pot, and tea bags to their table and a Coke for Chet.

"I've given you your choice of teas. So what are you all doing here? Just passing through on your way to Yellowstone for a vacation?" Irena had her order pad out and pen ready to take orders.

"We're with the Cougar Special Forces Division out of Yuma Town. We take down rogue cougars," Bridget said.

Irena whispered, "You're after Joe Sharp, aren't you?"

"What do you know about Joe?" Chet sounded like he was ready to bolt from the chair and grab the guy if the waitress knew where he was and he was close by.

"He's from here, if you didn't know. As far as everyone knows he has been caring for an aging mother until she passed recently. His dad died years ago of a heart attack. Not everyone in these parts believes he's guilty. Of course the police aren't involved in this because the murderer has only killed shifters so far and our kind have hidden the fact that we've had any shifter deaths and that the perpetrator is a cougar. It's all rumors and speculation though. He still owns his mother's home. But don't kill him unless you know for sure he's the villain in all this," Irena said.

Bridget was reading everything going through the woman's mind, that she'd dated him, that he had been involved in minor crimes. Irena had no thoughts about telling Joe that the CSF agents were looking to take him into custody for questioning. "Yeah, we'll give him every opportunity to give up so we can question him about the crimes. But if he tries to kill us, then all bets are off."

"Understandably. I've never heard of that organization—the CSF. But you might have some trouble capturing him before someone else does. There's another guy who is after him," Irena said.

"A cougar with the force? Or a boyfriend or family member of the dead woman?" Travis asked.

Though Bridget knew he couldn't be someone on the force or Chuck Warner would have told them about him.

"Not a cougar"—Irena leaned over closer—"the man who came in here for breakfast yesterday morning reminded me of a bear. Smelled like one too. I figured he was a zookeeper at the zoo nearby or a bear reserve, or owned a pet bear, despite how

dangerous they could be. He really was into honey and everything berry. It sure had me wondering. Have you ever heard of
bear shifters before?"

Bridget, Travis, and Chet exchanged looks. Some bear
shifters had helped some of the cougar shifters out up on the
North Shore. Not to mention the case of the two male bears and
the female bear running around their territory. Bridget could
see where they could have more trouble headed their way if
other kinds of shifters did exist and started causing problems
between the shifter kind.

"We have," Travis said. "Are you certain he could be a
shifter?"

Irena shrugged. "No. Just like he couldn't be certain about
me, but he was...curious. Smelling the air, smelling me."

"It wouldn't be hard to be a bear shifter living near Yellowstone," Bridget said. "Did he react strangely about you being a
cougar? If he was a shifter?"

Irena shook her head. "Then again, unless he visited a zoo,
he might not know what a cougar smelled like. Maybe he would
think I just owned cats."

"Unless he'd run into them in the wild. From the sounds of
it, he was surprised to smell that you were different," Bridget
said.

Travis began a Google search for bears in Wyoming. "They
have grizzlies in the area, though they don't usually like the
prairie habitats. And they have black bears."

The door to the diner opened, and Irena glanced in that
direction. "Well, speak of the devil."

They turned to see who she was talking about.

The man was about six feet, two inches tall, clean shaven, his
brown hair brushed neatly back but if the wind caught it, it
would be shaggy. If they hadn't heard what Irena suspected,

Bridget would never have guessed the man could be a bear. Not that he could ever guess they were cougar shifters either.

"Well, I'll be damned. That's Luke Bier. One of the bears who helped us with the rogue shifters in Ely, Minnesota," Chet said, already getting up from his chair to greet him.

Travis was on his feet in an instant too. And Chet introduced them, then asked him to sit with them. Luke eyed Irena, who was smiling at him.

"Here I thought you were a tiger," Luke said, winking at her.

Irena blushed and smiled and gave him a menu.

"Do you need a minute to look at the menu further?" Irena asked them.

"No, thanks. I'll have the ribeye steak, medium rare, mashed potatoes, and asparagus," Bridget said. "And a glass of water."

"I'll have the T-bone steak and fries, medium rare on the steak, and broccoli," Travis said.

"Roast tenderloin for me, baked potato with everything on it, and salad," Chet said.

Luke smiled at Irena. "I'll have blueberry waffles smothered in blueberry sauce, toast, with a side order of sausages. Wild berry tea and honey."

"Again. All right. Coming right up."

"Don't tell me you're looking for bad guys in the area," Luke said to Chet.

"Yep. And from what Irena says, you're looking for the same man," Chet said. "At this rate, we're going to have to have a combined shifter force. So how are you involved?"

"He killed a former girlfriend of mine, if we have the right suspect in mind. I finally had to end our relationship because she wasn't one of my kind, but I still cared deeply for her."

Bridget shook her head. "I hope we find him soon then."

## 11

Ava headed to Nina and Stryker's house for dinner of barbecued ribs, french fries, mushroom, onion, and bell pepper shish-kabobs, and watermelon. She knew her sister and her brother-in-law wanted to know just where she was going with Chet. If he were to be Ava's mate, they would also be his family.

Ava hoped she wasn't being premature about this, but she sure wanted him in her life—for more than just a date here or there.

As soon as she arrived at her sister and brother-in-law's home with the apple pie she'd baked, fresh out of the oven, Nina was handing her a strawberry cooler—fresh strawberries, sugar, lemon juice and ginger ale, the best!

"Stryker's got the barbecued ribs and shish-kabobs on the grill. I'm nearly done with the french fries, so just enjoy your drink and we'll start eating in a minute," Nina said.

But Ava helped to set out the silverware, plates, and ice water for everyone.

Then they sat down to eat. A light, cool breeze swept over them, making it delightful to sit outside tonight.

"How's the baking going?" Nina asked. "Now that you're certified as a master baker, any changes?"

"Oh, yeah. Florence is giving me so much more responsibility for managing the shop, planning for special desserts and baked goods, and she wants me to start teaching baking to a couple of teens to give them an idea on how to bake either for their families or become bakers like me someday."

"Oh, wow, that's wonderful," Nina said.

"Yeah. And she even wants me to take the kids on a tour of the bakery when fall homeschooling starts. That should be fun."

"I agree." Nina finished another bite of her shish kabob. "So tell us about Chet."

Ava smiled. "I was surprised you wouldn't ask about him first up."

Stryker laughed. "She has been dying to talk to you about him, which is the reason for this lovely dinner."

Ava shook her head. "I knew it."

Nina hit Stryker in the arm with her napkin. "It is not. We haven't had Ava over since she made master baker and I wanted to know what she was going to be doing now that she is certified."

"And you've been *dying* to ask Ava about the situation with Chet since the Fourth of July weekend." Stryker ate some more of his ribs.

"The meal is great," Ava said. "Thanks for inviting me over to have it with you."

Nina sighed. "About Chet?"

"Ohmigod, he is sooo virile and hot and sexy and yeah, we really hit it off great. I never expected that."

Nina's jaw gaped. Stryker chuckled. "You asked, Nina."

Nina clamped her mouth shut and then smiled and began eating some more of her french fries. "So, are you—"

"Mating him?" Ava smiled.

"Well? You can't leave us hanging." Nina bit into another french fry as if she were frustrated with her.

"Yes. If it works out, definitely."

Nina stared at her for a moment, then smiled. "Seriously. Well, wow, this is great news." Then she frowned. "You're not leaving us, are you?"

"No, I think he wants to move here and work with his whole team."

"Wow, here I thought we worked fast." Nina smiled at her. "I'm happy for you."

"If it works out. I mean, I'm not sure he's feeling the same way about me, but if so..." Ava shrugged. She would be thrilled.

Stryker drank some of his water. "Sounds like the family's growing by two more—Chet and his mother. That works for me."

Nina sipped from her drink. "Well, I...I can't believe it. That's wonderful."

"If it works out." Ava would hate for word to be back to Chet that they were going to be mated when it was the furthest thing from his mind. But she really hoped they would. She loved how he accepted her gift of sight without reservation. Not all men she had dated had and if it worked out between them, she wanted to make him as happy as he made her.

AT THE RESTAURANT IN CODY, Irena brought out two of their meals while Bridget was texting her mom. Travis had been surprised she wanted to go with him on this mission. But she'd wanted to finally go on an assignment now that the twins were two years old. He was glad to be working with her again though. They made the perfect team. Plus, when they could settle down for the night, they enjoyed all the benefits of being a mated couple. And with no little ones to worry about for now, it was like a second honeymoon.

Travis was glad Chet had called him on this mission. Especially after Chet was on his own and then wounded during the last one. Travis only wished Bridget's first mission back to work wasn't so dangerous.

Irena delivered the last of the meals. Luke poured honey into his tea and coated his toast with honey.

"Irena, if some people don't believe Joe did any of the killings," Chet said, "are there any other candidates who could have done the deed?"

Irena sighed. "Joe's brother Rob. Or their friend Hugo."

Chet hoped, if Joe wasn't the culprit, that one of these other men would pan out. "Do you have any idea where either of them are?"

"They live here," Irena said. "Hugo has a hot temper. Rob's a womanizer. Joe is the one with all the plans."

"Thanks, Irena."

"I've got to wait on some more customers. Holler if you need anything more."

"Okay, thanks," Bridget said.

Travis eyed Luke as he poured more berry sauce on his waffles. "You eat like a bear."

Luke was just eating his waffles, smiling a little, appearing amused. "We live everywhere, like you do. And just so you know, I'm a black bear, not a grizzly."

"Oh, of course, that's what Chet and Leyton told us," Bridget said. "Are you from here?"

"I grew up around these parts, but my twin brother, Nathan, and I ended up in Ely, Minnesota and call the North Shore our home now," Luke said.

"Oh, do you know a Jonathon Browning, per chance?" Bridget asked. "We met him in Yuma Town. He said he was chasing his sister, Ursula, to protect her from another bear. Blue?"

Luke shook his head and cut up some of his blueberry sauce-soaked waffles. "Yeah, I know Jonathon. He's my cousin and is interested in dating her. But she's not interested in either of the bears. I keep telling him that. He needs to look elsewhere. Sister, eh?"

Bridget smiled.

"What kind of work do *you* do?" Travis wondered why Luke would be down here, ready to take care of Joe Sharp on his own. Maybe because he had his bear strength to back him up, just like the cougars were stronger.

"I'm a special agent for Bear Relations in Minnesota. Gunnar Swenson is our sleuth leader."

"What does your leader think of you being here?" Bridget asked.

Travis wondered the same. He assumed that others in the pack would take up the slack though.

Chet finished his meal and sat back and was listening in to the conversation.

"He understands why I had to be here, though he didn't like that I'd been dating a human. That's who killed her. Joe Sharp. At least we believe. Supposedly, he's no longer here. I've had word he has gone to Loveland, Colorado. But I learned he owns a house in Cody, and since I am already here, I wanted to check it out just in case the other information isn't accurate." Luke took another bite of his waffles.

"Irena told us about his mother's house. But she also believes he's innocent," Chet said.

"It's certainly possible that he is." Luke finished his meal. "I want to meet up with a grizzly, Cedric Shader, who's in town. He has a special...talent for seeing future events. That's where I'm headed now. To see him. He's supposed to be working another case with the police here in town."

"Cedric Shader. He's psychic?" Bridget asked, and Travis wondered if she was going to share her own ability with Luke, but she didn't.

"Yeah, if you believe in those things." Luke smiled.

Chet smiled too. "We always have an open mind. Loveland. That's only a couple of hours from Yuma Town."

Travis suspected if Chet got that close to Yuma Town, he would make a trip there to see Ava.

"Meeting with Cedric sounds like a great idea. Maybe we can be there for the meeting," Bridget said. "If you give us your phone number, or email address, we can let you know when the man is history just in case we split forces."

The small smile Luke gave Bridget made Travis believe he had no intention of dropping the issue. They exchanged information though.

Luke sighed. "You can come with me to meet Cedric. I'll just text him to let him know you're coming." He pulled out his phone and texted him, then paused, got a text back and nodded. "He said the more the merrier when it comes to taking down a murderer."

"We appreciate that." Chet got a text, and he shook his head. "Ava just learned that you and Bridget came up here to help me take down a murderous cougar."

"We didn't tell her," Bridget said. "We didn't want to worry her. But a lot of people knew we were leaving and I'm sure the word finally reached her."

Chet texted Ava back.

Bridget and Travis finished their meals.

Luke got another text. "Are we ready? You can follow me to Cedric's hotel. He said he just finished his job here."

"Yeah, let's go," Chet said, and they all paid their dinner bills.

In Travis and Bridget's car, Bridget drove, Travis sat up front with her, and Chet sat in the back as they followed Luke to Cedric's hotel.

"I can't believe you keep helping each other out on missions," Bridget said. "I mean you and Luke, Chet."

"I know. I was really surprised to learn he was here searching for the same guy as we are. It would help if we could combine forces," Chet said. "But those who fund our operations might not be game."

"I'm sure if it involves bears too, they would help finance a joint venture if we ended up with one," Travis said.

"You know the wolf who came through Yuma Town said that there is a United Shifter Force that jaguars created and wolves belong to," Bridget said.

Travis looked at his mate in disbelief.

"Didn't he?" Bridget asked.

"Jaguar shifters?" Chet asked, never having heard of such an animal.

"Yeah, I guess"—Bridget sighed—"I read his thoughts and he was thinking of the wolf and jaguar united force and was wondering if some of our cougars could join them. He must not have voiced the idea aloud."

"United Shifter Force," Chet and Travis said at the same time.

"No bears?" Chet asked.

"No. Just jaguars and wolves. Maybe they've never heard of the bears," Bridget said. "We only just learned of them ourselves last Christmas."

"True." Travis smiled. "I'm so glad you can't read my mind."

She laughed. "Travis, I always know what you're thinking anyway."

When they reached the hotel, Cedric greeted them warmly in the lobby. He had dark brown hair and eyes and was tall like Luke, about six-two, then they headed up to his hotel suite.

Chet was hoping that Bridget would tell him about her ability so that Cedric would know they believed in him, but that was up to her to share that she had the ability with others. He would never tell anyone about Ava or her sister's abilities either. That was up to them.

Luke introduced everyone and then they sat down in Cedric's hotel suite in the living room. "I don't have any visions of this guy, Joe Sharp."

He offered them sodas and waters. Everyone opted for bottles of water.

"My good friend Luke always thinks I can see visions of any of these guys or gals that we need to apprehend and know just where they are," Cedric said, passing bottles of water to everyone, "but it's not an exact science."

"Right, but can you get anything from this?" Luke handed him a cell phone.

Cedric arched a brow.

"The scent on it."

Cedric took the phone and sniffed at it. "Your scent. And I smell a male cougar's."

"Which is Joe Sharp's."

"How did you manage to get his phone and not him?" Cedric asked, a sparkle in his eye.

"He slipped away from me," Luke said, disgruntled.

"But he left his phone behind?" Travis couldn't imagine leaving it behind when it might even be able to incriminate him if they could find anything on it that could help in their investigation.

"He might have left it behind on purpose to throw me off his trail if he thought I was tracking him through it," Luke admitted. "Do you see anything about him, Cedric?"

"I see Bridget and Travis going home to their kids and the happy reunion. I see you have words about Jonathon saying a she-bear named Ursula is his sister and Chet's got packing boxes in his house. Nothing about Joe Sharp."

"Do you want to help us with this investigation?" Bridget asked.

"I've got another one I'm working on back in Kalispell, Montana. The police are expecting my help up there as soon as I leave here. I'm sorry I couldn't be of more assistance."

"Do you see anything about Chet and Ava?" Bridget asked, glancing at Chet and smiling.

"Now *that's* personal." Cedric smiled.

"We're going to Joe's mother's home," Luke said to Cedric. "Do you want to go with us?"

"Yeah, sure, I can do that. Since my case is done and I won't be heading back to Montana until tomorrow morning." Cedric rose from his chair.

"Should we go in two vehicles?" Luke asked. "You can ride with me, Cedric."

"Well, it was great you were able to use your ability to know when and where the murderer would strike next on your last case," Bridget said.

Cedric turned to Bridget. "You can't see future events, can you?"

"No."

"But you have some kind of ability, don't you?" Cedric asked.

Travis was astounded Cedric recognized it.

Luke was studying Bridget, looking surprised and waiting to hear if it was so.

She nodded. "I can read minds."

Both Luke and Cedric looked surprised to hear the news.

"I'll be damned," Cedric said, then smiled. "No one, except the homicide detective I was working with, knew I was the one who had seen a vision of the killer and the location and time of his next victim."

"You were thinking about it," Bridget said.

"Bridget keeps you on your toes when she's around," Chet said.

"That must be hard on you, Travis," Luke said.

"I can't read his mind. That's why I mated him, among other reasons, of course," Bridget said.

Luke looked a little worried as if he had been thinking things he shouldn't have been. Travis was dying to ask Bridget, but she could turn off listening to other's thoughts or she at least didn't let on that she listened to them.

But Travis would love to know what Luke had been thinking.

THE BEARS and cougars split up and headed out in the two vehicles and after about twenty minutes they reached Joe's mother's one-story framed house. Curtains were shut on the two windows, a Beware of Dog sign was hanging on the gate to the wood fenced yard.

The yard was neatly trimmed, like someone was still living there.

They parked in the driveway and then they all got out of their vehicles. Chet, Bridget, and Travis went to the door. But the others held back, waiting to see what would happen and provide backup if they needed it.

Chet knocked on the door, and to his surprise, a woman answered it. "Yes, can I help you?"

"We are looking for a Joe Sharp. Does he live here?" Chet asked, thinking the woman was Joe's girlfriend, or maybe she was housesitting.

"That's my triplet brother," the woman said. "He has gone on a trip to Loveland, Colorado." She frowned. "What do you want to speak with him about?"

"We're just looking into a matter that he may know something about," Travis said vaguely.

"Can *I* help you with anything?" the woman asked.

"Is your other brother, Rob, about?" Travis asked.

"No. I have no idea where *he* is. I rarely see him. He comes and goes as he pleases. We all inherited Mom's house, so he's welcome to stay here, but he prefers not to. I have rules and he doesn't like them. Mom put me in charge of the home, and we can't sell it. I was always the more levelheaded of the three of us. I'm Nancy, by the way."

"I can understand that," Bridget said. "I'm Bridget and this is Travis and Chet."

"And the other two men?" Nancy asked.

"Cedric and—"

"Oh, that's Luke. I recognize him now." Nancy lowered her voice and said conspiratorially, "Do you know he is a bear shifter?"

They smiled. "Yeah, and so is Cedric," Chet said. "Do you know anything about Hugo, your brothers' friend?"

"No, I have no idea where he is."

"But you're dating him," Bridget said.

Nancy's blue eyes rounded. Chet suspected that Bridget had read her mind, or Bridget would have told them earlier about Hugo's girlfriend being the triplet sister to Joe and Rob Sharp.

"What is this all about?" Nancy asked again.

"You might have heard the rumors about the cougar women who have been murdered," Bridget said.

Chet assumed Bridget knew what she was doing. He was glad she was on their team again.

"Of course. Within the shifter community, we all have heard about it. It's just ghastly. No woman is really safe, you know. Wait." She frowned at them. "You don't think my brothers or boyfriend had anything to do with this, do you?"

"Joe's name keeps coming up, but others have said he isn't the culprit. That someone else is. That's when Rob and Hugo's name came up," Bridget explained.

"No way." Yet Nancy didn't seem convinced of it herself. Her face had turned ashen, and she was giving off a volume of anxious scents, her heart racing.

Chet hoped she was thinking about the men and was giving Bridget clues about the possibility that one of the men was involved. He and the others were letting it be Bridget's call to pursue the discussion with her further. At least, Nancy didn't just shut the door in their faces.

"If you don't believe that any of the men did this horrible business, does any other shifter come to mind?" Bridget asked.

Chet was amused at her choice of words.

"If you've smelled the crime scenes, you should know who was there at them, right?" Nancy seemed to be holding out hope that the men in her life hadn't done this.

Travis and Bridget looked at Chet since he was the only one who had been investigating this so far. Though maybe Luke had been at the crime scene where his former girlfriend had perished.

"I have," Chet said, "though I don't know which cougars the scents belonged to. That's one reason we need to speak with Joe. To help clear his name." Unless of course he used hunter's spray to disguise that he was at the scene of the crime. "But since some believe he's involved, we have to look into his story."

"He was dating one of the dead women," Nancy said, letting her breath out. "Her parents probably are the ones who believe he did it. But he wouldn't have. He was planning to mate her. But her parents didn't like him. They felt he wasn't good enough for their daughter. That he didn't earn enough money and he has been in trouble with the law before. Fights with men in bars, mostly. He's easily riled."

"We thought Hugo had the hot temper," Bridget said, at least based on what Irena had told them at the restaurant.

Nancy chewed on her lip. "Uh, yeah, he does. His temper is worse than Joe's any day. But neither of them is ever violent toward women. Only guys who give them grief. And believe me, you don't wimp out in a bar around here. If some guy gives you trouble, you stand your ground and ensure they know you're not worth the trouble. We're cougars after all."

"And Hugo? Doesn't he like the women a little too much?" Bridget asked.

Nancy narrowed her eyes at her. "That's in the past. Once he started dating me, he stopped chasing after other women."

Once a womanizer, always a womanizer, Chet was thinking. And if Nancy couldn't see the truth, she would most likely be in for a rude awakening some day in the future if not sooner.

"So if you're dating Hugo, where is he now? Does he stay with you?" Bridget asked. "And what does he do for a living?"

"He does stay with me, and he writes novels."

"A writer," Chet said.

"A novelist. He doesn't like the term writer because that could mean anything. He writes novels."

"Has he been published?" Chet asked.

"Five books."

"Under a pen name?" Travis asked, looking for Hugo, the novelist, on the internet.

"No, his own. Hugo Ransom."

Travis showed his phone to Bridget and Chet. "He writes horror fiction in the vein of Stephen King, he says."

"Right," Nancy said.

Which made Chet wonder if the guy was murdering women to use for story ideas to get rid of writer's block.

"Sure, he writes horror stories, but he's the most caring man I've ever met," Nancy said, defending him.

As long as she wasn't the subject of his murdering spree, if that were the case. "Was Rob meeting Joe in Loveland then?" Chet asked.

"I guess. Joe said he was going there for a job interview, though I was surprised because he loves it here. But I think he believed I might be marrying Hugo and he wanted me to be able to live with him and start a family here. Though my brothers could stay at the house anytime they want to."

Or Joe wanted to get out of the area because the heat was on.

"Can we come into your house so I can verify your brothers' and Hugo's scents?" Chet asked.

"No," Nancy said.

"If it's not them, we'll clear them as suspects at least."

"No. Did you visit all the places where the victims had died?" Nancy asked.

"Yes."

"Did you smell the same cougar scent at each?"

"I did. But there were lots of other cougar scents there too. Some have come forth to tell me they are family or friends, but none of the ones I interviewed had been to all the crime scenes." Which made Chet wonder, if one of these men did it, why they wouldn't have used hunter spray. They had to have known that cougars, not the police, would be looking into the deaths.

The killer, or killers, had purposefully left the bodies in the victims' homes, so that the general public wouldn't run across them. All of the victims had been found by family members who were cougars also. Except in Luke's case, Chet guessed. Which made him wonder if the police, and not just the bear shifter, were looking into Luke's former girlfriend's murder.

Chet had hoped Nancy would let them in the house so that they could continue to talk inside, and he could smell the men's scents. Not just Joe's. But now he knew why Nancy was reluctant to allow them to come in.

"That's all I have to say. I've told you where I think my brother is headed."

"Have you talked to Hugo today?" Bridget asked.

"I did. He said he was going to the coffee shop to write because I am too much of a distraction when he tries to write at home. It kind of annoys me because he lives here off my good-will. He doesn't pay for anything except meals occasionally."

Chet hoped that she was ready to turn him over to them should she learn he wasn't at the coffee shop, and she discovered he was hiding out.

"The Sunshine Coffee Shop," Nancy said. "Don't worry. I won't call Hugo to warn him you're looking for him. He gets really annoyed with me when I call him or text him when he's in the zone writing. So it's not my fault if I don't warn him." Nancy smiled.

Chet suspected there was some trouble brewing with their relationship. "Okay, well, if that's all you have for us, we'll be on our way." He glanced at Bridget to see if she had anything to add or ask, since she could read her thoughts.

"Thanks for your help," Bridget said.

Travis and Chet agreed. Then Nancy closed her front door and the group gathered.

"So we're off to the coffee shop?" Cedric asked.

"Yeah, unless someone wants to hang around here in case Hugo shows up." Chet said. "Oh, and are the police involved in the business with your former girlfriend's murder, Luke?"

"No. A mutual bear friend was checking on her at my request, since he was in the area, and found her dead in her home. The murder was the same as the others. Strangulation," Luke said. "And the murderer had been in her home. There was no sign of forced entry, and she had no self-defensive wounds."

"Like the women knew who he was, were unafraid, and let him into their homes," Chet said.

"Exactly," Luke said. "And I checked out her place and smelled the scent of a cougar, to my surprise. She didn't have any family and maybe that's why she was targeted."

"I'll stay here and keep a look out," Travis said. "But, Bridget, I want you to go with Chet in case Hugo is at the coffee shop and you can learn what you can from him."

"All right."

"Do you want me to stay with you for backup?" Luke asked Travis.

Chet thought it was interesting that Cedric didn't offer.

"Yeah, maybe that would be a good idea," Travis said.

"I believe so," Bridget said, in mate-protective mode.

"All right. Then it's agreed. We'll go, you two stay here. We'll let you know what we learn, either way," Chet said.

"And if he returns here, we'll let you know," Luke said.

Luke and Travis stayed in Luke's pickup and Bridget drove the others to the coffee shop.

"Okay, Bridget, what did you learn that we didn't hear?" Chet asked.

"Nancy suspects we won't find Hugo at the coffee shop." Bridget turned down another street.

"Because Nancy lied to us?" Cedric asked.

"No, because she suspects Hugo has been lying to her," Bridget said.

"Does she think he's guilty?" Chet asked.

"Of murder? No. Of continuing to play the field while he's dating her? Yes." Bridget made another turn and then they were at the coffee shop.

But would Hugo be there?

# 12

Ava was in the middle of baking a birthday cake for a special order when she got a text from Chet. She washed her hands and checked her phone. She was still miffed at him that he hadn't told her the danger he was bound to be in and that he had been concerned enough to call on Leyton to provide backup. She knew it wasn't really any of her business, but if she was to be his girlfriend, she wanted to know if he was putting his life in danger.

Still, she knew that was the case anyway because of the kind of work he did.

He texted: *I may be going to Loveland, Colorado on this case and if I am, I'll drop by and see you if I'm able to. That means if we've taken him into custody and are bringing him to the jail in Yuma Town.*

She texted: *Okay, thanks for letting me know.*

Ava was thrilled.

He texted: *I didn't tell you about the mission, not because I couldn't, but because I didn't want to worry you.*

She texted: *You know if we're going to date each other, I need to know I can handle you always being in danger.*

*Oh, hell, yeah. And you're right. Next time, I'll let you know.*

She texted: *What about this case?*

*We have three possible suspects we're trying to track down and clear them from our suspect list if we can.*

She texted: *Okay, then stay safe. I'll let you contact me when you're able to.*

*Sounds good.*

She wished she could have said more to him. But if she got a vision that showed he was in real trouble, she would call him immediately.

Florence came into the kitchen for some more pastries. "Was that Chet?"

"Yes."

"You know he just didn't want to worry you."

Was nothing sacred in town? No, Ava supposed not. As a retired CIA agent, Florence knew just what it was like to be chasing down bad guys.

"He'll be okay. So will Bridget and Travis, unless you see something differently." Florence put the pastries on plates and then waited to hear what Ava had to say before she took them out to the customers.

"I haven't seen any premonitions of anything," Ava admitted.

"Okay, well, good."

No, it wasn't good. It just meant Ava hadn't seen any of him. He could be in a world of danger any second and she wouldn't have a clue. She went back to icing a couple of dozen cupcakes to get her mind off Chet's job and hoping he would make it here to see her. This time, she would make sure her place was neat.

WHEN THEY FINALLY REACHED THE coffee shop in Cody, Wyoming, Bridget, Cedric, and Chet piled out of the car and headed inside, the fragrance of coffee making Chet think of Ava working at Florence's bakery in Yuma Town.

"Do you want a cup of hot chocolate?" Travis asked Bridget.

"You could read my mind."

Travis chuckled. "Not like you can read others. Unless you're rubbing off on me. I just know you well enough."

Bridget smiled. "If you could read my mind now, that would be cool. But we can get some hot chocolate if I still feel like it when we call it a night at the hotel. Hey, there's a man who looks similar to Hugo, don't you think?"

They all looked at the man sitting in the last booth. He was busy reading a paper and drinking coffee, a half-eaten, buttered bagel sitting on his plate. He wasn't typing on a laptop or writing in a notebook, so Chet didn't think it was him. He was a little taller, grayer haired than he thought he would be.

Chet suspected Hugo wasn't here. But where was he?

Cedric was looking at Joe's phone. "Hugo's on his way to Loveland to meet up with the brothers." He showed his phone to the others to show them what he meant.

"What?" Chet looked at it, but he saw nothing that would indicate Hugo was going to Loveland.

Cedric shook his head. "I guess I saw it on his phone in a vision. He's meeting up with Nancy's brothers in Loveland at the Park Hotel."

"Wow, are you sure you don't want to work with us on this case?" Bridget asked, sounding impressed.

Cedric laughed. "I have that other case, or I would take you up on it. But I want to wish you the best of luck on this mission."

"And we wish the same for you," Chet said.

But Chet was wondering about Ava's similar ability and if she could help them with the case, when he shouldn't be considering such a thing. She should be an agent, getting paid to go on dangerous missions, highly trained in combat and in weapons.

They drove Cedric back to the hotel he was staying at.

After they parked in the hotel lot, they shook his hand, and Cedric went inside. Then Bridget called Travis on Bluetooth. "Hey, Hugo's headed to Loveland. And he didn't tell Nancy. Cedric saw a vision of it. So do you want to meet at the hotel, and we'll stay the night and leave in the morning?"

"Yeah," Luke said, but Chet thought she was saying it to Travis and not Luke.

But if Luke wanted to go with them to track the three men down, Chet was all for it.

"Sure. See you in a few," Travis said.

Chet was thinking about how Travis and Bridget were going to spend their night and Chet wished he and Ava had the same arrangement.

"We'll get up early, have breakfast and head out of here in the morning then," Bridget said.

"Yeah, that sounds like a good plan," Chet said.

They parked at the hotel and headed into the lobby and waited for Travis and Luke to arrive.

"I told you Cedric was good," Luke said. "I only wish he had known earlier, and we could have gotten a head start."

"Well, sometimes someone with his abilities has to be in a place where the vision can be triggered. If Hugo had been in the coffee shop when he contacted Rob and Joe on his phone, then that might have helped Cedric to 'see' it," Bridget said.

Chet wondered if she knew because that's how it had to happen with Ava and her sister, Nina.

"Hey, I need to take all of you to the homes of the victims and see if you find anything I've missed," Chet said.

"Yeah, and we can smell the scents in the residences so we can help you with identifying the culprit if he didn't wear hunter's spray," Luke said.

Then Chet took them around to each of the victims' homes,

checking each of them over, looking for any clues that they could find, breathing in the scents.

"Humans and cougars," Bridget said.

They couldn't find anything that would indicate who the murderer was. Each of the women had been suffocated with a pillow. No forced entry. Nothing left behind.

After investigating the final house, they were ready to call it a night. Then they drove back to the hotel, and everyone said their goodnights. Travis was getting a hot chocolate for Bridget, and Luke and Chet went up to their own hotel rooms.

Once Chet was in his room, he called Ava. "Hey, our perps are going to Loveland. We're going there in the morning. It's a seven-hour drive. I'll let you know when we get in."

"Okay, I'll meet you there."

"All right. We had another person help us, a bear shifter who has future visions."

"Oh, wow. Is he working with you now?" she asked.

"No, he has another job to do."

"Could you use my help?" Ava asked.

He wished. He would like nothing more than to work with her like Travis did Bridget, but it wasn't something Ava was trained for. Now her sister could because she was a police officer. But that wasn't what she was paid to do either.

Still, if Ava was working behind the scenes and could see something that would help them, all the better. "Possibly. I have to admit I think about you all the time.

"Good. I wouldn't want this to be a one-sided affair."

"No way." Then Chet got a call from Chuck. "Hey, the boss is calling, probably for an update. I'll talk to you tomorrow."

"Night, Chet. Stay safe."

"Thanks, you, too." Then he answered Chuck's call. "We're headed to Loveland in the morning. We have Luke Bier joining us." Chet told him about Cedric too.

"That sounds like we're getting more involved in each other's affairs."

"We are. We might end up having to form a United Shifter Force." Chet explained about the jaguars and wolves working with each other.

"Yeah, there might be an issue with funding."

"That's what we were thinking. Okay, well, I'll let you know what happens when we get into Loveland tomorrow."

"Talk to you then," Chuck said and ended the call.

All Chet was thinking of when he finally retired to bed was about Ava and how much he couldn't wait to see her.

AVA SETTLED down for the night and she figured it might still take days for Chet to finish his mission, but at least he would be close to her home, unless the man he was after went someplace else and led him on a wild goose chase.

She hugged her pillow and thought of being with Chet again. Soon, she hoped.

The morning came too early, and she headed into the bakery to begin work. She wondered if Chet was still sleeping in Cody while he was on an assignment and figured he was. It was five in the morning. Sometimes, she went in at four, but she didn't have as much to bake first thing this morning, except for donuts and cheese and sausage kolaches for hungry cougars working early hours too.

What she hadn't expected this morning was to see a dark-haired, very pregnant woman wearing designer-looking clothes, a sequined jeans jacket and jeans, high-heeled boots, and a diamond necklace at her throat, approaching her from a souped-up Maserati. Ava had never seen her before, and then she smelled her scent. She was human. Suddenly, Ava recalled the vision of her—the woman who was coming to see Ricky—to renew relations.

"Hi, I'm looking for Ricky Jones," the woman said to Ava intercepting her as she was about to enter Florence's bakery shop to begin her workday. "I heard he moved to Yuma Town."

"Ricky Jones?" Ava asked the woman.

She looked like she could have the baby any day now. In her vision, Ava had only seen her face, not her whole body.

"Yeah. He loves donuts and it's a small town. I figured you might know him." Then the women frowned. "You had better not be dating him."

"Me? No. He's a deputy sheriff and already very happily married." If Ava could send the woman packing without anyone else having to get involved, she was doing it.

"Married?" The woman held her stomach and looked distressed as if she had just learned the father of her baby was a rat.

But Ricky and his brother had been living here for too long and before that he'd been dating Mandy in another town. This woman hadn't been in the picture. Ricky had been with Mandy once she had run him over with her car and he had turned her —accidentally—in Yuma Town. So he wouldn't have been seeing the old girlfriend in Cody. It just wasn't possible.

"Yes, and they have their own babies on the way. I need to get to work," Ava said.

Tears dribbled down the woman's cheeks. Ava wasn't buying her distress. She looked like she could cry on demand and get her way with the ploy.

"He told me he had dated you years ago," Ava continued, figuring she might as well let the woman know that no one would be taken in by any lies the woman thought to tell about the child she was carrying, whoever it truly belonged to. Mel might not even really know who the father was, and Ava suspected Ricky seemed like the perfect scapegoat. Maybe Mel had even tried to blame other guys and they didn't fall for it. Maybe she thought Ricky was such a softy—he certainly could be—she could coerce him into agreeing to marry her. Or at the very least—support her child. Who knew?

"Oh, you probably don't know about the rendezvous we had." Mel smiled slyly.

"He probably doesn't have a clue about it either. Look, Mel—"

The woman's eyes widened.

Whoops. Ava kept forgetting how she knew things when others hadn't told her about them. "Ricky said he'd dated you way before he met Mandy. So, the thing of it is if you think you're going to make things difficult for him, don't bother. You'll be wasting your time. If you tried to pin the baby on him, it won't work. He can file a paternity lawsuit, just like that." Ava snapped her fingers as an illustration. Then she frowned. "How did you even know Ricky was living here?"

"Irena, a waitress in a restaurant in Cody, Wyoming, learned that Ricky and his brother are living here now. She had dated Kolby and she knew I had dated Ricky."

Great.

Mel narrowed her eyes at Ava. "When my dad learns how you treated me—"

"How? By telling you the truth? Go ahead. Run by the sheriff's office. Believe me, you won't be causing an issue for Ricky. Everyone adores him and they all have his back. And his wife's too. But if you think you're smart enough to pull the wool over everyone's eyes, be my guest." Ava smiled. Then she went into the shop and locked the door in Mel's face. The woman was probably used to getting her way in Cody because everyone knew who her daddy was. But in Yuma Town? The cougars ruled.

Then the woman stomped off and Ava headed back to the kitchen, pulling her phone out at the same time, and calling Dan. Since he was Ricky's boss, she wanted him to know what was up first so he could protect Ricky.

"Hey, the Mobster's daughter, Mel, is in town and she looks like she's ready to have someone's baby any minute, Dan."

"Great. I'll let Ricky...wait. He's on his way to the bakery to get some donuts for the office."

Ava sighed. She should have already had them started and ready to eat by now. She went back to the front windows filled with summery displays and saw Ricky pull up in the police car. "Yeah. He just parked and Mel is following him back to the store. I guess I'll let them in and monitor their talk while I'm baking breakfast goodies."

"Okay, keep me apprised of what's going on if there's trouble."

"Will do."

She opened the door and said to Ricky, "I've got to bake those donuts. Come in and you can wait for them while I'm in the kitchen and have your talk with Mel."

"Yeah, sure, thanks, Ava," Ricky said.

Then Ava went into the kitchen to begin baking pastries for breakfast. She was so late doing it, but at least with her cougar hearing, she would be able to listen in on the conversation between Ricky and Mel and if he needed further witnesses or backup, she would call for it.

"Okay, what's this all about? You being here? Looking for me?" Ricky asked, sounding annoyed.

Mel rubbed her belly. "I told my dad the baby is yours. You have to marry me. That woman in the kitchen said you were married already—but if you know what's good for you and her, you'll divorce her and marry me."

Ava couldn't believe the nerve of the woman. She hadn't even said the baby was his because she could never prove it was. But to get poor Ricky involved in this? What a horrible liar. Poor Ricky.

"You know I'm a deputy sheriff," Ricky said, folding his arms across his chest. He was wearing his uniform so he hadn't really needed to tell her that.

"Right. So? My daddy has a lot of you in his coat pocket." Mel gave him a wicked smile.

"It's not happening. You'll have to square it with your dad and give up the baby's father's name on your own, if you even know who it is."

Mel frowned at him. "He is furious with you and he's going to have your head if you don't come back with me and marry me."

"No deal. For once in your life, tell your dad the truth."

"I can't go home without you."

"I have a job, a wife, and babies on the way. I can't help you."

"All right, but don't say I didn't warn you. You haven't heard the last of this." Then Mel stalked out of the shop.

Ricky ran his hands through his hair and glanced back at Ava.

"I got it all on my cell phone. You denying anything, that you are a deputy sheriff. I can't imagine her dad would believe her," Ava said.

"She has always had her dad wrapped around her little finger. He always buys what she's selling. So yeah, I'm sure he believes it, though if he had her watched at all, which I know he does, he probably has an idea who it might really be. I suspect though, he figures if she'll go to such lengths to say I'm the father, he'll go along with it, thinking she really wants to be with me. I never would have gone along with it. Not even if I had still been working as an informant and unmarried. Can you imagine what her father would have done to me if he had known I turned in bad guys to law enforcement?"

"Yeah, he wouldn't have been happy with you, worried you would do the same to him." Ava finished up the donuts and kolaches, placed them in a box, and handed it to him for everyone at the sheriff's department. "Dan's waiting to hear the news."

"You better believe Mandy is too." Then Ricky thanked Ava and headed for the door, his phone out, calling Dan. "Hey, hopefully Mel is on her way out of here. Ava recorded the whole thing."

"I'll send it to Dan and you," Ava said, and then went back to baking.

"Thanks." Ricky left the shop.

Ava just shook her head. She still couldn't believe the nerve of the woman to do that.

Then she got a call, and it was from Chet. She smiled, thrilled to hear from him so early.

"We're getting an early start and leaving now. We'll be in Loveland at one for lunch."

"It'll take me two hours to get there though."

"Yeah, unless we run into the men and have a time capturing them, if they're truly involved in any of this. If we are led on a hunt, we might end up going somewhere else."

"I'll chance it. Where do you want me to meet you?"

"At the hotel where they're supposed to be meeting up at." Chet gave her the address.

"Okay, I'll see you at three if you're able to hang around." She just hoped that she'd actually be able to meet up with him.

Then Mandy came in for donuts and kolaches for the

hospital clinic and Ava smiled and waved at her. "Got to go. I have another customer." She would tell Chet later about that crazy Mobster's daughter, but she wondered if Ricky had already told Mandy about it.

"See you in a few hours."

Then they ended the call and Ava wrapped up Mandy's box of pastries to go. "Tell me about her. This ex-girlfriend of Ricky."

Ava smiled. Ricky must have told her she had been here and talked to him, but Mandy must have believed he wouldn't tell her *all* about Mel.

"She's a spoiled rotten brat who gets her way because of who her daddy is." Ava showed Mandy the video she took of Mel and Ricky. Mandy could see for herself what she looked like, how she spoke, and all.

"Oh, Ricky didn't tell me she's about to pop one out."

Ava chuckled. "Yeah, a little too late to be hunting down a father for the baby." She was going to tell Mandy that she didn't have to worry about Ricky, but she figured Mandy already knew that. And that she had a whole ton of cougars to watch their backs.

"How are things going between you and Chet?"

Ava smiled. "We're missing each other. He's going to Loveland for a case."

"Oh, great. Then he'll be visiting you?"

"I'm going up there to see him."

"That's super. The nurses and doctors are waiting for me to get these over to the clinic."

"Here you go."

"Thanks." Then Mandy left the shop and Florence arrived.

"Morning." Florence said.

"Morning. We've been busy and I've got to get back to baking." Ava headed back to the kitchen.

More cougars came in for pastries and Florence took the orders.

Later that afternoon, things slowed down, and Ava kept wondering if Chet had reached Loveland yet when she got a call from him. She smiled.

"Hey, we're here, looking for the two brothers and a friend of theirs."

"Oh, good, Chet. Any luck?" Ava asked.

"We're headed to the hotel where they were supposed to be staying."

"Okay, well, you know Tracey is from there, so if you need her help, you should call on her to get you around up there."

"Yeah, we're good so far. We're parking now. You don't have any premonitions about this, do you?"

"No, but if I were there, maybe." She had the afternoon off so she could do it.

"Okay, meet us at the hotel." Chet gave her the location. "If you haven't had lunch—"

"Oh, I haven't. I'd love to have lunch with you all, but it's already one and it will take me a couple of hours to get there."

"We had a hefty breakfast. We'll wait for you. Everyone's in agreement."

"Okay, thanks, I can't wait." She smiled. "I'm on my way." She was elated she might be able to help them with their case. She'd never used it to help any kind of law enforcement before. It was too scary to think of what would happen if she couldn't see any visions in a situation and the police thought she was just a nutcase. But at least with the cougars, they knew she was the genuine deal.

"See you in a few."

She was ecstatic. "Heading out now." She gave Florence a hug. "I'm going to help Chet with his case."

Florence hugged her back. "Finally, someone has enough sense to put your talent to good use."

"Just for this case."

"Uh-huh. Good luck and stay safe."

"I will." Then Ava got into her car and drove to Loveland feeling like she could conquer the world. Chet made her feel that way.

## 13

B ridget and Travis were glad Chet had asked Ava to join them in Loveland for the case. Chet was thankful she could do it too and wanted to. Though he didn't want her to be in any danger. But they hadn't had any success in looking for the men. Just maybe she could get a clue for them. She just needed to be here if her ability would work, he figured. But he didn't want her to feel badly if it didn't work out.

"I didn't smell the men's scents in the hotel lobby," Chet said. "I doubt they would be running around wearing hunter's spray here, believing cougars were trying to chase them down."

"So they haven't gotten here yet or they decided to meet somewhere else?" Bridget said.

"Yeah, either case I figure," Chet said. "Or they've cancelled on the trip here."

They took seats in the café where they could wait for Ava while having some drinks. And still watch for the brothers and Hugo.

"I still can't believe you took down three cougars on your own on that last case," Travis said to Chet.

"You weren't there to help, or I would have given two of them to you."

Travis laughed and saluted him.

They took turns checking on the lobby to see if the men had arrived and somehow slipped by them, but where they were sitting right now was the perfect spot for surveillance.

Then they finally saw Ava drive up and park. Chet hurried out of the café to greet her. He hadn't exactly planned to jump off his chair and nearly upset their drinks, and he smiled when Bridget and Luke laughed and Travis said, "Go get her."

Then Chet hugged and kissed Ava before she'd barely left her car. "I missed you. I'm afraid we have an audience."

Ava kissed him and hugged him back. "I've been missing you and I'm glad we have an audience." Ava waved at Bridget, Travis, and Luke.

They smiled and waved back.

"I'm starving. Are you all ready for a really late lunch?" Ava asked as she and Chet joined them.

"Boy, are we," Bridget said.

Travis had already gotten the menus for them. Chet introduced Ava to Luke.

"I heard about how you helped Chet and the others up in Ely," Ava said.

"Yeah, we were after the same bad guy and his cohorts," Luke said. "Kind of like now."

"I'm having the grilled ham and cheese sandwich," Bridget said, looking over her menu.

"I'm going for the steak and cheese," Luke said, "with an order of berries as a side."

They all smiled at him.

"Hmm, the Reuben for me," Ava said.

"I'll have a Reuben also," Travis said.

"BLT for me." Chet waved at the waitress to take their orders.

Once their meals were served, Chet explained the case to Ava. "But they haven't arrived yet. Two people said they were coming here, and Cedric saw the phone conversation that Hugo and the brothers had that confirmed that," Chet said.

"But not for two more hours." Ava took a bite of her Reuben.

Luke, Chet, and the MacKays were staring at her.

"What?" Ava asked and took a sip of her iced tea.

Bridget picked up a potato chip from her plate and pointed it at her. "You sound like you know for sure that's when they'll be here. We thought they would be here sooner."

"I...I saw three men arrive who fit the description Chet gave me. They looked like good friends, and they were talking away to each other. I heard one say, 'Hugo, are we going to have dinner here?' And one of the men said, 'Yeah, we are. They have the best steaks.' As to the time, I heard the clock chime in the background—five times."

"In another two hours," Travis said.

"Yep." Ava ate one of her potato chips.

"We knew we needed you on the case," Travis said, the others agreeing.

"They're sitting at a booth in the steak restaurant. Well, in my vision. It's in the back of the restaurant," Ava said.

"Do you see anything about us talking to them?" Chet asked.

"Or them trying to elude us?" Travis asked.

Luke asked. "Or pulling a gun on us?"

"I don't see that much. Just that they ordered steaks and they're talking and laughing like they haven't a care in the world. Are you sure these guys did anything wrong?" Ava took another bite of her Reuban.

"We don't know for sure. That's why we need to talk to them and smell their scents. We have to learn if their scents match anyone that had been in the homes where the murdered women were." Chet hoped that the mention of any of this wouldn't be too upsetting to Ava. The CSF agents were used to dealing with crimes and crime scenes. Ava wasn't.

"What do we do in the meantime?" Ava asked. "After we eat lunch, we'll still have about an hour before they arrive."

"We can move to the lobby for a while and then when we see the men, we'll wait until they're seated in the restaurant and then approach them there. They won't be able to bolt if they're sitting in a booth," Chet said. "We can pin them in."

"What if they're not the ones involved in any of this? If you smell their scents and you don't recognize them as anyone that was in the homes where the murders were committed?" Ava asked.

"They could have used hunter's concealment. They would know that cougars would get involved in a cougar's murder," Bridget said. "Unless—"

"The murderer wasn't a cougar," Ava said.

"But all the women murdered were cougars. How would a human have known—" Chet frowned. "Maybe he gained the women's confidence and one of them spilled the beans, then he learned who all else was in her circle of cougar friends."

"Then what do these men have to do with anything?" Ava asked.

"The rumor has gone around that these men might have been one of the ones who committed the murders," Chet said.

"But one of the women wasn't a cougar. She had dated Luke and she was human," Bridget reminded them.

"Do we have a connection between the women?" Travis asked.

"They're cougars from a small town. They knew each other. They were friends. They were all about the same age—mid-twenties to thirties. Different hair colors though. Blond, brunette, redheaded," Chet said.

"It doesn't have to do with hair color like in some serial

killers' cases, but that they are all connected as cougars and friends, or maybe just friends," Bridget said.

"Then who has started the rumors that these men are involved?" Ava asked.

"Someone who actually did the murders and wants someone else blamed for them?" Travis asked.

"We could have been sent on a wild goose chase while the killer is still in Cody," Chet said. "Since we're here now, we'll check out the men's stories to see if they had any connection to the women, or alibis for the time the murders took place."

Ava told them about Mel coming to the bakery this morning and explained all that had happened.

"Poor Ricky," Bridget said.

"It just seems Ricky is always in trouble in one situation or another," Travis said. "In a way, I'm not surprised."

"Well, Dan knows what's going on, and I showed Mandy the video of Mel this morning so she does too," Ava said.

"A video?" Chet asked.

"Yeah."

"Very clever." Chet smiled at Ava.

When the time was upon them, Ava said, "There they are."

Chet couldn't believe Ava would see the three men first. He smiled at her and squeezed her hand. "Okay, let's go inside and get a table."

They found a table near the men and ordered dessert. They remained quiet while they listened in on the conversation. It was great having cougar hearing when they needed it for a mission.

Hugo said, "I'm glad we could get away like this. With all the rumors going around about us—"

"Yeah, by you know who. It makes me wonder if Langston had something to do with it," Joe said.

Langston? Chet wondered why no one had mentioned him to them when they were talking about who might have committed the murders. Had the men been setup to take the fall? But unless they had no alibis for the times of the murder, then maybe they had nothing to with them.

"I just can't believe anyone would think any one of us would have committed the crimes," Hugo said.

Which could mean they were innocent, or one of them was still guilty and was playing the game.

Chet and the others ordered pies and cakes, figuring they would be finished before the men were and could ask them some questions, but also, they wanted to know what Bridget could learn from reading the men's minds in the interim.

"Getting any clues yet, Bridget?" Chet asked.

Bridget shook her head. "Hugo is thinking about some woman that he wishes he was with instead of the brothers, and it isn't Nancy."

"The guy's a womanizer," Travis said. "But no thoughts about the murders from any of them?"

Bridget forked up another bite of her pecan pie. "No. I would think that if they're talking about the murders, if one of them had done it, I'm sure he would have feelings about them. His secret knowledge. It would be hard not to consider it."

"Okay. Then we...you need to just talk to them," Ava said.

"I'm going over there and start up a conversation." Chet finished up his apple pie.

"Do you want any of us to come with you?" Travis asked.

"Bridget?" Chet said. "Travis, you're backup if one of these guys bolts. Luke, you too, if that works for you." Since Luke was here on his own, not part of the CSF, he wanted to make sure Luke was okay with the division of roles. "Ava, you just sit tight."

Ava smiled.

He suspected she would try to block an escape attempt if one of the guys tried to leave and they thought he was the bad guy. Which he didn't want her to do.

"Sounds good to me," Luke said, taking another bite of his blueberry-topped cheesecake.

Then Chet and Bridget got up from the table and Chet introduced himself and Bridget to the three men. "We overheard the three of you talking about those murder cases in Cody. We wondered how much you knew about them and if you might have any clue as to who might have been involved."

Hugo frowned at them. "Are you reporters?"

"No. CSF." Chet showed his badge.

The men's jaws all dropped.

"We're looking into the cases because we believe a cougar did the killings and I'm afraid each of you have been implicated through rumors. We would love to clear you of any suspicions anyone has," Chet said.

"Well, I can tell you right now, none of us had anything to do with the murders," Joe said. "But we suspected it had to be a cougar also since the women were cougars."

"We figured it might be a cougar who has been jilted by his lover," Joe's brother said.

"That could very well be. Tell us your whereabouts on the nights of the murders." Chet listed the dates.

"We have to tell you we've talked about this before because of the rumors that we've heard about us. We have witnesses that can prove we've either been with someone at our homes or working or socializing." Joe shook his head. "We were as horrified over the deaths as anyone who knew them."

"Did you know the women?" Bridget asked.

"I knew some of them, but I was never involved personally with them," Joe said. "They were cougars, and it was a small town, so naturally we would know some of them."

"Yeah, it's like Joe said," his brother added. "It was awful, is awful. We even tried to come up with names of suspects who might have killed the women and who could have been spreading the rumors that it might be one of us."

"Like who?" Chet asked.

"Langston, Benny. He is a real womanizer," Hugo said, as if he wasn't one also. "He has no respect for women. And he has a beef with me because a lady I had dated had left him for me."

"One of the dead women?" Bridget asked.

"No. She's still alive. You can talk to her and learn I'm telling the truth about it."

"You're dating Nancy and giving her the impression she's the one for you, aren't you?" Chet asked Hugo.

"Uh, yeah. You guys are good."

"Thanks. So what about the two of you? What reason would Langston have to try and pin this on you?" Bridget asked.

"Really, Benny doesn't need much of a reason. He just needs to get the heat off himself, if he did it," Joe said. "Why not just start the rumors that any one of us did it? None of us have mates or girlfriends."

"Hugo has a girlfriend." Bridget frowned. "Nancy?"

"I haven't been seeing her all that long," Hugo said. "I mean, some of the killings took place before that."

"Why would he kill a human woman? All the rest were cougars," Chet said, playing along with what they were telling him.

"Are you sure he, or whoever did the killings, did that one too? We asked ourselves that but thought maybe it wasn't the same person," Joe said.

"One cougar had been in all the homes, even the human woman's. She had been dating a bear shifter," Chet said.

The men looked at them in disbelief.

"She'd dated some cougars too," Hugo said. "Not me," he hurried to add. "And I have an alibi for that murder too."

"We all do," Joe said.

Chet wondered about their professed alibis. So many times people had them, but their alibis were from girlfriends or family members, or set up to protect them from appearing to have committed a crime in the first place. Someone who had committed seven murders and not gotten caught yet had to be good at what he did.

Which made Chet think that Langston hadn't even come up on the radar for them.

Chet was writing down all the dates and times and places the men had been so they could check them out.

Of course Ava, Luke, and Travis were listening in also.

"I didn't do any of it," Joe said.

"Neither did I," his brother said.

Hugo shrugged. "I said the same thing. What else can we say to clear our names?"

"That's all the questions I have for the three of you," Chet said.

Bridget smiled. "I'm sure when your statements are proven to be correct, that will be sufficient."

"Good," Hugo said, but he sounded and smelled annoyed.

Not that Chet blamed him. Anyone who was being considered as a murder suspect could feel that way.

Chet and Bridget joined their companions and then they left the restaurant while the men continued to eat their dinner.

"What do you think?" Luke asked.

"I don't know," Bridget said. "I didn't 'hear' anything that the three of them were thinking that would indicate they had done any of the murders. All I could 'see' was that they were considering possibilities of who might have tried to frame them by spreading the rumors. And all of them thought of Benny Langston, who also lives in Cody."

"I say we return there tonight and locate him and question him," Luke said.

"I agree," Bridget said. "I think if we talk to him, we'll learn the truth."

"You will," Travis said. "If he's the one who was involved, I'm sure you'll learn all about it."

"She's handy to have on the team," Luke said.

"She is," Chet agreed. But he felt badly that he'd called Ava to come and join him and then not at least have the night to spend with her. He took Ava's hand. "I'm sorry that we aren't staying the night."

Ava smiled. "I wish I could have helped more, but I'm so glad that we had lunch and dessert together." She gave Chet a hug and kiss. "I hope we can see each other again soon."

"Absolutely." He planned on it.

Then he gave her a hug back and kissed her, not wanting to leave her, but he was glad she was so cheerful about it.

"Okay, I'm off and you catch the bad guy or guys." Ava hugged him again. Then she got in her car, and they all waved goodbye to her and she drove off.

"Let's go and see if we can find the new suspect on our radar," Travis said, and they climbed into the car and returned to Cody.

"That seemed like a long drive for not catching the culprit," Luke said, "though we might be on the right track now."

"I sure hope so." Chet wanted to finish the job so he could make some excuse to return to Yuma Town to see Ava.

Ava was so glad she had seen Chet, got to kiss him, hug him, and have lunch and dessert with him. And to see the others too but being with him had been like being on a date, so she was thrilled.

She really hoped they would figure out who killed the

women and take care of it soon. And she hoped Chet would be able to return to Yuma Town soon too.

She finally arrived home and entered her condo, thinking about the last time Chet was here and wishing they were chasing each other up the stairs.

## 14

E arly the next morning, Chet and the others had been trying to learn where Benny Langston lived and worked. Now they had his home address and knew he worked at Crawley's Bar where he was the bartender.

They all had a quick breakfast early, and then headed over to his home where they suspected Benny would be asleep. But when they knocked at the place, no one answered. They'd learned he was a bachelor and didn't live with anyone. When dealing with cougar shifter rogues, they didn't need a warrant to investigate if a cougar was committing heinous crimes. They put every shifter at risk.

Chet brought out his lockpicks, unlocked the door, and they went inside to search his place for any evidence relating to the murders.

They discovered jewelry that the victims' families and friends had said were missing from their bodies or residences in a box under the king-size bed.

Chet pulled out his phone and showed the pictures of the missing items someone had taken from the victims' homes, and everyone agreed they were the victims'.

"Of course, he could say he went into their places and stole the items *after* he found the women murdered," Bridget said.

"Yeah, you're right," Chet said, "but you will still know the truth."

Travis found some photos between the mattress and box springs in the master bedroom. "Hey, these are pictures of the seven victims. They're alive in these photos."

"It proves he knew each of the women." Luke examined them more closely while the others were searching for any other evidence in desk drawers, kitchen drawers, bedroom drawers, and closets. "He met them all at the bar. Crawley's Bar, most likely. He took the pictures when he was behind the bar."

Chet looked them over more carefully. "You're right. He picked up the women at the bar. It must be frequented by cougars."

They hadn't talked to anyone about him in Cody, not wanting him to get word they thought he was a suspect in the murder cases.

"He won't be at the bar this early," Travis said.

"Yeah, and that worries me," Chet said. "What if he's with another woman? Maybe even the one pictured here that we haven't discovered a body for yet?"

"Then we have to find him," Bridget said.

They'd checked all the rooms in the house. "You know it's odd that Benny was sleeping in the spare bedroom also. His scent is on that bed too," Bridget said.

"Good observation." Chet didn't detect a scent for any of the murdered women in the house. And no other males' scents either. Just Benny's.

Now Chet wished Ava had been with him if she could have seen something about him. "So what now?" Then Chet got a call from Ava, and he smiled. "Hey, we might have gotten a break."

"The one the men mentioned in Loveland?"

"Yeah.

"I called to tell you I had a vision when I was in the middle of making donuts."

"Of?"

"A black-haired man who works at a bar in downtown Cody?"

"Benny Langston?" Chet asked.

"I don't know his name from the vision. I just got a visual. He has a home near there."

"Okay, what did you see about him? Was he doing something?"

"He...he's with a woman. I don't know if she's a cougar or not. He might not even be one. But I just keep feeling this impending doom where he's concerned. If...if he's the one, you have to find him. The woman could be in danger."

"We didn't find him at his place. But we're searching it now. We found some evidence that we believe could be related to the murders." The thing of it was he might have taken pictures of the women, but there had been no sinister intent. Still, why only of the women they had found murdered? Except for the one and he was afraid she might be next.

"He's at her place. There's a yellow Ford Mustang sitting out front. There's a...mailbox, uh, house number—45012. The...the street sign says...Fanning Way."

"We're on our way, Ava. Thanks."

"Let me know if you find anything."

"I sure will. Thanks Ava." They ended the call and Chet told Travis where to drive to.

"How did Ava get the 'message'?" Luke asked.

"From what I understand, she could get a visual of something from a person who is in relatively close proximity, sometimes touch, or if it involves her in some way," Bridget said.

"But this time?" Luke asked.

"Maybe just hearing the men talking about Langston, if he's the one, she finally had a vision," Chet said. "She had one about Joe and his friends because she was going to be there, I figure."

"Okay, this is it, well, actually a couple of houses down," Bridget said.

Travis parked and they hurried out of the car to go to the house Ava thought the man was at. They saw the yellow Ford Mustang parked in the driveway at the home.

"Why don't two of us go to the front door, and the rest of us go around the back," Chet said. "Travis and Bridget in front, Luke with me around back."

"Hope they don't have any big dogs in the backyard, guarding the place," Luke said.

Chet smiled at him, then he and Luke sneaked around the back of the house, hoping that the owner of the home didn't see them and call the police.

Travis knocked on the front door.

No dogs were located in the backyard, and none were in the house barking up a storm either because they were intruding on the property, thankfully. Chet didn't smell any sign of Benny's scent out here.

Suddenly, the back door banged open, and a man bolted out of the house, black hair, eyes wide as he saw Chet and Luke, both running to grab him. He was definitely afraid of getting caught at the house. But it might have only been a case of him making love to a woman who already had a significant other— husband, boyfriend—and he didn't want to get caught.

Luke and Chet both took the guy to the ground and Chet hoped they wouldn't find a dead woman inside the house.

"Hell, get off me."

"We have some questions for you," Chet said, not moving off the guy as he confined his wrists with wrist ties. He definitely was Benny and he'd been in all the victim's homes.

"Let me go, damn it."

A woman came to the back door and watched them, looking shocked, her hand on her mouth, her eyes wide. Thankfully, she was alive and well and she was the same woman from the photo Langston had in his home.

Bridget and Travis came running around through the back gate to join them.

"Are you Langston? Benny?" Bridget asked.

"Yeah, hell, what's it to you?" Langston glanced back at the woman in the house.

"This is an FBI matter," Chet said, flashing a badge at the woman.

"Hell, CSF?" Langston looked ill to realize they were cougars who could take him down if he was the murderer and they were onto him.

"Yeah, we need to talk to you. You're coming with us," Chet said. They had to get him to a safe place where they could question him in privacy. "I'm going to talk to the woman first."

Luke and Travis stayed with Langston, while Chet and Bridget went inside the woman's house to question her and realized she was human.

"What's going on?" the woman asked.

"Langston is just a person of interest at this point." But Chet believed they had their man. He glanced at Bridget, and she nodded. He identified himself and Bridget and the woman told them she was Xenia Monroe.

Xenia's face suddenly drained of color. "You're investigating the murders of the women in town?"

"Yeah. Where did you meet Langston?" Chet asked.

"At Crawley's Bar." She motioned to them to sit on the seating in the living room.

"Have you ever gone home with him before?" Chet asked.

"No. I had just broken up with my boyfriend and Benny was

available. So I brought him home. He's always so friendly. Well, to all the women. God, how could I be so stupid."

"We don't know that he's the killer. We need to question him to learn if he has any alibis for the nights of the murders. Did he take photos of women at the bar?" Chet asked.

"Photos? Uhm, sure. I mean, I don't know about anyone else, but he took one of me. I thought it was cute of him. Not that I was going to take his coming home with me as anything that could develop into anything serious." Her eyes filled with tears. "Excuse me." She headed for a room down the hall, and they heard her throwing up.

"She was thinking he was charming and nice, a change from her former boyfriend," Bridget whispered to Chet. "She's sick from upset that he could be the murderer of the other women and she could have been next."

Then Xenia returned, her eyes red. "I don't know what else I can tell you."

"Did you frequent the bar?" Chet asked.

"Yeah, but I was always with my boyfriend. He bought the drinks, and I never really paid any attention to whoever was serving them. My ex-boyfriend had been so controlling. If I so much as looked at another man when I was with him, he would have exploded. You can see why I broke up with him. Benny was so charming, such a change in venue."

"I'm so sorry you've had to go through any of this, but we still don't know for sure if he's the real suspect or not," Bridget said. "I would just be careful who you go out with until this situation is resolved."

"Thanks. I should have told you that before. You might have just saved my life," Xenia said.

After they finished talking to her, she had nothing more to share, except she'd made love to him, and they had slept until they heard knocking at the front door, and he'd bolted. She thought he had been afraid her volatile boyfriend had come to see her and would kill him.

"Are you taking him to jail?" Xenia asked, seeing them out.

"Yeah, in Yuma Town, Colorado," Chet said.

Then they said goodbye and found that Luke and Travis had loaded Langston up in the car already.

"I don't know what you think is going on," Langston said.

"That you murdered seven women, six cougars and one human," Bridget said as she shut her car door, wedging Langston in between her and Luke.

Chet figured she said so because she was hoping he would confess what he'd done in his mind, even if he held his tongue during questioning.

"What the hell? You've got to be kidding."

"We know you have been at all the homes of the victims," Chet said.

He didn't say anything to that. What could he say? They were all cougars. They could smell his scent.

"I've been to cougars' homes, sure. I'm a cougar."

"Why kill a human?" Luke asked.

"I don't have any idea what you're talking about," Langston said.

"I suspect Langston didn't want to be with the woman, but there were no cougars readily available and so he figured he'd kill a human to see if he got just as much of a thrill out of it as he did with killing cougars," Bridget said.

"He's the one, isn't he?" Travis asked.

"Yeah, he's the one," Bridget said.

Travis said, "We'll question him on the way to the jailhouse."

"Sounds good to me," Luke said. "But I'm going to let you handle this. We have three vehicles. Just drop me off at the hotel and keep me informed."

"Will do," Chet said. After driving for a few minutes, Chet

parked at the hotel. They said their goodbyes to Luke, thanking
him for helping them.

"Thanks for nabbing the guy," Luke said, smiled and headed
into the hotel.

"Okay, so how are we going to work this?" Chet asked Travis
and Bridget.

"Two cars, one driver for each, and one of us takes a turn
sitting in back with the perp," Bridget said.

"Let's do it. I think we should leave him in your car though,
Chet," Travis said.

Bridget said, "I'll stay with the prisoner and you, Chet, and
then we can switch off later."

"Two hours' time," Chet said.

"Sounds good to me." Travis gave his wife a hug and kiss,
then he went to their car and got in.

Then they were on the road, Travis following behind, while
Chet drove, and Bridget questioned Langstone nonstop—asking
him about every victim, times, dates, murder locations, and she
was taking notes. She could be a one-woman CSF team.

It would be enough to drive a man crazy. Chet only smiled,
figuring that even when Langston didn't answer her, she was
gathering all the information she needed.

"I told you, I want a lawyer. I'm not speaking without a
lawyer."

"Rules are different when a cougar kills innocents," Chet
said.

"Besides, your scent and posture reveal all there is to know,"
Bridget said. "So don't mind me. I'll keep questioning you until
someone else does."

When they stopped for gas, Chet drove the MacKay's vehicle
and Travis sat in the back seat with Langston and he started the
questioning all over again. Only this time, Bridget was quiet,
listening in on the one-sided conversation.

When Chet took his turn in the back seat with Langston he asked, "How come the woman is always in the car with me? You think she intimidates me?"

"I think you like to have the upper hand with women, but in this case, she has got your number and all of a sudden, you aren't in charge," Chet said. And then he began the questioning again. Only when he was questioning Langston, the guy was giving him answers. Chet figured the reason he hadn't answered Bridget was that he really didn't like any woman to be in charge of him. Though he didn't trust Benny's answers either. They just weren't adding up.

"That's not what you told Travis," Bridget repeatedly said.

"I didn't tell him anything." Langston growled at her and if looks could kill, Bridget would be on his hitlist for certain, Chet was thinking.

During a switch off, Chet drove the MacKay's car again, getting close to Yuma Town, and he called his boss. "Hey, Chuck. We've got some evidence concerning the murders in Cody and caught the person we think is the murderer, Benny Langston. We still need to learn what his motivation was, but we think he's our man." He shared all they had discovered. "I'll call Dan as soon as we're off here so he knows he has got a prisoner coming in."

"Good job. You sure caught him quick. I heard you spent the weekend on your vacation at Ava's place."

"Yeah, the safehouse was under renovations and she had the only room available."

"Well, you let me know if you're putting in for a transfer, will you?"

Chet chuckled. "Yeah, I sure will."

"Yeah, well, first it was Leyton and Travis and Bridget. It's like a Shangri-la for cougars."

Chet agreed. Especially if a male cat connected with a

female there.

Then Chet called Dan, telling him that they had caught the suspect and they were bringing him in.

"Good show. And Addie will do some investigating to see if he has committed any more serious crimes. Bridget always comes in real handy for the interrogations with being able to read their thoughts."

"Yeah, absolutely."

"Do you have another job to do after this?" Dan asked.

"Not yet. Chuck hired three more special agents to work out of Cheyenne."

"That's a long drive here. You'll have to stay overnight."

"Yeah, I'm going to check in with Ava and see if she has room for me." Chet didn't want to take things for granted. "All right. I'm giving Ava a call now." Then they ended the call and Chet phoned Ava. "Hey, I'm coming in late tonight with the murder suspect. It might be too late by the time I get in"—he really should have thought of that first, but he wanted to see her so badly, he wasn't thinking of that—"but if it's all right with you—"

"I'll leave the light on for you. The spare key will be on the back patio under the table leg."

"Okay, thanks. I can't wait to see you."

"You didn't get bitten this time, did you?"

He smiled. "No, we arrested him as a human."

"Good. I'll see you when you get in."

"I'll try not to wake you."

"No problem. If I hear you coming in, I'm going to get up to make sure you're not an intruder."

"All right, and thanks so much, Ava."

"Is the safe house available?"

"Yeah, so if you want me to stay there and not trouble you tonight, I can do that."

She chuckled. "You can stay here with me."

That's just what he wanted to hear.

## 15

With rock and roll music playing in the background while Ava cleaned up the kitchen after having tilapia for dinner, she wanted to jump for joy that Chet was returning to see her, well, to drop off a prisoner, but he wanted to stay with her. She was glad they'd caught the man and she hoped he was the right one.

She did a little dance around the kitchen floor. She was going for a run for now. Chet would get in too late, and she still wanted to see if the she-bear was anywhere about.

She finished cleaning the kitchen, then danced out of her clothes, tossing her shorts, shirt, panties, and bra on the kitchen floor, then she shifted and headed out the door. She felt like she was on cloud nine.

While Ava was running, she found the scent of the she-bear again and wondered where the bear had been staying that she seemed so close by all the time. Had Jonathon or Blue found her? Or was she evading them still? Ava heard the flow of water falling from Rainbow Falls off in the distance and thought the she-bear had gone that way. At least from the scent trail she'd left behind, she had. Good. Ava was thirsty.

She should have had more water to drink before she left the house.

But then way up ahead she saw the bear. She was smaller than the male bears, and Ava smelled the same scent here that she'd smelled at the cabin and the night Jonathon ran into her after she was treed by a coyote. She was certain it had to be Ursula and she was gaining on her. The bear was eating some blackberries and hadn't noticed her coming yet. She didn't want to startle her or make her think that a cougar was coming in for the kill and have a big fight on her hands. Ava was so far from her yet, she didn't want to shift and call out to Ursula to tell her that she was a shifter, a friend, and she only wanted to help.

Ava wanted to get closer first, and she was when she heard something behind her off in the distance. Voices. Male, three of them and no one she knew. She didn't think they were the bears that had been looking for Ursula either. They'd been running as bears before when they tried to track Ursula down.

Who else would be running around at night other than cougar shifters like Ava or the bear shifters. The only thing she could think of was hunters. She raced toward the bear, wanting to warn her, and that's when the bear turned and saw Ava running at her. Ava quickly stopped, shifted, and said, "Hunters." But she whispered it to her.

Then she shifted and ran to close the distance between them. Thankfully, the bear waited for her. Ava knew the territory and she could help her reach the perfect hiding spot. She shifted again as she got close. "Come with me. I can take you to somewhere safe until the hunters leave."

Ursula shifted. "Let's go."

Then they both shifted back, and Ava led the way.

"I see something that way. Movement. A bear," one of the hunters shouted.

They must not have seen Ava ahead of the bigger bear now.

She was at the pool of water in front of the waterfall and jumped in, then swam across it. She finally reached the waterfall, climbed out on the rocks, and ran through the curtain of water.

Then Ursula splashed through the pond, swimming the rest of the way to the waterfall and pulled herself up on the ledge and ran through the screen of water.

They were standing behind the waterfall, watching for the hunters. Ava shifted and whispered, "Are you Ursula?"

The bear shifted. "Yes, how do you know that? And who are you?"

"Ava." She held out her hand to shake Ursula's. "I...I'm psychic and I'm an empath. Jonathon...came to see me at a fortune teller's booth, apparently having learned I could see visions. Anyway, I saw that you were at a cabin and another bear was after you. Blue? My friend and I met up with him later. He says you aren't Jonathon's sister."

Ursula laughed. "Hardly."

"So both bears are fighting over you?"

Ursula sighed. "Yeah. And I'm not interested in either of them."

"Well, we were worried about you. That something bad had happened to you since they couldn't find you. So I've been looking for you."

Ursula smiled. "Thanks."

"You know, I have room, if you would like to stay at my condo in the guest room for a while until you can sort out things with the guys."

"I might take you up on it for the night, anyway, if we can get ourselves out of this situation."

Then they heard the sound of men's voices and the women both shifted into their fur coats, feeling warmer and safer and they weren't going to talk right now, even though Ava figured the men wouldn't be able to hear them through the noise of the waterfall and how low they had been speaking. But the women could hear them with their enhanced animal hearing.

If the men did something crazy and went through the waterfall to see if they were on the other side of the falls, they could shift first. They would find two naked women, and hopefully wouldn't try to pull anything with them.

"I know that bear and cougar went this way," one of the hunters said.

So they had seen Ava. She thought they'd only observed Ursula.

"The cougar might have gone up on the cliffs, but I don't see it," another said.

"It's getting dark. We'll set up camp here," the one man said.

*Great.* Ava glanced at Ursula who looked just as disgruntled as Ava felt.

"You think that's safe here with a bear and a cougar nearby?"

"We'll all take turns guarding the camp."

Ava had figured they would slip out when the men went to sleep. Then again, if the men were on the lookout, surely they would be watching for any moment coming from every direction other than the pond and the waterfall.

For now, they would just tough it out until the other men settled down for the night and fell asleep.

Ava finally laid down on her belly and Ursula followed suit. At least they could see the men setting up camp, erecting tents, starting a fire, heating water. But the men couldn't see them in the darkness. Not without the cougar and bear's night vision.

"That cougar could be up on those rocks there observing us," one of the men said as they sat beside the fire and warmed up a pot of chili.

That meant they would probably watch in the direction of the cliffs and waterfall. The cliffs were exactly where Ava thought she would go, but she wasn't sure Ursula could climb that steep cliff. Though come to think of it, bears could climb trees so she probably could.

"I'll take first watch tonight and the last shift in the morning," one hunter said.

"Yeah, I'll take the next one," another man said.

"Where do you think they got off to?" the last hunter asked.

"They could have hightailed it out of here, if they knew what was good for them. Or they could be sitting around waiting to make a meal of us. Which means no sleeping on guard duty for any of us."

Ava wished she had her phone. She would have called Dan and had these men arrested for illegal hunting. No one would even know she was missing. Not until she had to go into the bakery at four in the morning. Chet might come in about two. He might not even check on her, thinking she had to go in so early, he wouldn't want to disturb her.

Of course, she had no intention of waiting until morning and the hunters went back to hunting. She and Ursula would be out of here as soon as two of the men went to sleep and only one man was on guard duty.

Ava figured both she and Ursula would need to decide who left the cave behind the waterfall first. And once one of them was out of there safely, the other would take off and they could meet up and Ava would have Ursula follow her home.

Ursula had to have left her clothes somewhere. They would need to go there first. Maybe she had a car parked somewhere close by. Ava wished they'd had more time to talk before the hunters had shown up.

The hunters talked forever though, and Ava didn't think they would ever go to sleep.

LATE THAT NIGHT, Chet and the others finally arrived in Yuma Town, and he called Dan. The sheriff and Ricky took custody of Benny Langston.

"Have you had any trouble with the ex-girlfriend yet?" Chet asked Ricky.

He shook his head. "She has been here already. But as far as I know, she returned home and that's the last of it."

"Good. I hope so. I'm going to get some sleep."

"Is Ava putting you up?" Dan asked.

"Yeah, she is."

Dan and Ricky smiled.

"All right, thanks." Then Chet said goodnight to Bridget and Travis also before they headed home, and he soon arrived at Ava's place. The first thing he noticed was it was dark. She had said she would leave the light on. Had she changed her mind about him staying with her? Or had she just forgotten to leave a light on?

He found the spare key under the patio table leg on the back patio and let himself in.

As soon as he walked into the kitchen, he saw her clothes strewn about the floor. It reminded him of the first time he'd been to her place to stay, and she'd dropped her clothes all the way to her bedroom because she wanted to hurry and swim the day of Fourth of July festivities. But she had said she normally didn't do that. And since she had known he was coming, he figured she really wouldn't have done it.

It made him think she had shifted and gone for run as a big cat. But at this hour? He headed for the stairs and went straight to her bedroom to make sure she was sleeping there. He hadn't planned to disturb her, though one of the steps on the stairs squeaked when he stepped on it. When he finally reached her bedroom, he peeked inside and saw that the bed hadn't been slept in. He checked the master bathroom, but she hadn't taken a shower in it recently and she wasn't there. He thought maybe she was sleeping in the guest room bed, waiting for him to come him. He sure liked that idea.

But when he didn't find her in there, that really worried him. Before he stripped and shifted and went into search mode, he called Dan as he hurried down the stairs. "Ava's not home. She left the spare key for me, but her clothes are on the kitchen floor near the cougar door, and it appears she went for a run, but she hasn't returned."

"Did you check with her sister first?"

"No."

"I'll call Nina first and get back with you. Don't go until you hear from me, just in case she's over there for some reason, or she told Nina where she was going."

"All right. But make it quick." Chet didn't want to have to wait a second longer than necessary before he took off after Ava. Yet, it would be foolish of him to take off searching for her if she was just with her sister or at the bakery or something and was all right.

He got a call back from Dan. "She's not at Nina's and now she's worried. We're organizing a search party now. We'll meet you at the condo."

"I'm leaving now. You can catch her scent." Chet wasn't about to wait a second more. He dumped his clothes on top of hers on the kitchen floor and then shifted and bolted out the door after her.

He prayed she was okay as he ran after her, following her scent. He had to find her.

He ran across a she-bear's scent soon afterwards and he suspected Ava had been after the she-bear, to learn her story. But he didn't think she would be out this late like this if she'd met up with the woman and had talked. Not when she knew he was coming in to stay with her and he would have worried about her. Which meant? She was in trouble, he was afraid.

Then he found the scent of three males—humans, following her. Following them? Who were the men?

Hell, they better not be hunters. He sprinted faster through the woods and thought all of them were heading toward Rainbow Falls. He figured if Ava was in trouble, she might have decided to hide behind the waterfall if hunters were after her and the bear. The she-bear might not know a safe place to hide like Ava did.

And then he finally saw the tents—three of them. And one hunter sitting with a rifle on guard duty.

So if the women were hiding behind the waterfall, they might not have been able to leave because of the hunter watching for them.

Chet wanted to pace. He wanted to snarl and tell Ava he was here if she was there. He wanted to shred the tents and scare off the hunters into the darkness. He wanted to join her behind the waterfall and let her know he was there for her.

But he needed to wait for the others to get here, to take these men into custody, while he remained here to protect Ava.

That's when she shot through the waterfall and headed up the face of the cliffs, leaping from one boulder to the next.

At the same time, the bright full moon helped the hunter sitting beside his fire see her and he began firing at her. Chet slammed into him, taking him down, then leaped onto the cliffs, and headed Ava's way. He thought she would have headed home, but she was sitting in a safe spot where the men couldn't reach them, and she quickly greeted him.

"I was worried about you," he said, shifting in the darkness where the men couldn't see them and giving her a hug.

She shifted and shivered in the cool night air. "Ursula is still in the cave," Ava whispered. "We need to stay here and get her out of there safely. But when the hunter shot at me, she'll know she has to stay put."

"I notified Dan that you were missing. He's getting a search party together and they'll all follow our scents. They'll deal with the hunters and we can take Ursula home with us."

Ava held onto Chet tight. "You are so my hero."

He smiled at her and kissed her. Then they shifted to stay warm in their cougar coats and laid down on the rocks, watching the one man leaving his tent, scrambling to get dressed, and readying his rifle.

"Up there," the one hunter serving on guard duty said as the last guy that was sleeping emerged from the tent, still pulling on his boots. "Two mountain lions. That's the way they went up there. Shoot them."

## 16

Ava couldn't believe Chet would search for her after he got into town and realized she wasn't in bed. She was afraid he would have just gone to sleep and not wanted to disturb her. She'd already decided Chet would sleep with her in the master bedroom, if Ursula stayed at Ava's place and she could use the guest room. Even if Ava hadn't found Ursula, Ava wanted Chet to stay with her in her bed anyway. If she had been waffling about it, which she hadn't been, his coming to rescue her cinched the deal.

For now, they were waiting for the troops to arrive to ensure their safety. At least she had Chet to snuggle with on top of the cliffs. Though the men fired off the shots, they couldn't reach them. The rounds pinged off the rocks, clipping at them, but well below Chet and Ava. She didn't think they could even see her and Chet up so high on the cliffs with only the moonlight shining on the scene. She was certain she and Chet blended in with the dark shadows of the rocks. Unless the men tried to climb up here, the cougars were safe. Ursula was also safe where she was at for the moment. But Ursula didn't have the benefit of knowing that the law enforcement officers of Yuma Town were coming to their aid, or that Ava was all right after the shooting the hunters had done, or even that Ava hadn't abandoned her.

"What the hell happened, man?" one hunter asked, looking up at the cliffs while Ava and Chet watched them move back to the safety of the campfire.

"The cougar came out of nowhere and before I could get a shot off, another attacked me."

"Did it bite you?"

"No, it just pounced on me and knocked me down. By the time I was able to get to my feet and ready my rifle, he was halfway up the cliffs. I fired a bunch of shots, hoping to hit him."

"So you're saying two of them are out here?" one of the other men asked.

"Yeah. One came out of the pond, and then the other came at my back, like it was protecting the other from me shooting it. Even though we only saw one earlier, there are two now up on the cliffs. We shot up there, and I was hoping if we didn't kill them outright, we would chase them off."

"Then a male and female? Or maybe a mother and a couple of kits that are still with her."

"They both looked like they were full grown to me," the hunter Chet had knocked down said.

Ava owed her life to Chet. If he hadn't thrown the hunter's aim off when he heard her come out of the water and whipped around to shoot her, she would have been dead. Upon death, she would have shifted into a human. If Chet hadn't pounced on the hunter, she wouldn't have stood a prayer of a chance. In retrospect, she should have stayed put.

But she'd worried someone running in their cougar coat would come along and then get shot—like Chet could have.

Then she finally saw lights approaching from the direction she and Ursula and Chet had run. Good. Whoever the rescuers were had to be in their human forms and were using flashlights to let the hunters know they were coming and not sneaking up on them so *they* wouldn't get shot.

"Hey, someone's coming," one of the hunters said.

"I'm Sheriff Dan Steinacker," one of the men shouted. "Lower your weapons now."

*Yes!*

"Two mountain lions are out here, up on the cliffs and they damn near killed us," the one hunter said.

"Did either of them bite you?"

"Well, no, but the one knocked me down."

"What are you doing out here? Illegally hunting?" Dan asked.

"We have a right to protect ourselves from bears and mountain lions," one of the other hunters said.

"Hand over your weapons. Pack up your stuff. You're coming with us," Dan said.

"You can't prove we were hunting anything," the one man said.

"We heard all the shooting from a mile away," Dan said.

"Yeah, for protection."

"We have really strict laws out here," Dan said. "And we have eyewitnesses who reported you were trying to kill a bear and a couple of cougars."

"No way in hell," one of the hunters said.

Ava figured Dan meant that she, Chet, and Ursula were the eyewitnesses. Not only was Dan there, but three of his deputy sheriffs, Nina, Addie, Stryker, and Chase, and the CSF special agents—Leyton, Jack, and Travis were also. All of them had to have smelled Ursula's scent and heard the shots fired.

Then Stryker, Jack, Addie, and Travis hauled the hunters off while Dan, Nina, Leyton, and Chase stayed behind. Others would gather any evidence of the shooting—shell casings primarily, in the morning at dawn, but for now, they were looking for Ava and Chet.

As soon as the hunters were out of earshot, Ava and Chet moved down the cliff, but that was when she smelled blood. Not her blood. Had Chet been hit?

Nina called out, "Ava, are you and Chet okay?"

Ava growled that she was.

When they reached the bottom of the cliff, she dashed into the water and swam to the waterfall, hoping that the men would take care of Chet if he'd been injured. Ursula wouldn't know that these men were safe to be around.

Ava went through the waterfall and she shifted. Ursula was still a bear. "Come on. You can go with us to my condo and stay with me and we'll talk after we get some sleep. My cougar friends in law enforcement came to our rescue."

Ursula shifted. "Are you all right?"

"Yeah, but my friend Chet, who came to my rescue, might have been hurt. He was the one who called the sheriff and alerted him I might be in trouble. Chet was supposed to come stay with me so he discovered I'd gone for a cougar run and hadn't returned home. The sheriff will charge the men with everything he can come up with and discourage them from coming here again."

"It's a good thing for us that Chet came after you then. I hope he's okay, and I'm glad the hunters will get what they deserve. We've got to get my clothes first though."

"Okay, you lead the way, and we'll get them and then go to my place. The guys will keep us safe."

Then they both shifted and headed out of the cave, through the waterfall, and swam across the pond.

Their rescuers probably wondered what Ava was doing, and they looked surprised to see Ursula. Nina gave Ava a big hug and Ava licked her cheek in greeting.

Ava nuzzled Chet who was now wearing a bandage on his hind leg. She hoped he hadn't suffered too bad of an injury, and it made her feel an even closer bond with him for putting his life at risk to rescue her. He nuzzled her back as if to say he was well. Though she didn't trust him when it came to telling her the truth about his injuries and how he was truly feeling.

"He'll be okay," Nina said, and Ava was relieved to hear it.

When they reached Ursula's clothes, Ursula shifted and dressed.

"Thanks for coming to our rescue," Ursula said, while Dan made introductions. "Ava told me you've been concerned about me. I just have to say that I appreciate your help. Both Jonathon and Blue are interested in dating me, but I'm looking for something else."

Then they all headed in the direction of Ava's condo.

Once they finally arrived at her home, the men said good night to them, and Chet and Ava headed into the house through the cougar door.

Ava shifted and she unlocked the back door for Ursula. Chet had shifted and was already pulling on his boxer briefs. Ava pulled her shirt on over her head and then slipped her shorts on. She wasn't bothering to dress in more than that because she would be removing her clothes shortly before she showered.

"Would you like something to eat or drink?" Ava asked Ursula. "What about you, Chet?"

"Just some water for me, thanks," Ursula said. "If you don't mind, I would love to take a shower and get some sleep."

"Yes, of course," Ava said and got all of them iced water.

"I'm with Ursula. I just need some sleep," Chet said.

Ava figured she'd change his mind about that in a hurry. "Okay, then. I'll show you to your room, Ursula." Ava led her upstairs and showed her the guest room. "And in there is the bathroom."

"Thanks so much for taking me in for the night," Ursula said.

"And thanks again, Chet, for the rescue." Then she disappeared into the bathroom and started the shower.

Ava figured his injury couldn't have been too bad or Nina would have insisted he went to the clinic. Ava took hold of Chet's hand and hauled him to her bedroom. "Shower first?"

"Yeah. Are you going to join me?" Chet asked, looking hopeful.

"Unless you're shy."

He laughed and yanked off his boxer briefs.

She glanced down at his bandaged leg. "You were shot. How bad is it?"

"Just a bullet that ricocheted off some of the rocks and grazed me."

"It's bleeding."

"Yeah, so we wash up and you can bandage me again."

She frowned at it. "Maybe you need to see the doctor."

"No way. They would have just bandaged me, nothing more. I swear it."

She sighed. "Okay. But if you start running a fever..." She pulled him into the shower and started the water. And then she began kissing him. "You are my hero, you know."

"As soon as I saw you were gone and at the hour you were out running as a cougar, I worried about you."

"Well, I'm glad you did."

They began soaping each other up, their mouths kissing each other, their tongues licking and stroking each other's as the hot shower water caressed their skin.

"*You* are delectable," he said.

"You are too. I'm so glad you caught your man and returned here with him to incarcerate him in the jailhouse. And to see me."

"Yeah, I told Chuck that's where I was taking him when I

found him. He accused me of wanting to return here and work with Leyton and his team."

Ava smiled up at him. "Was he right?"

"Yeah. I developed this real need to be with the old team."

She smiled.

"But mostly, I wanted to be near where you are."

"We only dated for a weekend."

"Yeah, but I want a hell of a lot more weekends like that with *you*. And evenings during the week, you name it. Taco Tuesdays. Monday Movie Nights. Friday Free-for-Alls."

She laughed and began kissing him again. "I wanted the same thing, but I didn't think a long-distance relationship would work out."

"I agree. That's why I needed to make a change. And Chuck has hired three new special agents."

"Oh, that's great news. But are you sure you want to be here?"

"Hell yeah. This is the happening place. I want to be with you and working with Leyton and the others."

"I heard they had a new female agent in Cheyenne."

"They do. But I want to be with you."

"Okay, well, if you're sure." She kissed him again. "I want the same." She hadn't had anyone like him to date ever. There was a possibility they wouldn't succeed as a couple, but if he was living and working here, they had a much better chance at it.

Then she was soaping him up further, his arousal already full blown and she wanted to take this to bed and feel the pressure of his erection filling her.

They rinsed off then and he and she grabbed towels and dried each other off. Lots more fun than just drying themselves. Then she removed his wet bandage and checked to see that his injury wasn't more than a bloodied scratch. There was no need for stitches, so she applied a new bandage over the wound.

He kissed her again, but before they got carried away, they headed into the bedroom and climbed into bed. She was tired, sure, but she felt revived now, just wanting to make love with Chet.

"You're so hot," she said to him and began to kiss him again.

"Oh, man, you make *me* feverish, all in a good way."

This was what she had needed in her life. Him, a hot cougar, who needed her as much as she needed him. He caressed her breasts, massaging, making her feel like she was in heaven, hot and passionate and needy. He was kissing her throat and mouth and cheeks all the while. And then she was kissing his jaw, neck, and mouth, their tongues tangling.

She ran her hands over his hard body and loved the muscled feel of him, remembering him dripping wet at the lake and all hers now in the moment. He was just perfect for her.

She surrendered to him completely, unlike how she'd ever been with any man before him—which was a rare thing for her anyway.

His five-o'clock shadow made him appear roguish, the bristle chafing her cheeks, intriguing her, totally cougar sexy. She could sure get used to this. To loving him, to having special nights together. Their nights. And shared nights with others where he was in her court all the way.

Besides making love to each other. Yeah, she could absolutely get used to this.

The ache between her legs intensified before he even began to stroke her there. She felt tense, eager for his stroking her as she rubbed her body against his, instinctively, like a big cat would her mate.

His dark brown eyes were filled with desire as he studied her for a moment and then he began to kiss her again. He swept his hand down her tummy to her short, curly hairs and then he began the incredible seduction, his finger finding her nub and stroking, fully arousing her. She was so ready for taking this all the way.

He kissed her again, his mouth lingering on hers, slowly, measured, and she savored his kisses, but he was continuing to stroke her between her legs the whole time, working her up.

Her heart was drumming in her ears, pounding with fervor.

"*So* hot," she mouthed against his lips. She was burning up and had an unquenchable thirst for him. Every bit of him.

He kissed her ear and pulled on the lobe with his lips and then began kissing her breasts.

She was feeling the end coming. The beginning. The climax building. The flow of emotions overwhelmed her as he pulled his mouth from her nipple and he whispered in a ragged voice, "Let it go."

She realized how tense she was, drawing on the passion of his touching her until her drew her over the top and she released, shattering, ready for him to take the plunge next.

He began kissing her again, readying himself to dive between her hot, slick folds. Then he was centered, pushing in, and she was ready for him, accepting him as he started to thrust deeper inside her.

She lifted her pelvis and met his thrusts, sweeping her tongue over his lips, his hips moving against her. She straddled his hips, wanting him deeper still.

She loved how much power she had over him, just as much as she loved how he made her think of nothing else but being with him like this. His passion fueled her need to come again and without a word, he moved her around him and continued to thrust between her legs, but now he was at her back. He reached over her hip and began wickedly stroking her nubbin again. Ohmigod, she was in heaven. He nuzzled her neck with his mouth, and then nibbled her earlobe.

But he was still thrusting into her, and she felt as though she was turning to mush, but at the same time, tensing with the wild expectation of coming again, feeling the high approaching. Oh, man, Chet was a godsend.

He started to hold back, and she was certain he was trying to suppress the need to finish before she could. He stroked her until she was about to come.

"I can't hold back, hon," Chet said.

"Oh," she moaned, "I can't either. Keep going."

He kissed her shoulder and climaxed, continuing to stroke her until she cried out. "Oh, man, you are a girl's best friend." She couldn't have been any more ecstatic than she was now.

He chuckled and pulled out of her, then she turned to face him and he took her into his arms. "*You* are amazing. And this is equally nice."

She licked his lips and he kissed her again, deepening the kiss.

Then she rested her head on his chest, her leg draped over his. "I'll say." And she was thinking how much she wanted to keep him and never let him go. She couldn't believe how much he affected her in a good way.

---

## 17

The next morning, Ava woke early, smelling the coffee in the kitchen brewing and since Chet, the hunk of a male cougar, was sound asleep next to her, she figured Ursula must be in the kitchen. Ava sighed. She had to get to the bakery to work. She grabbed her phone and saw she had a text from Florence.

Florence texted: *Take off this morning. I know you have the bear staying with you and need to learn what you can from her. Come in when you can.*

Ava texted: *Thanks, Florence.*

Ava was so glad Florence had given her some time off this morning. It was time to sit down and talk with Ursula. Ava yawned. Man, she was going to need a catnap this afternoon after all the loving she'd had with Chet last night and dealing with the hunters and chasing down Ursula. She slipped out of bed, trying not to disturb Chet and grabbed her clothes and hurried to dress. She left the bedroom and carefully shut the door.

When she walked into the kitchen, she found Ursula sitting

at the kitchen table eating an English muffin, coated in honey, and drinking coffee.

Ava smiled.

Ursula was watching out the window but heard her come in and turned and smiled at her. "I hope it was all right to eat a muffin. I was starving after that wild night we had. I didn't want to wake either of you."

"Oh, absolutely. It's fine. I'm usually up even earlier than this so I can get into the shop and bake. But Florence texted me and said not to come in until later so I could rest up after our ordeal last night." Ava didn't want to mention that knew she needed to question Ursula as to what was going on.

"Oh, good. I want to pick up some honeybuns before I leave town."

"Why did you come to Yuma Town? Or the surrounding area to get away from Blue and Jonathon?" Ava asked, popping an English muffin into the toaster. After seeing Ursula eating it, that appealed to her too.

"I didn't want them fighting over me. I tried to tell them that I wasn't interested in either of them without hurting their feelings, but they just weren't listening. Each was trying to outdo the other. Our sleuth leader said he wouldn't get involved in relationship squabbles and just to work it out ourselves. Just like bears do in the wild would. So I just drove until I found this neat, unoccupied cabin in the woods. But then they brought the trouble with them. The next thing I know, they're trying to locate me after I had made a few runs as a bear around the woods surrounding the cabin. I have no idea how they found me. Though I'd seen both of them at one point and neither of them had seen me. I packed and left the cabin before either of them arrived at it."

Ava felt bad about that right away since *she* was the one who had told Jonathon where to find her. "Oh, I'm so sorry. I was a fortune teller at a booth during the Fourth of July celebration at Pinyon Pines Resort on Lake Buchanan and Jonathon wanted to know where you were. That you were in danger because of another bear." She pulled her toasted muffin from the toaster and butted it, then added honey.

"How did *you* know where I was?"

"Sorry, I'm so used to everyone in Yuma Town knowing what I can do, sometimes I take it for granted that not everyone does. I see future visions." Ava figured Ursula wouldn't believe her. Most people who learned that about her didn't unless she could prove it.

"Oh, okay," Ursula said.

Ava was sure that meant Ursula didn't believe her. She fixed some berry tea for herself and sat down to eat with Ursula.

"I know a couple of bears like that." Ursula got a refill for her coffee.

That really surprised Ava. "Oh, okay. You know, you would think that Jonathon and Blue would realize you aren't interested in them, and they would give the whole thing up."

"It's a power trip between them. Competition between two males, and yes, I've dated each of them, so it isn't like I didn't give them both a chance. They're sure I just don't want to get them all riled up by professing my love for one and then the other is left out in the cold."

Ava suspected there was something more to it than that. "But there's somebody else you're interested in." She finished off half of her muffin and took a bite of the other half.

"Yeah. An investment counselor at a bank in Ely, Minnesota, but he barely knows I exist. I've had a lot of financial dealings with him, and he knows I'm a bear too, but he has never asked me out and the one time I asked him, he said he had other plans."

"Is he seeing another she-bear?"

"He broke up with one. Maybe my asking him out was too soon after he and the other woman broke up."

"That could be. What appeals to you about him?" Ava took another sip of her tea. She couldn't imagine wanting to date a guy if he wasn't in the least bit interested in her. She wondered if he was just shy with women though.

"Oh, he has the cutest dimples when he smiles, dark brown eyes and the blackest eyelashes, long and full, like I wish mine were. And his hair is dark brown, nearly black, cut just so for his professional job. Despite being a banker, he's well-toned, muscular, not bulky like a bodybuilder, but in great shape. I've seen him shift before in the woods."

Ava smiled. That could describe Chet, except for the coloration. "Were you stalking him?"

Ursula's face flushed. "Uh, no, I was just out for a bear run when I smelled his scent and went to see if he was out running as a bear too. I hadn't expected him to be getting ready to strip and shift."

"Did you run with him then?"

"No. I didn't want to intrude."

Maybe the one who was shy was Ursula.

"Did you watch him run, track him?"

"No, I went my own way. I didn't want him thinking I was following him. I ended up running into hikers and scared them to pieces and I called it a day. Do you mind if I get another muffin?"

"No, of course not. Help yourself. Would you like some bacon and eggs to go with it?"

"Oh, sure, thanks."

Ava rose from her chair to make them a more substantial breakfast.

"So what about you and Chet?" Ursula asked.

"He lives in Cheyenne, Wyoming usually, but I think he's

probably making a move down here to work with the Cougar Shifter Force in Yuma Town." Ava figured he still needed to call all the parties concerned—Leyton, who would be his boss here, and Chuck, who would need to approve the transfer.

"See? That's what I mean. If Dennis was in the least bit interested in me, he would follow me to the ends of the earth."

Ava turned the bacon and finished the eggs. "Well, we don't know if we were meant to be together forever, but we're having fun getting to know each other."

"And he came to your rescue last night."

"That's true." Having a male cougar who took it upon himself to wake up the sheriff while concerned for her safety said a lot about him.

"I hope it all works out for you."

Ava smiled and dished up the bacon and eggs.

"With your visions, have you seen anything else in my future?" Ursula asked.

"No, just that you were trying to get away from a bear. And Jonathon said you were his sister, so we were worried about you."

Ursula laughed. "He wants to date me, not be my brother."

Ava sat down to eat with Ursula. "What are you going to do now?"

"Go home. They'll have to get the message one way or another. I'm not dating them."

"Okay, good. But you're welcome to stay longer or visit me anytime."

"Thanks. You can visit me too. You'll have to keep me posted on you and Chet." Ursula shared her phone number and email address with Ava.

"Thanks. I will. But who knows where it will take us? Maybe just a dead end." Ava shrugged. She didn't think so, but where guys were concerned, it was always iffy for her.

"You don't see anything in your future about it?"

"Like Chet holding a couple of babies in his arms while we're going diaper shopping?" Ava laughed. "No."

CHET STIRRED awake and glanced over at the mattress in Ava's bedroom but found she had already left the bed. Man, he must have been tired.

He heard her talking to Ursula in the kitchen, and smelled eggs and bacon and coffee brewing.

He normally woke early, but after making love to Ava again during the night and the late night they'd had already, he had slept in. Then he heard Ava and Ursula talking and he didn't want to intrude. He got up and took a shower, planning to tell his boss he was transferring to Yuma Town though. He'd call Leyton first to see if he was agreeable to him working with his team. Leyton had always told him he should move here and work with them, but Chet had to make sure it was still okay with him.

He lifted his phone off the bedside table and called Leyton. "Hey, Leyton, it's me. Hope you got some sleep last night."

"Yeah, I did. Hope you got some."

"Some."

Leyton chuckled. "What's up?"

"Does the offer still stand for me coming to work with you and the others?"

"Hell, yeah. Chuck said you have three new agents filling our positions. Though I heard one of them is a she-cat," Leyton said.

As if Chet would be intrigued with anyone else once he got to know Ava better. "Not interested. I've been friends with you guys for years and I can't imagine working with another team like yours. And yes, I know you're the boss this time around. I have no issues with that."

"Besides, there's a she-cat here who has been missing you, I've heard tell."

Chet smiled. "Well, I've been missing her too."

"What about your mom?"

"She's not moving until she knows it's a sure thing."

"She's a smart woman. When did you want to start working?"

"I'll talk to Chuck, but he told me already that if I decided to transfer here, I wouldn't have to give him any notice now that he has a whole new staff working for him there."

"Okay, good show."

"I'll get a place lined up and move my stuff down. That's all I'll need time for. Then I can begin working."

"We'll help you move."

"I appreciate it, but I really don't have that much to move. I'll get back with you when I'm about ready to return here. And thanks! Talk to you later." Then they ended the call.

Chet called his boss next, who oversaw Leyton and his operation in Yuma Town also, so it wasn't like he was actually quitting his job. He would just be relocating. "Hey, I spoke with Leyton and he wants me to work with him and Travis, Bridget, and Jack. You've got your three new special agents in Cheyenne. Are you good with that?"

"Yeah, why do you think I hired three new agents? I knew, even before you began seeing Ava, that you would be joining your fellow agents since all of you get along so well."

"Thanks, Chuck."

"How are things between you and Ava?"

"Good. I'll get a place of my own temporarily and date her to make sure things work out between us, but I would say we are good for now."

"That's great. What about your mother?"

"She says she's staying in Cheyenne until I decide to truly settle down—with a she-cat. She's afraid I'll fall for some other cougar and move to a different location and she'd be here, and I'd be somewhere else with a mate."

Chuck laughed. "I don't blame her. We'll be talking and if I need you up here, I'll call on you."

"Sure thing." They ended the call and Chet needed to find a place to rent and then move there. He suspected Ava might offer to let him stay at her place in the meantime, but he didn't want her to feel obligated.

Before Chet could leave the bedroom to join the ladies, Travis called him right after that. "Hey, I heard the good news. Though it took you long enough."

Chet smiled. "Chuck had to hire some more agents to take our places."

"And you have other interests here which made it really worthwhile to move." Travis sounded like he was smiling when he said it.

"Uh, yeah."

"So, did you want to stay at the safe house until you figure out what you want to do?" Travis asked.

"Yeah, you know that would be perfect. I thought of renting a place, but I can do that anytime. The furniture belongs in the safe house in Cheyenne, so I just need to pack up my personal belongings. The other three agents will appreciate that they have more room at the house when they use it."

"Okay, that sounds good. I'll let you go, and I'll get the place tidied up for you. We're so glad you are joining us finally."

"Yeah, me too." Then Chet ended the call, and he took a quick shower and finished dressing and then he headed down the hall to the kitchen to speak with Ava and Ursula. He had to let Ava know his plans and he wanted to know about Ursula.

"Morning, ladies," Chet said, smiling.

"Thank you for saving us," Ursula said.

"You're so welcome."

"Morning. I'll get you some eggs, a muffin, and bacon." Ava started making breakfast for him while he got a cup of coffee. "I heard you on the phone."

"Yeah, taking care of business. I've got a job with Leyton and the team here. I called Chuck to say I'm joining Leyton and his team. Then Travis called and said I could stay at the safe house until I—"

"Figured out what you want to do with your life when you grow up?" Ava asked.

Chet smiled. She was cute.

Ava finished making breakfast for him and then she got another refill of tea and a cup of coffee for Ursula.

"What are you going to do about returning home, Ursula?" Ava asked.

"I've had a nice vacation. It's time to go home. If you could drop me off at the new cabin I was staying at, I'll pack and return home. Maybe Jonathon and Blue have had a long enough period of cooling off now and they'll behave themselves."

Chet hoped Ursula would be all right and the guys would get a clue. He couldn't imagine continuing to want to see a shifter who wasn't just as intrigued with him. It had to be mutual respect and interest in each other.

"And the other guy?" Ava asked. "Don't give up on him. He could be just the one for you."

The other guy? Chet raised a brow but didn't question them about the "new" guy.

Ursula smiled. "He could be. Thanks for everything."

"Do you have to work, Ava?" Chet thought she had to go in earlier today. He would volunteer to take Ursula to her cabin if so.

"No, Florence told me to come in later."

That was good that Ava's boss was so flexible with Ava's working hours if something came up and Ava had to take off. "Okay, so the issue with Blue and Jonathon you believe is resolved then?" Chet asked Ursula.

"As far as I'm concerned. I just needed to get away from their fighting with each other over me." Ursula smiled. "I hoped that they would get the message. I didn't expect them to come after me and cause all this trouble."

"I'll take you to the cabin," Ava said.

"If you don't mind, I'll come along." Chet wanted to talk to Ava about their future.

"The more the merrier." Smiling at Ava, Ursula picked up her dish and empty coffee mug and took it into the kitchen.

And then she helped Chet and Ava clear the rest of the dishes.

After that, they all got into Chet's car to drive to the cabin, and he hoped Ursula wouldn't have any more issues with the bears.

When they finally reached the cabin, they made sure Ursula didn't have any company waiting for her. She didn't.

"Are you sure you're going to be all right?" Chet asked Ursula.

"Yeah. You all are the greatest. I was really lucky to find you all." Then Ursula gave each of them a hug before she packed up her car and they followed her out of the park where the cabin was located.

Ava smiled at Chet. "I'm so glad you're moving here."

"I figured you might want me to stay at the CSF safe house while we're dating."

She nodded. "Sure that would be good."

He had hoped she might say she wanted him to stay with her, but he was good with living at the safehouse and seeing her after he was home from missions, and she was off from work—at least for the time being.

"Unless you think people will talk." She arched a brow.

"About dating you?" He hoped she didn't think he was stepping back from the relationship.

"About not staying with me."

He chuckled. He sure hoped that meant she was opening her house to him. "What do you want me to do so that the cougars won't have as much to talk about?"

She smiled. "Oh, I think anything we do will cause speculation. So you might as well as stay with me and end the speculation."

"Hot damn."

She laughed. "And then if we decide we need other arrangements, we can start tongues to wagging again."

He smiled. "I'm all for it." And he hoped they could get along satisfactorily. That was the thing about them staying in the same place together. They could see how compatible they were when it wasn't just for a date.

"So what are you going to do? Go home and pack up and then return?"

"Yeah. I want to be ready to start working as soon as I can so that if the guys need me, I'll be all set." He figured Ava couldn't take off that much time from work to go with him and he didn't want her to have to help him pack anyway.

"Okay, good. I'll make room for your clothes and anything else you'll be bringing with you."

"Thanks, Ava, I really appreciate it. I'll return to Cheyenne after I drop you off."

"I'll go into work then. Florence gave me time off to speak to Ursula and now we know what that was all about."

When they arrived at her condo, he kissed her, and she

hugged him back and smiled. "I can't wait for you to return for good."

"It'll probably take me a couple of days before I make it back."

"I'll be ready with steaks for you to grill."

He chuckled, kissed her, and hugged her, and then he got into his car, waved, and drove off.

## 18

Sighing heavily, Ava waved goodbye to Chet, then went inside her home and called her boss. "Hey, Florence, I'm on my way to work."

"You could have taken the day off. I've already heard Chet is transferring to Yuma Town."

"He sure is. He's going home to pack his stuff up and bring it here. I'll be there in a few minutes." Ava climbed into the car and headed over to the bakery, parked, and went inside. Chet was so virile and sexy and caring. She really needed him in her life. And he needed her—especially when he was wounded on the job, and he wouldn't take of himself.

The shop was already busy with afternoon customers. She smiled at everyone eating their pastries and she went inside the kitchen. "I'm here."

"Good to see you." Florence was getting ready to serve some more pies and looked a little harried.

"I'll take over the baking." Then Ava started making a couple of apple pies.

Florence returned to the kitchen, and they talked about Ursula.

"She dropped by here and picked up some honeybuns. The way I see it, she just needs to stand her ground with the male bears and let them know they can't intimidate her," Florence said.

"That's just what I was thinking," Ava said.

"And Chet? Where's he staying when he moves here?"

Ava smiled. "With me. It could be just temporary. We'll have to see."

Florence smiled. "Uh-huh." Then she went to take another order and Ava heard her say, "You're Jonathon, right?"

Ava glanced back to see the bear, Jonathon, standing at the counter to order something. Or maybe question what Ava knew about Ursula if he had a clue she'd been at Ava's house.

"Is Ava here?"

"Yes, she's in the kitchen working though. Did you want to order something?"

"The blueberry pie. Can I speak to her for a moment?" Jonathon asked.

"When she has a break."

"Which is when?"

"She just got to work. She has a break in three hours."

Ava smiled. Florence was saving her from an interrogation. Florence never would tell her she had to wait for three hours to talk to someone briefly.

Jonathon grunted. Then he took the pie to the table and sat down to eat it.

Ava didn't believe he would wait that long to see her. She sighed and finished putting the pies in the oven. Then she went out to talk to him. "You wanted to see me?"

Jonathon smiled. "Yeah. I found Ursula's scent trail went straight to a condo and she'd been running with you."

"Yeah, I was out searching for her last night and hunters came after us. We ended up at my place."

He frowned. "And?"

"She went home. For your information, if you didn't get the message, she's not interested in dating either you or Blue."

"Is that right?" Jonathon asked.

"Yeah, she's interested in someone else."

Jonathon raised his brows.

"I don't know his name, but that's what she told me. So you guys need to look elsewhere for a she-bear." She didn't intend to mention a name and cause trouble for him if Jonathon and Blue went to harass him about it and he wasn't even cognizant that Ursula was interested in him.

"Great pie."

"Thanks. Is that all you needed to talk to me about?"

"Yeah. Thanks for telling me the truth."

"You're welcome." Then Ava returned to the kitchen, glad she had the talk with Jonathon. Maybe she had convinced him to leave Ursula alone. To her surprise, she got a call from Ursula. "Hey, are you okay?"

"Yeah, I'm still headed home. I wanted to thank you again."

"I'm at the bakery working."

"Oh, I'll let you go."

"No, I just wanted to say that Jonathon's here eating a blue-berry pie, and he questioned me about you." Ava pulled out a couple of other pies and set them on the cooling rack and told her what she said to him. "I hope that's okay with you."

"Yeah, thanks. Maybe if someone else tells him, he'll finally get the message. Well, since you're busy, I'll let you go."

"You're welcome. I hope we can get together again someday."

"Invite me to your wedding when you get to that stage," Ursula said.

Ava laughed. "I will." Then they said their goodbyes.

Right after that, Ricky entered the shop and said to Florence,

"I've got to get Mandy some jelly buns. She has a real craving for them."

"Sure," Florence said. "Coming right up."

But then a couple of men wearing black suits walk into the bakery and they didn't look like they belonged in Yuma Town. "You're Ricky Jones, just the man we wanted to talk to," the fairer-haired man of the two said.

His nose was crooked like he'd gotten into a fight, and a scar cut across the lower part of his cheek that had only healed part way. He looked like a real tough guy, an enforcer for the Mafia.

"Bruno," Ricky said. "And Caruso. I didn't think I'd see you here."

"Yeah, we got business to attend to," Bruno said.

Ava called Dan right away in case the men caused real trouble for Ricky. "Hey, a couple of men are here because of Mel and are talking to Ricky. They're definitely thugs."

"We're in the vicinity and on our way. Bridget is with us."

"Thanks, Dan."

"What's this in regard to?" Florence asked. As a retired CIA agent, she was still a formidable adversary, and she didn't allow any nonsense in her bakery.

"He knows," Bruno said, jerking his thumb in Ricky's direction, his voice deep and threatening.

"You have the story wrong," Ricky said. "The baby Mel is carrying isn't mine."

"You're saying Mel lied. No one says she lies and gets away with it," Bruno said.

Florence said, "Okay, listen, if you're here to buy something to eat, you're welcome, but if you think to threaten my patrons, then you need to leave now."

Bruno gave Florence a dark smile as if he had no intention of leaving before he resolved this to his satisfaction.

But then Dan, Addie, Bridget, and Chase drove up outside, parked, and entered the shop. "Can I help you?" Dan asked.

The two Mob guys turned to scowl at them. "We came to speak to Ricky Jones. Why would the sheriff's department have been called?" Bruno cast a look back at the kitchen.

Ava wiped flour off her hands and gave him a little smile to say *she* had been the one to call them. They weren't without their resources here in Yuma Town.

"We don't want any trouble," Dan said. "If you're not going to buy anything from the bakery, then you need to leave. We don't allow loitering in the businesses."

The guy rubbed his whiskerless chin. "Ricky is the real source of the problem."

"Because you think he's the father of the baby Mel's carrying?" Dan shook his head. "Find another scapegoat. Someone closer to home. Someone who is the real father of the baby."

"Of course you would say it while you're trying to protect him," the man said.

"You know what a paternity test is? If we have to get one after the baby is born, it'll prove Mel has fabricated the whole story. If you know what's good for you, you'll leave well enough alone. Ricky hasn't been anywhere near Mel for years. It's in his past. It's in her past," Dan said.

"Oh," Bridget suddenly said, pointing to the darker-haired man of the two of them, "your friend is the father of Mel's baby."

Bruno glanced at his cohort.

"Ohmigod, yes!" Ava said as she saw a premonition of the Caruso having to come clean with Mel's dad. "That guy is the father." Ava pointed to Caruso. "Mel's daddy won't be happy about it at first, but then Mel begs him not to kill him, and this guy and Mel's dad are helping to bottle feed his fussy grandson. You're not dead, Caruso, but you're going to have to deal with the fallout and fess up." Ava smiled.

Bruno glowered at Ava, then at his cohort. Caruso looked like he would be in trouble not only with Mel's father, but Bruno.

Bruno whipped around and bumped into Dan as he and Caruso left the shop. "What the hell was that all about?" Bruno asked Caruso.

The door closed and Dan smiled this time.

Ricky looked relieved.

Florence said, "The two of you, Bridget and Ava, could make a winning psychic team."

"I'll say," Addie said.

Bridget smiled.

"It's a good thing that we're such a close-knit community," Chase said. "They're driving a black SUV and I've got their license plate number, so if they cause any trouble, or return, we'll know about it."

"I doubt they will. I think Bruno believed you and Caruso will now be on the hotseat. Mel should be also," Addie said. "I'm surprised they didn't ask how you knew about it. Then again, I think you stole their thunder with outing him." She smiled.

Dan and Chase chuckled.

"If you have any further problem with them, give us a call," Dan said.

"They had guns," Florence said.

"Yeah, I saw the bulges under their suitcoats. Chase and Addie had their hands on their revolvers at all times." Dan glanced at the glassed-in case of pies and cakes and he and Addie checked out the selection.

They picked out a chocolate cream pie.

Chase smiled at them. "If you're not eating that at the office but taking it home with you, Shannon will get word and wonder why I didn't bring her home one."

Dan laughed. "We're here now, so we might as well get whatever you want for dessert for supper."

Chase didn't need anyone to convince him of that and he picked up a pie too, and then the three of them left with their goodies in hand.

Bridget sighed. "Call on me if you need my help on any other cases."

Ava smiled. "Florence is right. We make a great team." She and Bridget hugged each other and then Bridget left. Ava went back into the kitchen and started to work.

They had some more customers then and Florence began taking orders.

"Hey, who were those men who came into town wearing suits and were driving in the black SUV?" Shannon asked, entering the shop.

"Oh, Mafia bad guys," Florence said. "By the way, don't make dessert for tonight."

Shannon smiled at her. "Oh?"

"Yeah, Chase bought a chocolate cream pie for tonight." Florence smiled. "As soon as Dan and Addie got one."

"Oh, boy, it's a good thing Chase got one too then."

In the kitchen, Ava smiled. Then she got a call from Chet. "Hey. You must have another four hours before you get home."

"I do. It's a long drive. But unless I have a case to work on in this area in the future, I won't be having to make the trip too often."

"What about your mother?"

"I'm going to have to convince her to move here. It won't be easy. Not unless I mate you."

Ava laughed.

"I'm serious."

"You had better not be proposing a mating to me when you're on your way to Cheyenne."

He chuckled. "Yeah, I'm proposing to you. And I know I'm not doing it the right way, but if I didn't do it right away, what if you found someone else before I returned?"

"You're not afraid you'll change your mind and think you better propose before you do, are you?"

"No way, honey."

"Okay, well, that means you need to pack up in a hurry."

"You betcha. I might even leave some things behind."

She laughed. "I've got to get back to work."

"I'm so glad we're going to do this. I love you."

"I love you too. Talk to you later." Then they ended the call and Ava did a little dance around the kitchen.

Florence caught her at it and laughed. "Good news, I gather."

"The best. Chet and I are mating."

"Oh, that is the best news ever. So you're not going to have any trial living arrangement."

"He was just going to pack and move in with me, but he was afraid I might find someone else in the meantime before he returned to Yuma Town. Silly cougar."

Florence smiled. "Well, the two of you will be good for each other."

"There's no sense in delaying the inevitable." Ava was ready to go home now so she could make room for Chet so he could move his things in. She glanced at the clock. Only a couple of more hours to go and she would go home and do it.

Florence gave her a hug and then she returned to the seating area to wait on customers.

And Ava gave another little twirl around the kitchen. She was so happy.

## 19

Chet dropped by his mother's house to tell her the news, figuring she would choose to move to Yuma Town now and he wanted her there. But he also needed her to meet Ava soon too.

"Hey, Mom, I have good news."

She smiled at him. "You're mating Ava."

"I sure am. How did you know?"

"Every time we talk, you've been elusive about mentioning her, but you couldn't wait to see her again. I don't have to be a mind reader to know she meant something special to you. Did you want to have dinner with me? I made beef brisket, potatoes, and carrots in the slow roaster."

"Yeah, sure. That would be great."

"When are you moving?"

He came into the kitchen with his mother and helped her dish up the food. "As soon as I can load up the car. Leyton said he'd help, but I told him I wouldn't need it."

"They're a great team there."

"They are."

"I knew you would be joining them soon, even if you hadn't

found Ava to be your mate." His mother smiled at him. "I'm so happy for you." She gave him a hug and then they sat down to enjoy their meal. "So tell me about the case. I hear you solved it, though there will be no headlines telling of how well you did in the hunt of this man because it's all being kept secret."

"That's for sure." Chet explained how they caught the culprit.

"Oh, I hate cases like that where you have to drive all over the place to learn that you needed to be where you were in the first place. Good job to you and the others. And Ava, wow. We could have used her and Bridget on the team when I was a special agent with the force or when I was in charge of the operation."

"I know. They can be a real help on a case." Not that Chet planned to use Ava for that purpose, though if she had any premonition about something that could aid them, he would be eager to learn of it.

"So now, what do I do?"

"You join us out there. You can get a place and be close by." Chet would help his mother with all the arrangements, though he knew she was perfectly capable of doing it on her own.

"Okay, I'll certainly do that."

"I'll help you with any arrangements that need to be made, moving, selling the place—"

His mom smiled. "I can manage, but if you want to help, sure. I definitely won't turn you down. But you better be sure you're moving there for good."

He smiled. "This is for good. Just like with you and Dad."

"Okay, I just wanted to make sure. I know when you make up your mind to do something, you do it, but this is a big decision."

"Yeah, it is. I love her."

"Good. I can't wait to meet her. Do you want me to help you with your packing?"

"Yeah, sure, if you don't mind."

"Not at all. Once you return to Yuma Town, you'll be a mated cougar. So I would love to spend more time with you before that happens. Though it's about time you got mated and I'll be glad for it."

He figured his mother would be.

After dinner, he helped her clean up the dishes, and then he took her to his place, and she began helping him pack. He was glad she was here to assist. He always enjoyed spending time with her.

"Then the kids will come," his mother said. "And I'll be there for them too."

"Yeah, you'll be a great grandmother."

Two days later, Chet had packed up everything and his mother was coming with him. Ava was glad she had asked Chet's mother to come and see her. Even though they planned to mate when Chet reached Ava's place, she wanted his mother to know she had a place with them too. And his mother wanted to look for a home while she was here.

Travis and Bridget said Wendy, Chet's mom, could stay in the safehouse as long as she wanted, and the whole family of CSF special agents intended to wine and dine her, which Ava was looking forward to. Though Ava had thought they might mate before the big barbecue the CSF family was having for them.

When they arrived in town, the whole CSF bunch, Jack, Leyton, Travis and Bridget, and Leyton's wife, Kate, and Jack's wife, Dottie, were there to help celebrate Chet and his mother moving into the area.

"And a mating between cougars," Bridget said, giving Ava a hug.

Everyone agreed.

"I guess we're celebrating the capture of the serial murderer in Cody also," Wendy said.

"About that," Bridget said, sounding so serious, Chet got the distinct notion that they had the wrong man. How was that even possible? What had changed Bridget's mind since he'd left to return to Wyoming? "I'm having serious doubts that Langston killed the women," Bridget continued.

"Hell, why?" Chet asked as they all sat down to eat ribs, corn on the cob, and potato salad and drink margaritas.

"He's not talking about anything, but when I read his mind, he knows too many details about the murders not to have been involved in them somehow. But he's also not seeing them as in he committed the murders. I mean, think about it. If you, well, let's say fish all the time. And I asked you about fishing, you would tell me some general details, but while you're telling me about them, you're thinking of fishing. Of catching certain kinds of fish. You're not going to tell me every miniscule detail, but you're thinking about some of them."

"So you think someone told him about the murders. The murderer himself," Chet said.

"I think so. Langston could still be an accessory to the murders," Bridget said.

"What if we ask him questions that would encourage him to think of who told him about the murders?" Leyton asked.

"Sounds good to me," Chet said.

"But Benny had pictures of the women at his place," Kate said.

"What if he doesn't live alone?" Ava said. "Maybe whoever lived with him took the photos of the women."

"That could work," Bridget said. "I imagine he would think of the murderer when we questioned him about that."

"The woman at the home where we apprehended Langston said he took the photo of her at the bar where he works," Travis said. "We saw that all of them were taken at that bar."

"Maybe his identical twin brother did it," Ava said.

"Twin brother?" Chet asked. "We hadn't found anyone like that."

"They would smell the same unless they use different soaps and deodorants, etcetera. As to how I knew about it, I thought you had mentioned it to me. His name is Marty and he's furious that we have Benny incarcerated in Yuma Town." Ava pointed her barbecued rib at Chet. "He's going to be coming for his brother."

"You saw this in a vision?" Chet asked.

"I guess. I just thought you had mentioned him to me. I must have dreamed it—well, had a vision when I was half asleep this morning. I'd...forgotten about it...until now."

"When is he coming?" Leyton asked. "We need to be prepared for it."

"I would think right away. Though he'll have to get a scope of the situation before he can break his brother out," Ava said.

"Is he coming alone?" Jack asked.

"Now that I don't know." Ava buttered her corn.

"But Benny is a womanizer," Bridget said. "Which was why we thought he could fit the murderer's profile—easily puts the women under his spell. If he's not the one, what's the real murderer's issue?"

"He doesn't like women," Wendy said.

Everyone agreed that could be the case.

"If Benny isn't the killer, but Marty is, then the murderer is still out there on the loose, and women are still at risk. We need to get him now," Jack said.

"Well, you don't have to return to Cody. Marty's on his way here," Ava said. "I'm sure of it. And if he's the murderer, you'll have him in custody soon."

"You saw that in the vision?" Chet asked, hopeful.

Ava shook her head. "I just know you can do it."

"You ought to hire her," Wendy said.

Ava smiled. "My visions come and go. Sometimes I think they're just dreams. They're not all that reliable."

"You've given us so much to go on already, I would say they're pretty reliable," Chet said.

"One other thing, Chet," Bridget said, "we were at the jailhouse talking about that case you were on where you took those three cougars down because of the murders they had committed, and Benny knew who they were. Benny was glad he hadn't been with them when you took them down. He hadn't known what had happened to them though. To his way of thinking, they had just vanished into thin air."

"Courtesy of our cleanup crews." Chet dished up some more ribs. "But it sounds to me that he was involved in those murders."

"Well, he did have the thought that if he'd been there, you wouldn't have gotten the upper hand with the men. Of course, he never spoke a word about it. He was just thinking about it—the whole situation running through his thoughts. And yeah, he thought of killing one of the men they had murdered. That's why he needs to remain in jail too. But it's also why I didn't think he'd murdered the women. He doesn't have a clear picture of the women's murders. He had witnessed the murders in the earlier case you had but he hadn't taken part in them until they made him, or they would have killed him. They needed him to be just as guilty as they were, or he might have told on them. But he hadn't done any of the *other* murders and so it really made me question whether he was our real suspect in the women's case."

Ava squeezed Chet's hand and he suspected she was telling him she wanted to be with him tonight and she didn't want him to go to the jailhouse and interrogate Langston, but it was his job. He wanted to be with Ava more, but he had to learn something further about Benny's involvement in the murders in the other case he'd dealt with earlier. And he had to know more about Benny's twin brother. He did consider that Benny wasn't going anywhere, but with the issue of his twin coming to rescue him, he felt he had to talk to him tonight.

Chet felt disquieted though. Here he thought he'd wrapped up the earlier case in one neat little bow when instead one of the men involved—Benny—had gotten clean away. Chet just hoped Ava would continue to see visions of Marty to assist them. Benny was probably protecting his brother, if Marty had killed the women.

Ava leaned over and kissed Chet's cheek. "You have to go and question Benny. No problem. I'll see you at the condo later. I would do anything for you because I love you."

"Are you sure? I mean, I feel the same way about you."

Ava smiled. "Yeah, it's your job and I know you have to learn about his involvement in the other case too. I'll be working at the bakery early in the morning, but I get off at three and we can have brunch at ten. You and your mom and me."

"That sounds good. I promise this won't take too long."

Ava shook her head. "You take as long as necessary. You have to find closure and you need to learn what you can about Marty before he gets here."

"Thanks, honey." Chet had to know that she would be a partner in this because he never knew how long it would take to finish a mission or where one might send him.

They continued to eat and enjoy their visit with one another, though Leyton called Dan with an update about the trouble they might have with Marty coming for his brother.

"Okay, Dan's putting extra guards on the prisoner," Leyton said when they ended the call. "If we need to, the CSF agents can help with guard duty. In the meantime, the whole force will be on the lookout for Benny's twin brother."

That's what Chet loved about their team. They were always ready to help the regular law enforcement with criminal cases affecting the townspeople and do their own missions too.

By the time they finished eating and visiting, Jack took Wendy to the safehouse to stay. Ava and Chet kissed each other, and she gave him a spare key to the condo. Then he rode with Bridget and Travis to the jailhouse.

AVA WANTED to go with Chet, but she knew this was his job and he had to do it without her and not have her always be there with him. If it hadn't been ten at night already, she would have had Wendy come over to the condo and visit, but she figured she would be off to bed. Ava didn't want to go to bed when she wanted to make love to Chet.

But this was past her bedtime because she had to go into the bakery so early. She dropped her purse on the kitchen island, pulled out her phone, and plugged it into her charger. She headed upstairs to the bedroom, stripped off her clothes, and walked into the bathroom to take a shower. While she was washing up, she was trying to think of any more details concerning Marty and his brother that would help her learn when Marty would arrive and where they might catch him so they could interrogate him next.

She finished washing up and grabbed a bath towel. She was just drying off when she heard the front door open downstairs. *Chet?*

She couldn't believe he would get here this quickly. She was certain he would still be questioning Benny. Unless he got the information out of him that he needed right away, or he was just too eager to see her, or everyone goaded him into leaving and joining his mate.

She didn't have a gun and her cell phone was downstairs where she'd left it on the kitchen counter charging, so there was no way to get ahold of anyone if someone had broken into her house. She could think of only one way to get out of the bind she was in. She shifted into her cougar and took off down the stairs. She hoped she was wrong, but when she saw a man walking into her kitchen, the light on in there still and smelled his cougar scent, she tore off through the cougar door. It didn't take long for him to follow her as a cougar. And she recognized him from the vision she'd had during the Independence Day celebration.

She ran toward Rainbow Falls, but she knew he would be able to follow her scent wherever she went, and she suspected the cougar was Marty and he was coming after her to take her hostage as a bargaining chip to force Dan to release his brother.

No way was he going to use her to release Benny, when he had murdered someone himself. Benny might have had to be convinced to do it, but he had still been one of the gang. Coercion or no, he killed for them, to be accepted by them.

But Marty, he was a different brand of murderer.

She ran her heart out and hoped she would reach the river ahead of Marty so he would lose her scent once she was swimming in the water. If she'd been a wolf, she would have howled to the pack, to gather them together, to get assistance so she could help them capture the bastard.

But on her own as a female cougar against a male, she didn't stand a chance.

## 20

Chet, Bridget, and Travis arrived at the jail to find Nina and Stryker serving on guard duty and they greeted each other.

"Dan told us about the brother," Stryker said. "And about Benny's involvement in the last case you were on. Oh, and congratulations for moving here and joining the rest of us in Yuma Town."

"Thanks, I'm glad to be here. And so is Mom." Chet was afraid she would have had major heartburn over leaving Cheyenne for as long as she had lived there, but she was excited about having a daughter-in-law and nothing beat that.

"And we hear other congratulations are in order," Nina said, smiling at Chet.

"Yeah. I couldn't be happier."

"They would be at it right now if it wasn't for this," Bridget said.

Everyone laughed.

"Then you better get to the business of interrogation." Nina gave him a heartfelt hug. She would be his sister-in-law and he was glad for it.

Chet went in with Travis and Bridget to speak with Benny. Nina and Stryker remained in the office holding down the fort.

"Okay, tell us about your twin brother, Marty," Chet said, ready to grill him all night, though he wanted to go home as soon as he could to be with Ava.

"I don't have a twin brother."

"So you want to go down for the murders he committed? Because we have you and we're not releasing you," Chet said. "You know what we do with cougars who commit murder. You can't go to jail. Not when you're a shifter."

Bridget was quiet and Chet knew she was just reading Benny's thoughts. Chet realized if he spoke to Benny about the other case he was involved in, Benny would know his goose was cooked. There would be no reason for him to implicate his brother in the other murders, if he wanted to save his life.

"He's not going to squeal on his twin, no matter what we say to him," Bridget said.

"All right. Benny goes down for the murders. It was his place, the photos were there, he's the bartender who went home with the women, and they ended up dead. His scent is in every one of the murder victims' homes. He has answered enough of the questions that tells me he was there and knew only details that the murderer would know," Chet said.

"But his twin told him about the murders and that's how Benny learned the details," Bridget said.

"Benny said he doesn't have a twin. That means Benny did them." Chet was sure Marty had killed the women based on what Bridget had said. Chet had played this game with her on interrogations before. He hoped the twin, when they caught him, would confess and not let his brother take the rap for it. Though they were both dead men for the other murder Benny had committed.

Nina rushed in to join them, and Chet was afraid they had trouble out front.

"You have to come with me," Nina said, and rushed back out of the confinement area.

"What's wrong?" Chet asked.

"It's my sister. I had a vision of a cougar chasing Ava. He's not a cougar I recognize."

"Where is she?"

"Headed for Rainbow Falls. Knowing Ava, she's trying to hide her scent in the river if she can reach it in time."

Chet rushed out of the sheriff's office, but Travis hurried after him. "I'm coming with you. Bridget will be going home to the kids and is leaving Benny to stew further about the situation he's in."

"Let's go then."

"I called Dan and they're meeting you over there," Stryker said. "I wanted to go too, but Dan wants two of us to be here at all times, just in case Marty slips back this way."

"Marty, hell." If he hurt Ava, Chet would kill him. No bothering to question him about the murders. Did Marty think he could use her as a hostage to release his brother?

They couldn't let either of the men go. Not if they were both murderers.

Travis drove them over to Ava's condo, parked in her driveway, and then they jumped out of his car and raced to the front door. It was unlocked. Chet smelled that the shower had been running. She must have been in the shower when the guy broke in. Had he used lockpicks? Had to have been because there was nothing that indicated he'd broken the lock and Chet was certain Ava wouldn't have just opened the door to a stranger. Not when she knew Marty was coming for his brother and could be dangerous.

Chet stripped off his clothes and Travis was doing the same.

They found men's clothes in the kitchen, and they smelled just like Benny's scent.

"I don't know how you feel about this, but I'm ready to kill him," Chet said.

"Yeah, I'm with you there. He's not going to hurt another woman if I can help it," Travis said, and then they both shifted.

Chet bolted out through the cougar door and Travis followed.

They ran off, neck to neck, following Ava's scent and the male cougar's. He was aggressive and angry, and they had to get to him before he could reach Ava. They knew he was still trying to catch her because they were still running.

They finally reached the riverbank near the falls, but there was no one there. They sniffed at the bank and smelled both cougars' scents. But the male's scent continued along the bank of the river. They lost Ava's scent and Chet was sure she was swimming, or maybe she had crossed the river and ran into the woods.

Chet began to swim across the water. He wanted to see if Ava had gone to the other side, meet up with her, and protect her. Instinctively, Travis stayed on the side where they had still smelled Marty and ran along the riverbank to track him. Chet continued along the opposite bank, trying to smell any sign of Ava, but it appeared she had swum downriver with the current for some time.

Wouldn't Marty have joined her in the water? Maybe not if he could run along the bank faster to catch up with her and just wait for her to get out on the other side, swim across, and chase after her again.

Then Chet finally found her scent way downriver and snarled at Travis. Travis was sniffing around, but he shook his head. He'd lost Marty's scent. He had to have crossed there.

Chet tore off into the woods after the two cougars. He

couldn't wait for Travis to reach him. Then he heard shouts off in the distance. Chase, Dan, Ricky, and Hal were on their way.

Out of his peripheral vision, Chet saw Blue headed toward him as if he knew what was going on. But Chet couldn't stop to talk to the bear about it. Chet had to reach the cougar before he could hurt Ava.

Suddenly, he heard Ava snarling and Chet's heart about gave out. He had to reach her now.

He swore both he and Blue ran even faster to rescue her. And then they saw her leap into a tree and Marty was about to jump up there and fight her. But then he saw Chet and Blue coming for him. At first, Marty just stared at the bear as if he couldn't believe his eyes.

Then he must have figured he'd better get the hell out of there and he tore off away from the tree and deeper into the woods.

Chet wanted to take care of Ava, but he had to catch this bastard, or he might come after her again. Or any other woman too. And Chet knew the other law enforcement officers would follow and at least one would stay with her.

But the next thing he knew, Ava was running after them. He wished she would wait for the others to show up, but then again, she didn't know anyone else was coming to aid them.

He was damn glad Blue was still hanging around the area.

Then he heard another cougar approaching. He glanced over his shoulder. Thankfully, his friend Travis was right behind him.

The sheriff and his deputies wouldn't be able to catch up to them as humans, though he suspected one or two of them would shift to help out.

Then they were out of the woods and Marty was running full out to reach the cliffs. Chet would track him down to the very end. When he had a mission to do, he did it, though Benny was a surprise as far as being involved in that earlier case Chet had so he hadn't completely finished that job.

Marty finally reached the cliffs and bounded up them.

Chet was right behind him and to his surprise, Blue was climbing the cliff after him. Though the bear wasn't as fast as the cougars and Travis quickly passed him by. Blue grunted.

But when Ava jumped up onto the boulders and was instantly past him, Blue growled.

His heart thundering, Chet was on top of the cliffs and leaping from rock to rock after Marty.

He heard snarling below the cliffs and glanced down to see six more cougars on their way. The cavalry was here and if Marty thought he had a prayer of a chance to escape them, he was wrong.

Chet was nearly within leaping distance of the cat. He hadn't expected the cougar to whip around and pounce on him instead, as if Marty thought taking out Chet would be the end of his troubles. Now Chet knew, as angry as the big cat was, that he couldn't control his temper, and both tore at each other with claws and teeth.

Ava was trying to get around them on the narrow ledge, but she couldn't easily, and he was afraid she would fall while trying, but she was pacing like crazy, wanting to help him. Then Travis leaped over them and landed on the back side of Marty. The two male cougars were no match for him.

Yet he wasn't giving up and Chet figured he planned to fight to the death. That he had nothing to gain by turning himself in, though they wanted him to confess to the crimes. Chet suspected Marty wasn't going to do the honorable thing and confess either.

That was the way it was going to be. Marty would go to the grave with his secrets. He wasn't getting off the cliffs alive.

Both Chet and Marty were bleeding and Travis leaped at

Marty's back and bit into his neck, killing him. Chet didn't need the kill to feel satisfied that the cougar wouldn't hurt anyone else. Ricky crested the top of the cliffs and just stared at the dead cougar, and glanced at Ava, but she appeared to be okay. Hal was up on top next to Ricky right after that.

Dan and Chase leaped onto the top of the cliffs at the same time, though it was getting a little crowded up there.

Dan shifted. "We'll get his body down to the base of the cliffs and take him into town. You get yourself looked after, Chet." He glanced at Travis.

Travis shifted. "I'm not injured." Though his mouth was bloodied from biting Marty fatally. Then he shifted again.

Blue finally poked his head above the cliff and looked at all the cougars standing there. He shook his head. But Chet was grateful that he'd made the effort to come to his aid.

Ava was licking Chet, rubbing her face against him where he wasn't wounded. He was afraid he was going to need to recuperate from this ordeal now too. But he was making love to Ava. Mating her. Showing her just how much he loved her.

He nuzzled her, telling her to go down the cliff and he'd follow her.

She started down it and poor Blue began the descent. It would take him a while.

As soon as Chet and Ava were at the bottom of the cliff, they ran toward the river. Travis was right behind them, and Chet figured he wanted to get to Ava's home to call Bridget and tell her he was all right.

The others with the sheriff's office would stay and take care of the body, while Blue? Chet had no idea what he was going to do.

They finally reached the river and swam across. Man, he was going to be sore tonight. Every muscle ached, and of course all the fresh claw marks and bite marks were burning like crazy.

They finally reached the riverbank and he stumbled. Damn it. He didn't want Ava to think he couldn't make love to her tonight. She nuzzled him, making sure he was all right. Travis was right there too, ready to carry Chet home if he needed to. Not that Chet needed that.

Then they loped upriver to where they would go back through the woods and head for her condo. Travis had to go with them because he'd left his clothes and vehicle at the house.

When they arrived at the condo, Ava went inside first, Chet following, and Travis bringing up the rear. Ava raced up the stairs to the bedroom and Chet assumed she was shifting up there and getting dressed.

Travis hurried to pull on his boxer briefs, then grabbed his phone and called Bridget right away. "Hey, sweetheart, I'm fine. Marty is dead. Chet's a bit chewed up." He glanced at Chet. "Yeah, he'll live, but it looks like Ava will be taking him to the clinic. Ava is fine. Can you relay the message to Nina and Chet's mother? Thanks. I'll see you in a few minutes." He ended the call and finished dressing while Chet was trying to dress, attempting not to groan too much. But his wounds were beginning to really hurt.

"You're going to see one of the doctors," Ava said, hurrying down the stairs.

"I don't need to. I'll be okay."

She frowned at him. "You'll go or I'm not mating you."

Chet smiled at her.

"I'm serious."

Travis chuckled. "I'm getting out of your hair, and I'm heading home. In the morning, we can interrogate Benny further."

"Yeah, sounds good, Travis." Chet let out his breath. "Okay, so I'll go to the clinic, Ava. But I'm not staying overnight there."

"See you tomorrow," Travis said, and headed outside.

## 21

Ava was wiping down all Chet's injuries, bandaging him, and then helping him get dressed. She knew he hated that she had to assist him in getting dressed when he wanted to prove he was the one who would take care of her. But he *had* taken care of her.

"How did you know that I was in trouble?" She hadn't expected anyone to come after her like that. She was sure she had been on her own.

"Your sister told us you were in trouble. She saw it in a vision. Travis and I dropped everything to come to your rescue. Marty has murdered so many women, we were worried sick about you. I'm just glad Nina had the vision of you. We would never have known what had happened to you otherwise, unless he had used you as a hostage so we would free his brother."

"This was the vision I had over the July 4th holiday weekend."

"Oh, then it's done."

"Yes. Let's go. I called the clinic and Dr. William is on duty right now. He said he's ready for us."

"I really don't need to go in."

She knew he would say that. "If you got sick, it would be my fault because you came to my rescue, and I know you want to do *other* things. Which, in your condition, you might need to wait until tomorrow anyway."

"No way."

She smiled at him, then frowned. "Do you need to question Benny further?"

"I do. But like Travis said, we'll do it in the morning while you're at work. He and Bridget need to be home for the kids and when we question Benny, Bridget needs to be there to 'listen' in on the truth of what's going on," Chet said, walking out with Ava to his vehicle.

They drove the short distance to the clinic and parked, and then headed inside.

Mandy was the nurse on duty, and she took them back to an exam room. "Ricky told me what happened. At least Marty won't be hurting anyone again. And congratulations you two on deciding to mate."

"Thanks, Mandy," Ava said.

"Yeah, thanks."

Then Dr. William came in. "I hear you took the murdering bastard down. Good work."

"Thanks." Chet removed his shirt. Most of his wounds were bites around his neck where Marty tried to grab hold to kill him. Chet had bite marks on his shoulders also and claw marks where the cougar had dug into his shoulders for purchase to keep Chet from biting him back. A couple of bites were on Chet's arms, but he'd kept his backside and legs relatively injury free, concentrating on Marty's teeth and trying to get the advantage.

"I'm going to administer a shot, give you some antibiotics to take, and I'll stitch up the worst bites."

Chet opened his mouth to object, but Ava said, "Thanks,

Doc. I need him back to normal as soon as possible and that will do it."

Chet smiled then.

"Okay, well, I think that's about it," Doc said, finishing up the last of the stitches and then he gave him a bottle of antibiotics. "The shot will be good for tonight and you can take the medicine starting tomorrow afternoon."

"Thanks, Doc."

"Congratulations are in order for the two of you also," Dr. Williams said.

Ava and Chet smiled. "Thanks."

Then Chet's mother hurried into the clinic and gave them both hugs. "Bridget called to tell me you'd been injured, Chet."

"Yeah, we're okay. I didn't want to call you this late to tell you we're all right, but then Bridget said she would." Chet gave her a hug back.

Then they said good night to Doc and Mandy, gave his mother a hug, and then dropped her off at the safe house.

They drove home after that.

"You know," Ava said, getting the door, "we're only going to be getting about four hours of sleep." Then she checked her text messages, hoping Florence might have gotten word about all the trouble they'd had, and that Ava would have barely any sleep before she had to work. She smiled when she saw the text message from her boss. "I have tomorrow off as a mating present."

Chet laughed. "Good show." He acted like he was going to carry her up the stairs, but she put her hand on his chest.

"Don't even think of it. You are wounded, and if you don't hurt too badly—unless you want to wait until later after we sleep and we can do it then—

"No way. I will never be too injured."

She chuckled. "Then come on, let's go to bed."

She ran up the stairs and he raced after her. In the bedroom, he was pulling off her clothes as quickly as he could. She kicked off her sandals and he worked on her shirt, bra, jeans, then her panties.

She worked slower on removing his clothes though, not wanting to hurt him. Shoes were tossed, socks, jeans removed, boxer briefs. But when she came to his shirt, she unbuttoned it slowly, then pulled it carefully off his shoulders. He was trying not to moan, but he was tensing enough, she knew he was hurting.

They really should wait until later, but she didn't want to wait, and she figured he didn't want to either.

"Thank you for coming to my rescue again," Ava said, then kissed him soundly on the mouth, savoring the softness of his lips.

He kissed her back, entrapping her with his arms, giving her a warm hug, and intensifying the kiss. "I love you, Ava. It probably would have taken me forever to finally decide to pack up and move to join the team here in Yuma Town, until I met you. You were all the incentive I needed to convince me to make the change."

She laughed. "I wasn't happy I had to take you in, but that weekend I spent with you was the best time I'd ever had, and I knew then that I was missing so much in my life without you in it. I love you too."

He continued to kiss her, his hands cupping her face with tenderness, and she felt lost in his love.

Their hearts were pounding wildly, and their pheromones were out of control. Blazing hot passion erupted between them. She was enraptured by the feel of him as he moved his hot naked body against hers, rubbing, titillating. She brushed her leg between his and then he lifted her onto the bed and joined her.

His cock was already full aroused from rubbing against her and she loved the feel of his hard body pressing against hers. His mouth moved from hers to her breasts and he kissed one and licked and sucked her nipple. She caught her breath with the delicious sensation.

He licked a path to her other breast and began sucking again, arousing her to the nth degree. And then he was kissing her mouth again. His hand swept over her body, down, lower, until his fingers found the center of her and began rubbing her aroused nub, building the pressure, stroking faster. She was so ready for him, wet with need.

And then he was stroking her to completion, and she felt so good, like she was on a runner's high. She suddenly peaked, the climax rippling through her, making her feel wondrous. In the same moment, he slid his arousal into her, and his penetration felt amazing. He was filling her, expanding her, the intimacy between them so special, she thoroughly loved him.

The urgency of his kisses made her feel as though he was about ready to explode into her, and she was ready for it too. She hoped he was okay, that his injuries were healing all right, but as long as he wanted this as much as she did, she wouldn't have stopped this for anything.

And then he was coming, pumping into her like a cougar possessed with a mission, and then he filled her with his seed.

"Holy..., ah, man, you are the only she-cat for me," he said, his voice drenched with lust. He collapsed on top of her and hugged her tight.

"Yeah, you better believe it. And you're the only one for me." She hugged him back, loving how he felt heavily pressed against her.

Then they kissed and he moved off her.

"How are you feeling?"

He smiled and kissed her. "The bite and claw marks hurt."

"Aww, honey. Well, no more of this until you're feeling better."

"No way."

She smiled and hoped by tomorrow he would be feeling better. For now, it was time to snuggle and sleep.

CHET AND AVA were nestling together and had fallen asleep when his phone rang from the floor where he'd tossed his pants. At this hour, it had to be important. He got out of bed and fished his phone out of his jeans pocket. The caller ID said it was Dan and he knew it was trouble. Now what?

"Yeah, Dan?"

"A woman came into the jailhouse sobbing, saying her daughter had been taken from her at the service station at gunpoint. As soon as Nina grabbed a phone to call an alert, the woman tased her and Stryker and freed Benny. They took off in light blue Tahoe."

"Hell." Chet started yanking on a pair of boxer briefs.

"Dr. William is taking care of Nina and Stryker and we're putting all our law enforcement officials on alert to search for Benny and the woman. Nina heard the man call her Xenia."

"Hell. Where do you want me to go?" Chet asked.

Ava was getting out of bed and pulling on her panties.

"Since Ava was targeted before, you stay there," Dan said. "Watch over her."

Ava frowned. "He's here," she whispered. "In the house. Downstairs."

Chet couldn't believe it. He hadn't heard a thing. Then again, he and Ava had fallen asleep. "Ava says he's here."

"We're on our way."

"All right." Chet left the phone line open and set his phone on the bedside table so Dan would hear what was going on if they ended up in a fight with Benny.

"What are we going to do?" Ava whispered.

"That woman, Xenia, who was with Benny when we caught him broke him out of jail." Chet grabbed his gun.

"What? She was terrified that Benny might have killed all those women. Bridget told me so."

"Evidently, Xenia changed her mind. Is she in the house too?" Chet asked.

"No, she's waiting in the getaway car. But when I saw her house number in the earlier vision, I also saw her blue Tahoe. Benny wants revenge for you killing his brother," Ava said, her voice hushed.

"*Travis* killed Marty."

"*You* were in charge of the investigation. He blames you."

"We'll stay here and—"

"Okay, by me." Ava yanked off her panties. "I don't have a gun so if he gets past you, I'll take him down as a cougar." She shifted into her cougar.

Chet hadn't expected that, though it was a good idea. He thought of throwing on some more clothes, but then he heard the one stair creak—at the same place where Chet had made it creak before.

Ava tensed.

Was Benny in his cougar form or his human? Had Xenia armed him with a gun? Hell, if they'd knocked out both Stryker and Nina with tasers, they could have their guns.

"Good night, honey, pleasant dreams," Chet said as a ruse to see if he could draw Benny out before the troops arrived.

Ava had to shift back to her human form, gave Chet an annoyed look—and he figured it was because she hadn't wanted to shift to speak to him—but to continue the charade, she said, "Night, sweetheart. I love you." Then she shifted back.

It seemed as though they waited forever before Benny made a move though Chet knew they hadn't. Benny might have wanted to wait for them to fall fully asleep, but he had to assume the deputies would come too soon and alert everyone there had been a jail break.

Then as if Benny couldn't hold off any longer, he rushed for the bedroom, his paws nearly silent on the carpeted hall floor, but Chet could make out a cougar's four footfalls not a human's two.

Chet yanked off his boxer briefs and shifted. He wanted to rush forth and take on the big cat, but he held fast, waiting for Benny to move into the bedroom and give the other officers a chance to get here.

Chet suspected Bridget was right. That Benny didn't really have it in him to kill without being forced to do it. But this time he wanted revenge.

Suddenly, Benny flew into the room and landed on the bed, but Ava was near the bathroom and Chet was by the closet, waiting for Benny to make his appearance.

Benny pawed at the bed, evidently so sure Chet and Ava had been in it that it took him a minute or two to register they weren't in bed.

Then Benny turned his fluorescent gaze on Ava and before he could attack her—if he planned to—Chet tackled his flank, knocking Benny off the bed.

Benny snarled and rounded on him, his actions reminiscent of his twin brother's movements in Chet's fight with Marty, most likely because they'd play fought with each other over the years and practiced the same attacks and counterattacks.

To Chet's surprise, he heard Xenia calling out from the front door, "Benny, did you do it?"

Kill them?

Ava looked like she wanted to confront Xenia, but she not in her cougar coat.

Chet was having enough trouble fighting Benny because of his recent wounds from his earlier fight tonight with Marty.

Ava shifted and pulled on her jean shorts and a T-shirt.

Chet didn't want her going anywhere near the woman. What if Xenia tased Ava? What if she was carrying a gun?

But then Ava dashed around Chet and Benny and grabbed Chet's gun off the bedside table. She waited, ready to shoot at Xenia if she entered the room.

Couldn't the woman hear the snarling cats and know how dangerous confronting them would be?

They heard Xenia's footsteps as she ascended the stairs and stepped on the creaking one. Ava ran out of the room and down the hall to the stairs.

Chet couldn't turn his back on Benny or open himself up to a fatal attack. But he damn well didn't want to leave Ava on her own with the woman either.

Shots were fired from midway down the stairs and more shots rang out from the top of the stairs, this time from Chet's gun.

Then everything was deathly quiet.

"Ava!" Chet wanted to shout. He bit at Benny's muzzle, digging his claws into the cat's shoulder, trying to reach his throat.

He heard car doors slam out front, but he worried about Ava most of all. He would never forgive himself if she were dead.

Then he heard running footfalls in the hallway—cougar style.

The front door slammed open, and Ava charged into the bedroom, snarling, her hindleg bleeding but that wasn't stopping her from coming to his aid.

He was cheered to see her alive, injured, but alive and her

charging into the mix gave him another shot of adrenaline. He snarled a blood-curdling cougar cry and attacked the cougar as viciously as he could.

Ava attacked Benny's flank, just as angered that the cougar would attack her mate.

The cougar didn't stand a chance and Chet took him down once and for all, biting into his neck and killing him.

Nina was running up the stairs with Dan and Chase. Ava was lying down, panting with exertion.

Chet was surprised that the doctors would have cleared Nina to come to Ava's aid, but Chet figured there would be no stopping her to help her sister and brother-in-law in the fight.

Chet shifted and checked Ava's leg and hurried to tell them, "There's a first aid kit in the bathroom. Though at this rate, I think we'll need to refill it with bandages." Then he said to Ava, "What happened to Xenia?"

Chase said from the bathroom where he was looking for the first aid kit before Ava could respond, "Xenia is dead."

"She panicked when she saw me, and her bullets were scattered about me. For the most part. Nina and I used to shoot at the range and despite being just a baker, I know how to use a weapon," Ava said.

"Thank God for that." Chet held onto Ava's wound until Chase brought him the first aid kit. Then Chase bandaged her leg. "Let's get her to the clinic."

She shook her head.

"Yeah, now you know how I felt." Chet hugged her, but he had brand new wounds also and he was beginning to hurt all over again.

"You too, Chet," Nina said, giving Ava a hug.

"Hell, are you even supposed to be here, Nina?" Chet asked.

Stryker walked into the bedroom, looking like hell. "No, she's not."

"And neither are you, doctor's orders," Nina said to her mate.

Leyton and Jack arrived. "We'll take care of the mess. The four of you need to go to the clinic," Leyton said.

Chet hurried to get dressed while Nina petted Ava.

Bridget and Travis showed up then. "Bridget's parents are with the kids. Here we thought we would be spending all night helping everyone track down Benny and his accomplice."

"What I don't get is why Xenia came after him to free him," Chet said, as he carried Ava to Dan's car, since it was blocking his own.

"Initially, she thought he had murdered all those women. Then she was intrigued that he seemed to really like her when the other women had died at his hand," Bridget said. "Though she didn't realize that Benny wasn't the one who murdered the other women. I didn't mention it before because I never suspected she would pull something like this."

"It doesn't pay to commit crimes against our kind," Jack said.

"She learned that the hard way." Nina climbed into the car with Dan and Chet.

"I'll go with Travis and Bridget," Stryker said.

Then they drove to the clinic where Docs Kate and William were waiting for *all* their patients.

"I thought we were going to have less trouble in town with you joining us," Kate said, making Chet strip out of his clothes in an exam room while Doc William took Ava into surgery.

Even the vet, Vanessa Vanderbilt, showed up to help with the surgery while Mandy monitored Nina and Stryker for any after-effects from being tased.

Chet got a call from Hugo then and he wondered what he had to tell him at this hour of the night.

"Hey, I just learned that Benny has an identical twin brother, and they trade places all the time, even working shifts at the bar. No one knew about it until Nancy told me she'd dated Benny before she started seeing me and she had seen Benny's identical twin brother coming out of the master bedroom. Before that, she had wondered why Benny slept in the guest bedroom. Anyway, if Benny isn't the suspect in the women's murders, you might check out the twin. Nancy didn't know his name and Benny didn't offer it. That had been a couple of years ago."

"Thanks. It's all been taken care of."

"Oh. Permanently?" Hugo asked.

"Yeah. That's how we deal with murderous cougars." Chet wasn't about to whitewash the truth for anyone.

"Oh, well, good. I'll just let you go then."

"Treat Nancy right."

"Yeah, I plan to."

Then they ended the call and Chet frowned at Kate. "I need to see Ava."

"You need to sit still while I disinfect and stitch up the worst of these wounds." Kate looked up from one of the locations she was sewing and said, "Ava will have to remain here overnight. Do you want to stay with her?"

"Yeah, sure, thanks, Doc." No way in hell would Chet ever stay in a clinic willingly, except if he was on death's door—or, to be with the woman he loved.

After Ava had recovered from her surgery and was groggily lying in a bed next to his, Stryker and Nina hugged them and finally managed to be released to go home. And Chet's mother, Wendy, had come in to see them too, giving them gentle hugs and kisses.

"This is like the wild west," Wendy said softly.

"Yeah, but it all started in Cody, Wyoming," Chet reminded her.

All the others who had come to their aid hugged them also and then Wendy and the others left them in peace. He knew beyond a doubt his mate was the only one for him.

But sometime during the night and in the hazy world of dreams he found himself in, he was freezing in the cold Arctic north, then stranded in a hot, muggy tropical forest. And lying next to him in that little bed was the she-cat he loved, snuggling against him, chasing away the nightmares.

"He needs another towel," Ava whispered.

Mandy whispered back, "You are making him hotter."

Ava sighed. "But when he's chilled, I'm warming him up."

When he finally woke, he was feeling—well, sore, but seeing a sleeping Ava half on top of him, cozily nestled against him, he was in seventh heaven and despite being in the clinic, he couldn't have been in a better place. Not when he was with Ava.

"How are you?" he asked Ava, worried about her wound.

She gave him a big smile. "We're going home to recuperate—and whatever else we can manage to get ourselves into."

He chuckled. "I'm ready. I love you."

"I love you too."

# EPILOGUE

Chet was grateful he'd gone to Yuma Town for the Independence Day celebration with his friends and ended up with the cougar of his fantasies. She was real and as beautiful inside as she was out. Here he thought he would end up sleeping on someone's sofa, so he couldn't have lucked out more that the safehouse was under renovations when he arrived and had to stay with a reluctant she-cat. He couldn't be happier that he had fallen in love with her and that she'd felt the same about him.

His mother adored both Ava and her twin sister and had taken them under her wing. And both Ava and Nina were thrilled to call her family. Stryker too, of course.

Even Chet's brother, Kenneth, had come into town to see who Chet had mated, giving him a hard time about doing the impossible.

The wedding was to be on Labor Day weekend. They couldn't wait. And a honeymoon in Hawaii was after that. Snorkeling, swimming, running through the tropics as cougars at night? Something new and fantastical for the both of them.

But for now, he and Ava were having a blast staying at

Pinyon Pines, their cabin retreat win, and Florence had delivered their pastries for breakfast and then it was a day of swimming, lounging, and making love. Who knew when they won the stay at the resort that they would be mated cougars, building their dream house, and going forward with their lives in Yuma Town and the rest of the wild cats there?

AVA REALIZED BEING with Chet didn't wear her out as far as her special abilities went like she thought being around him would. In fact, he energized her and made her wish she had gotten to know him sooner. Plus, she'd even helped him with more of his cases.

She loved him as her mate. Not to mention Wendy had fast become one of her best friends.

Both she and Nina were always asking about the cases Wendy had worked on as a CSF agent, and she was eager to tell them all about them.

Wendy adored Ava's lavender and turquoise-decorated condo and bought it while Chet and Ava were delighted to build a bigger home suitable for a family and family get togethers.

Ava loved how when she and Nina were off from work, Wendy was delighted to be one of the girls too and shop with them at the mall in Loveland or enjoy lunch out or in with them. Wendy had them over too and she was making friends with lots of the ladies in town.

Now that Ava was mated to Chet, they had bigger family gatherings—barbecues at their home or Nina's and Ava was no longer a third wheel. Even their Aunt Grace and Uncle Geoffrey Robinson came to the gatherings when they weren't on world tours.

But what Ava and Chet were looking forward to now was the

wedding in September and a trip to Hawaii before Halloween, because none of the cougars wanted to miss that.

Even Ursula had resolved the situation with Blue and Nathan, and the bears were all back home. She still hadn't made any headway with the other bear she was interested in. But they were all invited to the wedding.

"So do you see anything in our future?" Chet asked Ava after they had a day of boating and swimming and were heading back to the cabin.

"I do," Ava said, pulling off his shirt in the living room of the cabin. "I see you making love to me and me making love to you and dreaming about a trip to Hawaii. The wedding first, of course."

He chuckled and slipped her shorts off her hips.

"Good, that's just what I'd hoped for." Then he chased her into the bedroom, and she squealed, not meaning too, but he always brought that out in her.

He was so much fun to be with no matter where they were or what they were doing. And to think she had believed in the beginning that he'd just wear her out—senses-wise.

But boy, had she gotten that wrong. She loved how considerate he was of her special ability, trusting in them even when she didn't trust in them herself.

Then they were in bed, making love to each other, culminating another beautiful day of mated bliss and looking forward to so much more.

# ACKNOWLEDGMENTS

Thanks so much to Darla Taylor and Donna Fournier, who are so much fun. I love that both garden like I do, and they are a great help in finding all my goofs in the books! Thanks, ladies!!

# AUTHOR BIO

USA Today bestselling author Terry Spear has written over eighty paranormal and medieval Highland romances. In 2008, Heart of the Wolf was named a Publishers Weekly Best Book of the Year. She has received a PNR Top Pick, a Best Book of the Month nomination by Long and Short Reviews, numerous Night Owl Romance Top Picks, and 2 Paranormal Excellence Awards for Romantic Literature (Finalist & Honorable Mention). In 2016, Billionaire in Wolf's Clothing was an RT Book Reviews Top Pick. A retired officer of the U.S. Army Reserves, Terry also creates award-winning teddy bears that have found homes all over the world, helps out with her granddaughter and grandson, and she is raising two Havanese puppies. She lives in Spring, Texas.

# ALSO BY TERRY SPEAR

### Adult Titles

**Romantic Suspense:** Deadly Fortunes, In the Dead of the Night, Relative Danger, Bound by Danger

\*\*\*

**The Highlanders Series:** His Wild Highland Lass (novella), Vexing the Highlander (novella), Winning the Highlander's Heart, The Accidental Highland Hero, Highland Rake, Taming the Wild Highlander, The Highlander, Her Highland Hero, The Viking's Highland Lass, My Highlander

**Other historical romances:** Lady Caroline & the Egotistical Earl, A Ghost of a Chance at Love

\*\*\*

**Heart of the Wolf Series:** Heart of the Wolf, Destiny of the Wolf, To Tempt the Wolf, Legend of the White Wolf, Seduced by the Wolf, Wolf Fever, Heart of the Highland Wolf, Dreaming of the Wolf, A SEAL in Wolf's Clothing, A Howl for a Highlander, A Highland Werewolf Wedding, A SEAL Wolf Christmas, Silence of the Wolf, Hero of a Highland Wolf, A Highland Wolf Christmas; SEAL Wolf Hunting; A Silver Wolf Christmas, SEAL Wolf in Too Deep, Alpha Wolf Need Not Apply, Between a Wolf and a Hard Place, SEAL Wolf Undercover, Dreaming of a White Wolf Christmas, Flight of the White Wolf, All's Fair in Love and Wolf, A Billionaire Wolf for Christmas, SEAL Wolf Surrender, Silver Town Wolf: Home for the Holidays, Night of the Billionaire Wolf, You Had Me at Wolf, Joy to the Wolves, The Wolf Wore Plaid, Jingle Bell Wolf, The Best of Both Wolves, While the Wolf's

Away, Christmas Wolf Surprise, Wolf Takes the Lead, Wolf on the Wild Side, Her Wolf for the Holidays, A Good Wolf is Hard to Find (2024), Mated for Christmas (2024)

**SEAL Wolves:** To Tempt the Wolf, A SEAL in Wolf's Clothing, A SEAL Wolf Christmas; SEAL Wolf Hunting, A SEAL Wolf in Too Deep, SEAL Wolf Undercover, SEAL Wolf Surrender

**Silver Town Wolves:** Destiny of the Wolf, Wolf Fever, Dreaming of the Wolf, Silence of the Wolf; A Silver Wolf Christmas, Between a Wolf and a Hard Place, Home for the Holidays, Jingle Bell Wolf

**Wolff Family Lodge Wolves:** You Had Me at Wolf, Wolf on the Wild Side, A Good Wolf is Hard to Find

**Highland Wolves:** Heart of the Highland Wolf, A Howl for a Highlander, A Highland Werewolf Wedding, Hero of a Highland Wolf, A Highland Wolf Christmas, The Wolf Wore Plaid, Her Wolf for the Holidays

**Billionaire Wolf Series:** A Billionaire in Wolf's Clothing, A Billionaire Wolf for Christmas, Night of the Billionaire Wolf, Wolf Takes the Lead

**White Wolf Series:** Legend of the White Wolf, Dreaming of a White Wolf Christmas, Flight of the White Wolf, While the Wolf's Away, Mated for Christmas

**Red Wolf Series:** Seduced by the Wolf, Joy to the Wolves, The Best of Both Wolves, Christmas Wolf Surprise

**Wolf Novellas:** Day of the Wolf, Seal Wolf Pursuit, Wolf to the Rescue, Night of the Wolf, United Shifter Force

\*\*\*

**Heart of the Jaguar Series:** Savage Hunger, Jaguar Fever, Jaguar Hunt, Jaguar Pride, A Very Jaguar Christmas, You Had Me at Jaguar, The Witch and the Jaguar, Dawn of the Jaguar

\*\*\*

**Heart of the Cougar Series:** Cougar's Mate, Call of the Cougar, Taming the Wild Cougar, Covert Cougar Christmas, a novella, Double Cougar Trouble, Cougar Undercover, Cougar Magic, Cougar Halloween Mischief, Falling for the Cougar, Cougar Christmas Calamity, Catch the Cougar (Halloween Novella), You Had Me at Cougar, Saving the White Cougar, Big Cat Magic

\*\*\*

**White Bear Series:** Loving the White Bear, Claiming the White Bear, Bear of a Halloween (coming)

**Grizzly Bear Series:** Bear in Mind

\*\*\*

**Wolves of Old:** Wolf Pack

**Vampire romances:** Killing the Bloodlust, Deadly Liaisons, Huntress for Hire, Forbidden Love, Deadly Liaisons, Vampire Redemption, Primal Desire

**Vampire Novellas:** The Siren's Lure, Vampiric Calling, Seducing the Huntress

\*\*\*

**Comedy Romance:** Exchanging Grooms, Marriage, Las Vegas Style

\*\*\*

**Science Fiction:** Galaxy Warrior

**Young Adult Titles**

**The World of Fae:**

The Dark Fae

The Deadly Fae

The Winged Fae

The Ancient Fae

Dragon Fae

Hawk Fae

Phantom Fae

Golden Fae

Falcon Fae

Woodland Fae

Angel Fae

\*\*\*

**The World of Elf:**

The Shadow Elf

The Darkland Elf

Warrior Elf

\*\*\*

**Blood Moon Series:**

Kiss of the VampireMy Book

Bite of the Vampire

**The Vampire Chronicles Series:**

The Vampire in My Dreams

**Demon Guardian Series:**

The Trouble with Demons

Demon Trouble, Too

Demon Hunter

**Non-Series for Now:**
Ghostly Liaisons
The Beast Within
Courtly Masquerade
Deidre's Secret

**The Magic of Inherian:**
The Scepter of Salvation
The Mage of Monrovia
Emerald Isle of Mists